A SIGN FOR BATTLE . . .

A tangle of voices coursed over the road and, as usual, my uncle Dougal's voice rang loudest of all.

"It's come!" he was shouting, pointing to the west, then making the sign of the cross over his broad chest. "The summons has come."

His family followed his lead, gasping, crossing themselves, while his wife, my aunt Fiona, cried, "Oh, oh, oh!" over and over again as if she were more afraid than pleased. The other neighbors cried out as well, an infection of fear and awe.

Then I saw where he was pointing. There on the dark hillside above us blazed a cross of fire, like a sword that had been heated to a crimson glow. Flames danced along the outstretched arms and the fire swayed from side to side as the messenger who had borne it trotted onward to the next village.

"*Creau toigh*," Da breathed. "The Cross of Shame."

I knew then what the burning thing was: the Fiery Cross that summoned the men of clan Donald to follow our chieftain into war. Any man who failed to answer the call would live with the shame forever. I smiled slowly. No man of our village would ever fail in his duty to the clan.

ALSO BY JANE YOLEN AND ROBERT J. HARRIS

Girl in a Cage

Queen's Own Fool

PRINCE ACROSS the WATER

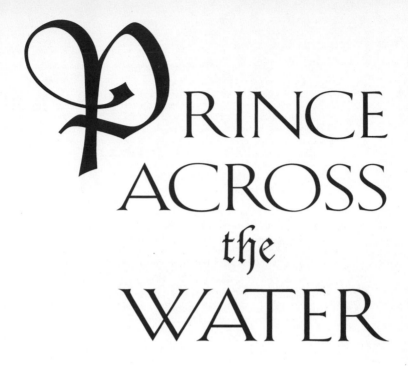

PRINCE ACROSS the WATER

JANE YOLEN & ROBERT J. HARRIS

speak

An Imprint of Penguin Group (USA) Inc.

SPEAK
Published by the Penguin Group
Penguin Group (USA) Inc.,
345 Hudson Street, New York, New York 10014, U.S.A.
Penguin Group (Canada), 90 Eglinton Avenue East, Suite 700, Toronto,
Ontario, Canada M4P 2Y3 (a division of Pearson Penguin Canada Inc.)
Penguin Books Ltd, 80 Strand, London WC2R 0RL, England
Penguin Ireland, 25 St Stephen's Green, Dublin 2, Ireland
(a division of Penguin Books Ltd)
Penguin Group (Australia), 250 Camberwell Road, Camberwell, Victoria 3124, Australia
(a division of Pearson Australia Group Pty Ltd)
Penguin Books India Pvt Ltd, 11 Community Centre, Panchsheel Park,
New Delhi - 110 017, India
Penguin Group (NZ), Cnr Airborne and Rosedale Roads, Albany, Auckland 1310,
New Zealand (a division of Pearson New Zealand Ltd)
Penguin Books (South Africa) (Pty) Ltd, 24 Sturdee Avenue,
Rosebank, Johannesburg 2196, South Africa

Registered Offices: Penguin Books Ltd, 80 Strand, London WC2R 0RL, England

First published in the United States of America by Philomel Books,
a division of Penguin Young Readers Group, 2004
Published by Speak, an imprint of Penguin Group (USA) Inc., 2006

1 3 5 7 9 10 8 6 4 2

THE LIBRARY OF CONGRESS HAS CATALOGED THE PHILOMEL BOOKS EDITION AS FOLLOWS:
Yolen, Jane. Prince across the water / Jane Yolen & Robert J. Harris.
p. cm.
Summary: In 1746, a year after the Scottish clans have rallied to the call of their exiled prince,
Charles Stuart, to take up arms against England's tyranny, fourteen-year-old, epileptic Duncan MacDonald
and his cousin, Ewan, run away to join the fight at Culloden and discover the harsh reality of war.
1. Culloden, Battle of, Scotland, 1746—Juvenile fiction. 2. Jacobite Rebellion, 1745–1746—Juvenile fiction.
[1. Culloden, Battle of, Scotland, 1746—Fiction. 2. Jacobite Rebellion, 1745–1746—Fiction.
3. War—Fiction. 4. Epilepsy—Fiction. 5. People with disabilities—Fiction. 6. Cousins—Fiction.
7. Scotland—History—18th century—Fiction.] I. Harris, Robert J. II. Title. PZ7.Y78 Pr 2004
[Fic]—dc22 2004044628
ISBN 0-399-23897-2 (hc)

Puffin Books ISBN 0-14-240645-7

Printed in the United States of America

❧ *To David,*
who has shared all my Scottish
sojourns and stood with me
on Drummossie Moor.

—JY

❧ *To Kirsty and Mark, to Nik,*
and to Elspeth,
the next generation.

—RJH

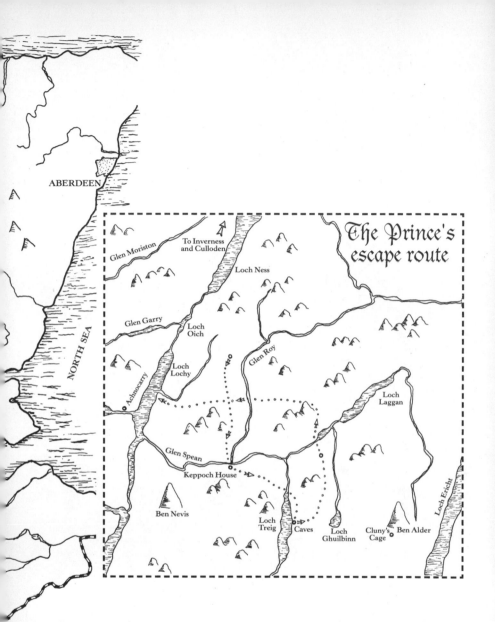

❧ CONTENTS

I. RAISING THE BANNERS

◈ *August–September 1745*

Ah, who will play the Silver Whistle?

When my King's son to sea is going?

As Scotland prepares; prepares his coming!

Upon a dark ship on the ocean.

—Scottish folksong

1 ❧ CROSS OF FIRE

Mairi was the first of us to see it. She came flying into the cottage, her yellow hair streaming behind her like straw in the wind and the fringe near covering her eyes. Her ankle-length skirt had torn halfway from its belt so that she was all but running in her petticoats.

"There's fire on the mountain," she cried. "They're coming! They're coming at last."

She bumped into Ma, almost spilling the plate of fresh-baked bannocks all over the floor.

"Take care, lass!" Ma said. "When the horse is at the gallop, the bridle's over late." She meant to chide Mairi, who was always moving before thinking, but as usual Mairi hardly noticed the scold.

Andrew and Sarah started giggling so hard that crumbs of cheese fell from their mouths onto the wooden table. Da silenced them with a hard look and took a swallow from his ale cup. His looks were worth two times Ma's old "says," but that never stopped her from using them.

"Where's she been off to now?" growled Granda from his place at the hearth. "It's night and not a time for lassies to be off alone. Not disordered the way she is. Look at the state of her clothes. For shame, lass." He took a deep breath before going on. "Catriona, ye should keep her on a bridle, or she'll be away into the mists before ye can stop her."

But Mairi was listening to none of them. Instead she leaped up and down, her bare feet scarcely touching the floor. "But they're *here!*" she cried in a pleading voice, turning to me, who was ever her champion. "Just as I always said. Duncan, tell them."

My mouth was full of bread and I had to swallow before I could speak. "Who, then?" I asked at last. "Who's here?" Though I feared I already knew what she would say.

She slid to her knees at my feet. "The *Sidhe,* Duncan. The faerie folk. Come here from the other side of the water. And their prince will be riding at the head of them all, mounted on a butterfly, with jewels flashing in his hair."

"Shush!" Da growled, since the look had clearly not worked. "I've told ye before to wheesht with that nonsense, girl."

"But it's *true!*" Mairi insisted, still looking at me, waiting for me to support her. "I told ye he'd come for me one day."

We all knew Mairi was soft-headed, a daftie they called her in the village, a girl who saw faeries under every leaf and flower. Usually I was ready to humor her harmless fancies. They hurt nobody and there were already enough people willing to make fun of her. I protected her when I could.

"Dinna *ye* believe me, Duncan?" she asked, turning her petal face up to me. Her green eyes had the sheen of a holly leaf.

Da was about to warn her again when Ma raised a hand. "Listen, Alisdair," she said to him, "there *is* something going on." She put the plate of bannocks down on the table and cocked her head.

Ma was right. We could all hear the voices outside, now. I stared down at Mairi, her face aglow, her eyes huge in the flickering firelight.

Could it be true? Could it really? The faerie folk riding down the mountainside into our village, all the bells a-jangle on their horses' bridles? Then I shook my head. I would be crazy myself if I believed in my sister's nonsense.

Da was up now and, in three great strides, out the door. Granda hauled himself to his feet, moving stiffly after.

Jumping up, Mairi pulled me off the bench. "Come, Duncan, come! Before the fey folk all disappear!"

She dragged me to the open door so quickly, we tripped over Andrew and Sarah as they scampered in front of us. Mairi shooed them on like a dog after straggling sheep, all the while belting up her plaid again.

Outside the stars were bright in the clear August sky and there was a tang in the air from the stacks of peat we'd stored to keep our fire burning through the winter.

A tangle of voices coursed over the road and, as usual, my uncle Dougal's voice rang loudest of all.

"It's come!" he was shouting, pointing to the west, then making the sign of the cross over his broad chest. "The summons has come."

His family followed his lead, gasping, crossing themselves, while his wife, my aunt Fiona, cried, "Oh, oh, oh!" over and over again as if she were more afraid than pleased. The other neighbors cried out as well, an infection of fear and awe.

Then I saw where he was pointing. There on the dark hillside above us blazed a cross of fire, like a sword that had been heated to a crimson glow. Flames danced along the outstretched arms and the fire swayed from side to side as the messenger who had borne it trotted onward to the next village.

"*Creau toigh,*" Da breathed. "The Cross of Shame."

I knew then what the burning thing was: the Fiery Cross that summoned the men of clan Donald to follow our chieftain into war.

Any man who failed to answer the call would live with the shame forever. I smiled slowly. No man of our village would ever fail in his duty to the clan.

Granda broke into a craggy grin. "At last," he said, his old voice breaking with a kind of pride.

"Nae, nae," Ma scolded, adjusting the plaid over her head for she'd had no time to find her white kertch. "The devil with ye men. All ye live for is war and glory. Well, hope is sowing while death is mowing. War is no respecter of families. Is it no enough we've children all but starving and nae crops in the field? And three years in a row a ruined harvest?"

"Hush, woman," Granda said. "What do ye know of honor? We fight for our clan and because our laird calls us out to do our duty. And our duty is to put the rightful king back on the throne."

The rightful king! James Stuart. My heart nearly burst in two thinking about him across the sea in exile while that usurper, that German lairdie, ruled in London. When everybody knew it should be a Scot—and a Stuart—on the throne. Granda was right. What did Ma, or any woman, know about honor, or about the glory to be won for the MacDonalds when we helped bring the rightful king home?

"Ye see, Duncan," Mairi squeaked, tugging on my sleeve and dragging me far from the cottage, "they're coming." She pointed after the burning cross. "That's the sign. The whole host of the Sidhe are on their way. And my faerie prince will be at their head, ready to take me to his palace in the west."

"Nae, Mairi," I told her, trying to be gentle, even though I was annoyed with her, "come away." She was acting just like Ma. She did not understand a thing. "It's got naught to do with faeries. Who's coming is a real live man, the bonnie prince from across the water—Charles Stuart, son of the rightful king of Scotland and England. He's coming to win the war that will bring his father home and we're to help him, we MacDonalds and the other Scottish clans. The prince is here to get his throne back. He's no here for ye."

Mairi's lower lip trembled. Her green eyes shuttered. Any minute she would start to cry. "I dinna mean the prince of the Scots," she said. "I mean the prince of the Sidhe . . ."

Losing patience with her, I said, "This is too important for any of yer games, Mairi. This is men's work. The Stuart has landed. The chief has called. Clan Donald is going to war."

2 ❧ THE KING ACROSS THE WATER

Men's work? What do ye know of men's work?"

Suddenly I was grabbed from behind and shaken violently from side to side. I wrestled free and spun round to see the familiar face of my cousin Ewan.

"Just testing yer mettle," he said, stepping out of range of my fist. "Maybe in another year or two ye'll be strong enough to lift a man's sword."

Ewan was only a year older than me, fourteen last winter, and already he'd been on a cattle raid with his father and the others. Last summer they had brought back six cows from the land of our enemies, the Campbells, a necessary theft with the harvests so bad. Ewan never tired of reminding me of his part in that triumph.

"Dinna ye worry, Duncan," he would say, patting my head as if I were a *bairn,* a wee child, "yer too young yet for a man's part. Ye must stay here and tend to the milking."

Milking! Girl's work!

After a whole winter of his head-patting, I'd finally turned and without warning punched him in the nose. We'd fought for a long time, kicking and gouging and rolling in the dirt, until finally we fell apart, too exhausted to go on. After that, he'd stopped calling me a bairn, stopped patting me on the head. But he'd yet to call me a man.

"If ye want to test my mettle again, then step closer," I challenged him. "I'm sure ye remember my fist." His nose surely did, for it was still askew from my winter punch.

He took another step away, laughing. "Oh, I willna fight ye, cousin, for I have to save myself for the true king's enemy, the English redcoats and the German upon our throne." His voice was mocking. "You wouldna deny me that, would ye?"

Mairi whirled round and stared intently at him. Then suddenly she jabbed a thin, wee finger toward him and spoke in a strange crooning voice I'd never heard her use before.

"There's blood on yer head, Ewan, Dougal's son," she said. "I see it as clear as if ye were wearing a scarlet bonnet."

A deadly hush fell over the three of us. I felt an awful shiver go up my back as sharp and fast as lightning.

Then Ewan shrugged. He tried to make light of it, but his face was pale and a deep line creased his forehead. He opened his mouth twice before he could speak and then he said, "Ye had best keep a tight hold on her, Duncan. She's so light in the head, she's going to blow away like thistledown."

I wanted to give him a joke back, but Mairi's voice had frightened me. She may have been a bit daft, but she'd never had the sight before, never seen past the dark curtain of time and into the future. An old woman named Granny Mags who lived in the next village was said to tell fortunes for a coin or a basket of milled rye, but I'd never believed in her power.

"Dinna say such things, Mairi," I chided her. "It's bad luck." I took her by the shoulder and led her gently back toward the cottage, where Da was looking grim and Granda elated.

As we got to them, Granda was saying, "Ye know what to do, Alisdair."

"Aye, I know well enough," Da responded grimly, his fingers

sawing through his beard, "though I dinna have to like it. And the men will like it even less. Catriona is right. The crops are all stunted again, and the children go to bed hungry most nights. The Stuart has picked a bad time to come back."

Granda gave him a startled look. "I never thought to hear you say such a thing, Alisdair. We Scots have been waiting thirty years for the Stuart's return. I know. I fought back in the '15 for the prince's father."

I was startled, too. "Da, surely this is a great thing, the prince come home . . ."

He ignored me and spoke directly to Granda. "Dinna fear, old man, I'll do my duty. I'm a loyal clansman after all, as ye brought me up to be. The MacDonalds hold my heart and hand and I know what we owe our laird. But I still have the right to speak my mind to my family. And I tell ye again, the prince has come at the wrong time."

I was stunned hearing him say anything against the Stuart prince. It brought me immediate shame. That a MacDonald should speak this way, and my own da. My cheeks went flame red while something awful and cold squatted, like a toad, in my gut.

But Da turned from the two of us and signaled the rest of the village men with a raised fist. "MacDonald! MacDonald!" he cried. Then he turned back and said to Granda, "Honor satisfied?"

Granda spit to one side as if to deny it, though he said nothing more.

But the other men had heard nothing of this exchange, and cried back at Da, "MacDonald! MacDonald!" for Da was the leader of our village since he was married to a woman who was the closest in blood to our chieftain, MacDonald of Keppoch. "MacDonald! MacDonald!"

The sound of the shout touched the hills and sent it back to us. I felt the cry like a strong wind off the mountain's slope.

"And God help us all," Da muttered. He waited until the men disappeared into their byres and cottages. Then he turned, saying, "Granda, Duncan, Andrew, come. Catriona, ye and the girls stay out here for now."

We followed him into the cottage. Once inside, Da closed the door behind us. Then he brought over a stool, stood on it, and pulled out a long stone from over the lintel of our door. He handed the stone over to me without a word. It was a heavy grey thing, as big as a child's coffin, and I nearly dropped it. Setting it on the floor carefully, I straightened up with equal care. Da had reached into the hollow space over the lintel and was drawing out a long bundle.

"Mark this well, Duncan," he said to me. "And ye, too, Andrew. For ye are my boys who will one day soon be men. Ye must know where we keep the family's great weapon of war, the one we use only to fight for our king." He stepped off the stool, then unwrapped the linen, and there lay a great basket-handled sword. He gripped it and held it up, one-handed. In the firelight, the blade glowed silver and red.

I watched in awe. In all my thirteen years I had known nothing of that hiding place, nothing of that sword.

"So now ye know, boys," Granda said. "Be proud of yer name and be worthy of that sword. I carried it in the '15 when I fought for our king, and now it's come out of hiding again to do its work once more."

"I will, Granda," I said.

"Me, too," Andrew echoed.

Da wrapped the sword back in its linen shroud and set it on the table. Then he picked up the stone, stepped on the stool, and slotted the stone back in its place. "Now ye can open the door to yer ma and the girls. But not a word to them about the hiding place, hear?"

Andrew and I put our hands over our hearts. "We swear," we said together.

In what seemed like moments but must have been an hour at least, the men of the village all gathered again at the crossroads, this time in a tight circle, two dozen of them, ready to unwrap their own treasures. Granda was already there.

I stood at the door with Ma and Andrew.

"Come," Da said to me.

"I want to go, too, Da," Andrew complained, and Ma cuffed him.

Da stopped and looked over his shoulder, saying, "Andrew, yer time will come, but it isna now."

We started again for the crossroads, but Andrew complained a second time.

Ma called out, "As the auld cock craws, the young cock learns. Watch what ye teach yer sons, Alisdair MacDonald."

This time Da turned and I turned with him. He spoke in a low voice I barely recognized. "Scotland has waited thirty years for this day, Catriona. We were children then, ye and I, and didna need to know what the kingdom meant for us. But we know now. And well ye ken I have nae choice in the matter. We owe service to the laird."

"There's always a choice," she countered. "We need ye at home. Three bad harvests in a row and the man gone when he's needed most? How will I manage?"

"Ye'll manage," he said curtly, "ye always do." He gave me a look.

We turned our backs on her and walked on.

When we got to the crossroads, I looked around the circle of men who I had known all my life. My uncle Dougal, big and dark and as bullheaded as Ewan, who stood by him, both on Da's right hand. The twins Robert and Ronald, who shared a single farm, next to them. Then their father, Andrew, who, it was said, was half their size and twice as hardy. The farrier MacKinnon, who had married into the clan, stood across from us. John the Miller, his son and apprentice Alan, and all the rest, right round to Granda, who stood by my left. Men who had lived around me forever. Men who suddenly seemed bigger and stronger than I could account for.

They were silent, waiting for Da to speak, yet for some reason he was still brooding.

"Why is Duncan here?" Uncle Dougal whispered to Da, though I could hear him. "Ye know he's not able . . ."

"He's a right to see what we do here," Granda said. "He's Alisdair's oldest son. His mother is second cousin to the Keppoch."

Uncle Dougal looked away, shrugging.

And still Da did not speak. Instead, he unwrapped the sword from its linen sheath.

Then one by one, the men shook dust and earth loose from bindings that had been undisturbed for years. What they brought out to show were pistols, muskets, axes, and even a few long baskethandled swords like Da's, a harvest of gunpowder and steel.

I recognized them, for they were as fine as Da's sword. These were not the day-by-day arms for cattle raids and skirmishes. They were weapons for the king's war.

I shivered, though it was not really cold. Overhead a partial moon stared down at us, like a broken shield.

The men passed the weapons around the circle without comment, except for an occasional grunt of approval. The axes I found heavy, unwieldy. The pistols sat easy in my hand. But when I held my father's great sword, I felt a kind of strange power shoot up my right arm. I looked up at Da to tell him, tried to catch his eye, but his face was grimmer than before and he was staring at the dark hills.

I handed the sword back to him, hilt first, and his eyes settled on the blade.

"That'll do," he said. Then he lifted the sword high overhead. He spoke quietly, but there was as much steel in his voice as in his right hand. "We owe a duty to our clan chief, the Keppoch MacDonald. We owe our loyalty to the King Over the Water. Remember, men, that the king on the throne, German Georgie, is nae our king."

"He's a usurper," I blurted out, then bit my lip as Da glared down at me. Suddenly I felt as daft as my sister. I vowed to never say a word more.

Da leaned into the circle of men, his arm still holding the sword high. "That which has been thrust upon us can be thrown off."

"Aye!" Dougal was the first to cry out in his loud, grave voice, and then the other men echoed him. At the last I shouted it, too, unable to keep quiet. "Aye!"

Da waited for the shouting to be done. "We'll gather back here at dawn," he said, "and march to join the Keppoch. Every man owes him that duty and by God I'll see us all delivered." He smiled at them slowly, a thin, humorless smile. "And if God is on our side, we'll be home in time for the harvest."

As he walked away, Granda said to his back, "Even so, that was well done, Alisdair."

Da did not look back.

• • •

"So, it's come then," said Ewan with a wolfish grin as we went toward our cottages. He elbowed me sharply. "Nae cattle raid this time."

"Nae cattle raid this time," I repeated. And in my deepest of hearts, I was suddenly sure that I would acquit myself well.

3 ❧ FIRE AND MARSH

In the morning, I said as much at the table, my porridge spoon held like a dirk in my hand. "I'll do my duty as well as any man."

"There's nae place for ye on this venture, son," Da said bluntly. He took a sup of his watery porridge and slowly shook his head. "We are talking war here, nae quick in-out cattle raid. Ye'll soon be old enough for that. But *war*, lad, that's no for ye. Cannon and muskets and trained soldiers. Why, ye can hardly lift the sword."

"But I'm nearly fourteen," I protested. "I am well able to fight in a battle line. I've practiced for years, Da."

"Yer barely thirteen and beardless, and ye have held only a wooden practice sword," my father countered flatly. "The only battle line ye have fought against is the line of gorse on the high hill." His voice dropped as if to soften this blow. "Whatever yer age, Duncan, ye know full well why I canna let ye come."

"But Da . . ." I said, my voice rising to a whine, "Ewan's going. And we're the only two boys of an age in the village and—"

"Do ye know he's going for a fact?" Da asked.

"*He* says he is. And if he can go . . ."

Da shook his head. "I didna want to say this aloud, but ye force me to it, son. I canna have ye fainting in the middle of battle."

He was right of course, but that only made things worse. I pushed my bowl away. There might as well have been bile in it as porridge for all the appetite I had then.

"Eat," Ma said softly, her face shadowed by the firelight. "Keep up yer strength, Duncan. Ye'll have to do yer da's work on the farm while he's gone. Likely ye'll also be bringing the harvest in, what there'll be of it this year. And shooting any deer or grouse that come near."

"Well, if I can shoot deer and grouse and work the farm, why am I no fit enough to march with the men?" I asked sourly. "Besides, I've never been further away from our village than when I bring the cows up to the summer pasture. Why can ye no let me go to see something beyond our door?"

She only echoed Da. "Ye know full well, Duncan."

Suddenly it all seemed so unfair. I was the oldest, and strong in every way but one. By rights I should be going off to fight for our king. To share in the glory. To uphold the MacDonald name. To see a bit of the world. Like Granda and Da. Part of me wanted to pout about it, like a child. But that would not have helped. And then I had an idea.

"Granda's going . . ."

"Yer granda wants to see the prince, nae more than that," said Da. "Then he'll come home to keep an eye on things here."

"Aye," Granda said, "I fought for his father and I'll cheer the son, even if that's all I'm able to do."

His words made an ache start somewhere in my chest, for I longed to see the prince from across the water as well. "I'd walk across fire and marsh to go," I exclaimed. "And I'm stronger than Granda. I could help him along the way."

Just then, Andrew flicked some porridge at Sarah and she poked him with her spoon. Like a fire flaring out of nothing, they were suddenly slapping at each other until Da skelped them both on the head to quiet them.

Mairi started crooning a song, something about the faerie folk keeping the peace, but Da shushed her. "Eat up, lass. There'll be more chores for ye as well from now on." He looked at her softly. She'd always been his favorite.

After that, breakfast was carried on in silence. No one had answered my question. And my treacherous eyes began to threaten tears. To cry now would only prove that I was still far from being any sort of man.

And what sort of a man *could* I be, what sort of warrior for the clan? Da was right. And Ma. I never knew when the fits that had plagued me since childhood might take me. Never knew when my body would start to tremble till I collapsed on the ground, pale and shaking, pain driving through my skull like an iron spike. Never knew till long after how anyone who saw me lying there, foaming and twitching, would draw back in horror, making a sign against the evil eye.

The others in the village often viewed my fits with horror, though Ma always told them, "He was born at midnight, and ye know a child born at that hour can see the ghosts of the dead. It's the terror of the sight that makes him shake so."

Ghosts of the dead? I'd never seen any. Or anything else of interest. So I had to try, just once more. "Ma, please . . ."

She stared at me for a long moment, as if she could read my heart as easily as she could read her Bible. Then suddenly she turned to Da, saying, "He could go with ye, Alisdair, and come back with the old man. *After* they've seen the prince."

I could scarcely breathe waiting for his answer.

"And what would be the point in that?" Da said. "Ye need him here. Did ye nae say that a moment before?"

"It's only for a few days. Just a few days," Ma said, then added,

"Duncan has never been beyond Glenroy except to take the cows up to the *shieling,* the summer pastures. He could help yer father along the way so you dinna have to worry about him. Andrew could take Duncan's chores. And maybe Duncan could meet the bonnie prince, and then . . ." Her voice trailed off before my father's bleak, angry gaze.

"And then what?" I asked, stupidly getting in between.

Ma turned to me and held out her hands, hands as veined as rivers running down the hills. "A prince's touch can cure all manner of ills, they say," Ma poured out in a rush, before Da could stem her words. "Just one touch."

"No more of that blether," my father declared, cracking his spoon on the edge of his bowl. "Have we no tried enough of yer cures? Heather soaked in water bound to his head, an animal's tooth on a thong around his neck, water brought all the way from the Holy Well at Eigg to be drunk down on the waning moon. For all the good any of them did. Leave him be, like ye do poor Mairi."

My mother locked her fingers before her and met my father's gaze. "Will ye no take a chance for the sake of Duncan's future?"

"Future?" The way he said it made me shiver. As if he thought I had but a small future ahead of me.

"He'll be nae bother," Granda added. "He and I have always worked well together. I'll watch him all the way and see him safely back."

"Ye'll be lucky to find the way back yersel'," said Da, who was clearly unhappy that Granda was coming along.

"All the more reason for Duncan to go, too," said Granda, smiling slyly. "Catriona is right. Duncan can see I dinna get lost in the mist or stumble into a bog."

"I'll guide Granda through forest and fog," I added, my enthusiasm making my voice and right hand suddenly shake. I forced myself to calm down. If I had a fit now, Da would never let me go. But the shaking turned out to be only eagerness, and I set my lips together in a thin line lest I grin like a daftie at everyone.

Da looked around at us all with narrow, suspicious eyes, as if he'd been caught in an ambush. "Fine then," he said at last. "But a glimpse of the prince then straight back home for the two of ye. As soon as the English hear the Stuart's returned, the hills will be swarming with redcoats, buzzing around like wasps kicked out of their nest. I'll no have an old dodderer and a boy who takes the fits around me then." He pushed away his porridge bowl. "If I'm to get the men back by harvest time, I'll need no distractions."

I winked at Granda and he at me.

Ma turned back to the hearth, but I could see her smile, just a wee one, as she stirred the pot.

4 ∂ FAREWELLS

The morning was cool for August, with a stiff wind bending the hedges. Layers of clouds scudded across the sky. *Good marching weather,* I thought as I came out the door.

I had kissed Ma and the girls good-bye inside the cottage. No need to make a fuss like a child off for the first time. Andrew was sulking on the bed we shared and had not even given me a nod. Da and Granda were already outside.

Looking over to the crossroads, I saw that all the men of the village were mustered for the march. Uncle Dougal's deep voice, like the drone of the bagpipes, was grinding away at something.

Ewan stood apart from them, staring at the ground. I was about to go and ask if he was waiting for me, when his da broke off whatever he was saying and went over to him. Uncle Dougal jawed at Ewan for a moment or two and then Ewan's head hung even lower than before. He clenched his fists tightly but didn't answer back. Then his da waved him toward the women, before going back to take his own place with the departing warriors.

So then I knew. Ewan wasn't going to march off after all and I was. What a change of fortunes.

I walked over to speak to him, glad of the soughing wind. It would mean no one could overhear us.

"Ewan," I began, but he turned and strode away toward his cottage. He was going so fast, I didn't catch up till we were well behind the stone byre where their three cows were kept. There, Ewan whirled about with such red anger printed on his face, I pulled up sharply.

"So they're taking *ye* along, are they?" he said sourly. "Dressed in yer best bonnet and plaid with a brooch pin ye only wear on holy days, and yer plaid stockings halfway up yer knee. Aye, yer a fine sight, Duncan MacDonald."

"I'm just going to see the prince," I said. "And a wee bit of the world outside of Glenroy."

Ewan turned abruptly and kicked the side of the byre so hard, I thought he might break his foot against the stone wall. From inside the byre, the cows lowed restlessly. "Well, I'm no going, as ye can bloody well see. My da says this venture may well fail. And if he is forced to turn outlaw, I must be free to care for the family and land."

Fail? I didn't know what to say to him. *How could anyone suppose we would fail?* And then, all in a rush, it came out. "How can anyone suppose we will fail? With all the might of Scotland behind the prince? They'll march down to London and God help any who stand in their way." I took a deep breath and in my mind's eye I could see them. The MacDonalds and the Frasers and the Douglases and the Camerons and . . . "Everyone knows the Scots are the best fighters in the world."

"Not *all* Scots are great fighters," he said, glaring at me.

"Well, I'm not going to fight. At least not yet."

"Then why *are* you going? I suppose they need somebody to muck out the prince's midden. Or maybe your da is hoping ye'll die on the march and save him further shame."

I felt as if an icy hand had run its finger down my spine. Ewan was supposed to be my friend as well as my cousin and neighbor. Then my anger began to rise, melting the ice of my spine. I cocked my fist and might have swung at him, too, but I saw a tear welling up in his eye.

"Och, Ewan, dinna be such an ass," I said. "I'm only going for a sight of the prince, nae more than that. Then I'll be returning with my granda. He needs minding, ye know, and that's why I'm allowed to go. Da wants him out of his way."

"I willna have even that much," said Ewan, his voice dropping. "My father wants me free of any taint of . . . of treachery." The last word fell strangely from his lips.

"Treachery?" I repeated. "How could any man call us traitors when we simply follow our duty to the *laird*?"

"King George will call us traitors, Da says," said Ewan, "and that's how he'll treat us if he wins. As traitors. He'll send the redcoats to take away our land. And burn our women in our houses. And spit our babies on their English swords."

The German lairdie win? I had never even considered the possibility that King George's redcoats might beat us. I shook my head violently. "He canna win. He willna win. The bonnie prince will be victorious. He *has* to be. After all, he has God on his side. And all the Scottish clans."

Ewan nodded, the redness on his cheeks now a paler pink, the tears gone, resolution replacing sorrow. "With God and all the might of Scotland, the bonnie prince canna possibly lose!" He gave a high yell that set the cows in the byre lowing again.

We both grinned at that. Nothing could stand against Highland warriors with their great swords and their sturdy targes and their skirling pipes behind them. Nothing!

"And when ye come back, will ye tell me what ye saw?"

"Aye, I will," I promised.

"Every bit of it?"

"Every bit."

"You swear."

"On the head of the bonnie prince himself."

Then we grabbed hands and clasped shoulders, friends again. Our quarrel was forgotten, the harsh words blown off in the wind.

5 ❧ THE MARCH

oon the Donald men were on the march along the road that wound down through our glen. On each side of the path, tall red-barked pines stood guard. I looked up, hoping for an eagle, seeing none. It would have been a good sign. And then I thought: *Who needs a sign? Everyone knows the Highlanders will win.*

Da and Uncle Dougal were at the head of our column of men, while Granda and I took up the rear. We were to stay in the back with the *humblies,* the poorer village men who were armed in the simplest way—with a dagger or hatchet or scythe.

Beside us, tossing flowers and singing in her sweet, wavery voice, came Mairi. "Tell the prince to come quickly, Duncan," she begged. "Tell him I'm waiting for him." She grabbed up my left hand.

I tried to shake her off, though gently, but she would not let go.

"Away, Mairi!" Granda said firmly. "Yer brother's marching with the fighting men of Donald now. This is nae place for a lassie."

Reluctantly Mairi let her fingers slip from my hand. I glanced back and saw her waving good-bye. All at once, she seemed to waver in the air, like an image reflected in water. I couldn't move. It was as if I had become rooted to the spot.

"Granda," I began, turning to find him, to tell him what I had seen, for surely he would know what it meant. But he was already well ahead. Tearing myself away, I ran to catch up, startling a hare off the path. It loped out of sight, its great ears wagging.

"There ye are," Granda said, when I got to his side. "I was afraid ye had decided to stay at home with the girls."

I laughed. "Not I, Granda. I'm off to see all I can see."

He laughed as well. "I didna really think so. After all, yer *my* blood."

We marched on together, he limping and me careful not to excite myself so much that I fell into a fit.

As we went along, I had time to really look at the weapons my companions carried. The humblies, of course, had little of interest. But a few of the men further ahead of us carried great Lochaber axes, long poles crowned at the top with a broad blade. Others—like Da, Uncle Dougal, John the Miller—were armed with broadswords and targes, leather shields each with a wicked-looking steel point sticking out of the middle. Da also had a dirk that he had honed to an edge so sharp, it could cut a single hair in two. Oh, he had a musket as well, but I doubted he'd use it. He liked to say, "A *man* goes hand-to-hand. Only a coward kills without seeing his foe's face."

Of all those on the march, I was the only one without a weapon of any sort. Nothing. Oh, I knew I was just going along to see the prince. But a Highlander off on a march without a weapon? I felt worse than useless. Even Granda had an old pistol and a dirk stuck into his belt.

I'd said nothing to Da. I feared that if I complained, he would send me home alone. But Granda must have seen me eyeing the weapons, and especially the dirk in his belt.

As the march rounded a deep bend in the heathery hillside, we were momentarily out of sight of the others. Granda reached over and put a hand on my arm.

"Slow a moment, lad."

"Is your leg bothering ye, Granda?" I asked.

"Aye, my leg," he said. "And also my heart."

This was a new and worrisome thing. "Yer heart?"

Overhead a kestrel hovered in the clear air, its wings beating furiously. Granda handed me his dirk. "My heart hurts seeing ye so unarmed," he said. "And I told myself, Duncan better have this. After all," he finished with a twinkle, "ye never know what sort of trouble we might run into. Even if we're only going to see the prince and no going to the actual war."

"Thanks, Granda . . ." I began and could say nothing more.

"And remember this, lad: Hold that dirk before ye when ye charge. A Highland man makes his charge from strength. We want high, solid ground and the wind at our back. Will ye remember that?"

I nodded. Then, with a delighted grin, I slid the dirk into my belt, feeling a man indeed.

We caught up with the others after a bit, but remained in the rear, for Granda was really quite lame. But so long as I had that dirk stuck in my belt, as solid as a knife in cheese, I was happy wherever we marched.

The familiar rocky cliffs of the glen soon gave way to more open land where prickly yellow gorse marked the roadside. Great scrubby fields of green lay all around. But without those familiar cliffs to guard me, I suddenly felt exposed and unprotected. At least the Roy, that lovely, lazy river, still ran along beside us. I longed to stop and fish for some speckled trout, but I longed even more to meet the prince.

As if he understood my homesickness, Granda started to talk. "Did I ever tell ye, lad, about the Sherramuir fight? About the glorious days of the '15 when we fought for the Stuart King?"

"Once or twice, I think." Dozens of times more like, but I was happy to hear the tale again now that we were on the march.

He smiled, the gap between his teeth as broad as a king's highway, and launched into his familiar tale. "We followed the Keppoch then as now," he said, "though he was a younger man in those days."

"As were ye, Granda," I said.

That made him laugh. He touched his sparse grey hair, where one strand had to do the work for ten. "As was I."

We were both so engrossed in the tale of the clans' last rising in 1715 against the first German George that we weren't watching where we were walking, and suddenly I looked up to see that we had fallen well behind the rest of the men. Taking a tight grip on Granda's arm, I quickened our pace. He took a deep breath and let me drag him along.

"It must have been a grand sight," I said, knowing what was coming next but never tired of hearing it.

"It was that, laddie," he said, never letting on that he was winded. "The pipers played a pibroch, the cry went up, 'Claymore!' and forward we all charged—the brave MacDonalds, and with us the Stuarts, the MacKinnons, the Camerons, and the rest."

As he spoke, I could almost see the clansmen charging, their swords raised, their targes at the ready, plunging right into the redcoat line.

"The English fired," Granda said, "a sound deafening to the ear and shattering to the eye. Clouds of smoke enveloped us all around. When the smoke lifted . . ."

"I know this part," I said, though indeed I knew it all. "Ye turned and saw yer best friend, Murdo, dead beside ye, a musket ball right through his head." I tried to picture it and failed.

Granda nodded, adding as he always did, "And I didna think, 'Poor Murdo,' I only thought, 'Thank God that isna me lying there.'" He put his hand on his forehead, marking the place where Murdo had been hit.

I could almost feel the pain driving through my own head as he spoke, and even raised my hand above my eyes, as if I, too, had been shot. But, of course, there was nae blood. This was but a story after all. "So what did ye do then, Granda?"

"What could I do?" He shrugged. "I said a quick prayer for Murdo but I couldna stop. No there. No then. I was a warrior, and we didna stop for our dead till the day was won." His face looked graven, like a headstone.

"So . . ."

"So we ran on, and a stone's throw from the enemy, we pulled up long enough to loose off a volley of our own."

"Did ye kill many?"

"I didna take time to see. The heat of battle was on us. We threw away our muskets and drew our swords. Some even flung off their heavy plaids. Another shout of 'Claymore!' and we charged the redcoats like crazed bulls."

"I'll bet it was a braw fight, Granda."

"Well, some of them fled like frightened doves, and some stood to face our steel. I skewered one man while he was trying to reload his musket. Another I smacked in the face with my targe, then threw him on his back."

I had my dirk out now, shoving it into an unseen enemy, acting out my granda's story as we strode along.

"So it went," he said, "hack and hew and run the man through. There was blood—aye, there was blood everywhere—like a flood in the gutter it was. And the awful, pitiful cries from the wounded lads."

"Did they cry out for their sweethearts?" I had never asked any such question before.

He was quiet for a moment, then said, "They cried out for their mothers," which surprised me. His jaw got strangely slack for a moment, then he blurted out, "And a pitiful sound it was, too."

Pitiful crying? What happened to Scots courage? It was hardly a comforting thought. So I stopped thinking about it at all.

Just then Da dropped back to see how we were doing. His face was slick with sweat though the day was cool for August. It was as if the coming war was a fever raging within him that had not yet broken.

"How's the leg, old man?" he asked, swiping a hand across his brow. If he noticed my dirk, he didn't comment on it.

"What is a leg when we march to glory," Granda said.

"Och, ye never change," Da told him, shaking his head.

I stared at Da, suddenly wondering: *If he were wounded in a coming battle, would he cry for Ma or his own mother?* Then I gave a short grunt, almost a laugh. Da knew his duty and he was a great fighter. He would have the courage the lads of the '15 lacked.

"Can I march up front with ye a wee while, Da?" I asked.

He cocked his head to one side and looked at me with a steely gaze. "I'm no yer da on the march," he said, "I'm yer leader, lad. Leader of the Upper Glenroy villagers. And dinna ye forget that." Then his eyes went soft, the color of a dove's breast. "Besides, yer here to keep an eye on yer granda and keep him out of trouble. Can ye manage that?"

I nodded.

"That dirk in yer belt should see you both safely through," he added, and ruffled my hair with his big hand.

6 ❧ THE KEPPOCH

So we came down the last part of the glen, the soft purple of heather turning an odd brown in the shadows. Beside us the Roy still ran its old course over a rocky bed. A black cock, startled by so many men passing, rose up in noisy flight.

Just as the gloaming was spreading its red glow over the hills, we reached the Keppoch's house at the foot of the glen where all of us were to meet. There we were joined by marchers from other villages, armed men in dark tartans and caps, all running together down mountain paths like brooks flowing into a rushing river, some three hundred of us in all.

I had never been to the Keppoch's house before. It was the grandest place I had ever seen. Not like our village's wee stone cottages, with their two rooms and a byre attached, the Keppoch's house was two stories high, made of huge grey stones. It had at least a dozen windows with real glass staring down on us like the eyes of giants. An orchard planted about the house was heavy with apples and pears, some ripe and some not yet ready for eating.

What must it be like, to live here? I thought. I couldn't begin to imagine it.

Our fellow clansmen, there before us, gave a whoop of welcome as we funneled down into the orchard. Some called out to Da and Dougal by name, others just raised a hand. Big men they were for the most part, broad and brawny, thick-bearded, in tartans as varied as the weavers could make them, and blue bonnets. I saw but a few young lads, though none as young as I. Even the smallest of them already had the beginnings of a beard while I was still as soft-cheeked as a girl.

And then the Keppoch himself came out of the house to greet us. He looked splendid, his fine red-and-black plaid fastened round his waist with a leather belt and over it a tartan short coat. From the belt hung his sword, dirk, and pistol, while a horn of gunpowder dangled from the sash that was flung over his shoulder. He took off his blue velvet bonnet to reveal a mane of snowy white hair, and when he waved his bonnet in the air, a cheer went up.

I called out loudest of all.

"Welcome, my brave lads," he announced in a hearty voice. "Ye've answered yer chieftain's call and the honor of that will shine bright on ye and yer sons for years to come." He put a hand out to a young man of some twenty years near him, who had a new beard like a clipped hedge. "My son Angus Ban and I offer ye welcome three times over."

Angus grinned and nodded at us. Even from the back of the tangle of men, I could see he hadn't his father's striking looks, for he was plain-faced, with deep pocks on his cheeks that spoke of some childhood sickness. But nevertheless he stood tall and proud in his black-and-red plaid and I soon forgot that he was a homely man.

Just then some of the Keppoch's womenfolk appeared from the house, offering cups of whiskey to drink a toast, and offering us sprigs of heather for our bonnets that would mark us as MacDonald men. The women were dressed in fine green gowns with gold trimmings and white roses pinned to the front. One of them was huge with child. She was quite young and I wondered whose wife she was.

Close by, a half dozen freshly slaughtered bullocks were roasting on spits over enormous bonfires. The smell of it filled my nostrils. My stomach began to grumble, like a spring torrent running down a hillside, for I hadn't eaten more than a handful of oats since morning, being so excited to be on the march.

"Here, laddie," Granda told me as the Keppoch made the toast, "To the King Over the Water." I took a sip of the whiskey. It nearly knocked me over, the taste bitter and sweet at once, and the sharpness like a second breath in my mouth. I coughed and coughed until I could catch my own breath again.

Granda laughed. "The Keppoch's whiskey is better than our poor stuff. Never mind. Ye'll get used to it once yer a man."

It was long past my dinnertime, though of course the summer sun was still high. The night birds, though, had just begun making passes across the sky.

Soon we were all settled on the grass, enjoying platters of meat and sweet ale. I had found a place near my father, though I was careful not to speak to him. Granda joined me, but he was quiet, too, I guessed for much the same reasons.

Da looked well at ease among the men, though I couldn't forget his sharp words with Granda about doing his duty. Yet he seemed to be enjoying himself here. It made me wonder.

Then the Keppoch and his son walked amongst us, congratulating each man on his loyalty and on the state of his weaponry. The Keppoch was our laird, and his son would be after him, therefore they were far above us in station. Yet here they were, speaking with all of us as if we were equals.

"Eat heartily, lads," the Keppoch boomed with a wide grin. "Ye'll no feast like this again till we set the rightful king on his throne." He lofted his tankard over his head. "To the King Over the Water!" It was the second time we had had that toast.

"And to his son, the bonnie prince!" Angus Ban added.

"The king!"

"The prince!"

The men's voices rang across the valley, and mine along with them.

I am not ashamed to say I had three portions, for walking starves a man. After, there was laughing and singing, led by the laird's piper. He played loudly, his cheeks puffing like a bellows, as he walked around the encampment. The men were all seated in circles at each campfire, and as the piper neared them, they raised their voices in song. Of course I sang along with them. Ye would have thought the prince's victory already won.

My father alone didn't sing but sat staring into the flames of a campfire where he sat unmoving.

"Come, lad," Granda said to me, "let's give yer da a bit of cheering up." I think he'd been made bold by the beef and the whiskey and—to tell the truth—I had been, too. Besides, the crackling fire was making more remarks than Da. So we got up and went over to Da and sat down on either side of him.

The singing had quieted a bit by then, but the piper was still playing pibrochs and the men at their small fires were still laughing and occasionally humming along.

"Yer stinting on yer food, Alisdair," said Granda, pointing to the half-finished beef. "It will be a long march before we get as good. Is something ailing ye?"

It took Da some time to answer and I couldn't tell if that was because he was angry with us or didn't know himself why he was in such a black mood. But at last he said, "All this cheer seems a bit beforetimes. Does nobody see anything but a good romp ahead?"

Even three helpings of beef had not lost me my senses, and I knew better than to say anything in answer. But Granda plowed ahead, making a furrow where there should have been none.

"These men have come at the call of their chief, and we should have joy in that," said Granda. "It was that way in the '15, too."

"And well ye remember how that turned out," Da said. "Yer own best friend, Murdo, killed and nothing gained by it." He threw the last bit of whiskey in his cup at the flames and for a moment the fire flared up, sizzling loudly. "A German still sits on the throne of England and Scotland, son of the one ye wanted to overthrow, and it's thirty years later."

Granda was as silent as if Da had slapped him across the face. Then he answered, "Aye, men died. But we all die in time. I believe it's better to die in battle fighting for the rightful king than to live on, as I have, to a troublesome old age."

"Granda," I suddenly put in, "if ye had died in the '15, I wouldna have known ye."

He laughed, but Da didn't. He turned away from us to glare into the fire some more.

"These are good men and brave, here to fight for their king," Granda persisted. "Do ye deny it?"

"Good men, yes. Brave, yes," Da said quietly, speaking more to the fire than to us. "But why they are here may no be why ye are here, old man. Yer still seeking some sort of glory in war. But dinna forget that if these brave men hadna come, the Keppoch would have burned them out of their homes."

I think my jaw dropped then. I wanted to say something, anything. For surely my da was wrong about that. We men of Donald had come to fight for the prince because of courage alone, surely.

Granda looked grim. "And the Keppoch would be right to treat them so. We owe him our fighting arms in exchange for our cottages and land. There's no room for cravens in the Highlands."

Da glared. "I'm no arguing with that, old man. I know full well what we owe the laird. But these men of Glenroy, we're farmers and millers and farriers and barrel makers. We can go on a raid against the Campbells. But we are no soldiers. We havena been paid to drill and parade and prance about in a single line like the redcoats. We marched here to give our time as pledged, but it's as much out of fear for homes and families as out of honor. Mark me, the time will come when the men of Glenroy will go back to their farms, whichever way the winds of war blow."

"A diet of victories will keep them all marching," said Granda, "more than shillings or the lash. That's what the English soldiers fight for—nae us."

"Aye, but a Highlander willna fight on and on if he disna see the sense of it." Standing, Da gathered up his plaid and moved a few paces away from us, as if to be alone again with his own brooding thoughts.

Granda and I sat for a while by Da's fading fire. He put his hand on my arm. "Duncan, lad, dinna let yer da's grim mood fash ye." He shook his head. "Yer father's as bold a man as any. He'll fight right enough when it comes to that. But he's got into such a habit of worry through the years, he canna let off."

I knew that much was true. My father worried about the health of our cattle, the state of our crops; he worried about Mairi with her fancies and me with my fits. *Maybe it was better to be a soldier,* I thought, *and only have to worry about yerself and the man in the line guarding yer side.* Maybe it *was* better to die gloriously in battle than to live on in a small village, worrying about too much rain or too little.

We wrapped our plaids around us and settled down for the night. The smoldering embers of the cook fires took the edge from the chill air, and soon, weary from the day's long march, I took off my plaid, rolled myself in it, and sank into a deep sleep.

7 ❧ REDCOATS

he Keppoch's piper roused me from my slumber with a high-pitched skirl. The smell of fresh-baked bannocks got me to my feet. Many of the men around me had been similarly awoken. But Granda was still dozing, probably because of all the whiskey he had drunk.

I shook him awake.

He sat up abruptly, groping about for a weapon. "What's the alarm?" he demanded. "Are we under attack?"

"No!" I laughed out loud. "Unless German Georgie's men are fetching us breakfast."

For a moment he looked confused, then gave me a laugh back.

Our meal was rushed, for the Keppoch was determined we were to be off to Glenfinnan before the sun had cleared the hills. Glenfinnan—where the prince would meet us.

"He'll raise the Stuart standard there," the Keppoch said, his voice clear in the morning's bright air. "And we'll show him the loyalty of the Highlanders, my lads."

We cheered, a sound so loud, doves flew off their roosts with a great flapping of wings, which only made us cheer louder.

The Keppoch held up his hand. "Let us not be shamed by the McKinnons or by the MacGregors," he said. "If they reach Glenfinnan before us, they will take pride of place and say that the MacDonald men are as slow as pigs in a bog."

There was laughter all around then, but I turned to Granda, a bit puzzled. "Where is this Glenfinnan?"

"At the head of Loch Shiel," he told me, as if that made things clearer. Then he knelt and smoothed a place in the dirt to draw a map with his finger. "We are here, at the Keppoch's," he said, "at the foot of Glen Roy." Then he drew a long line to the left. "We walk this way, to the west, crossing the River Lochy." He drew a squiggle. "Then we turn south." The line dropped toward his knees. "Then west again along Loch Eil." He drew an eel-shape for the loch. I tried to envision it filled with dark, peaty water but my mind didn't stretch that far. "And here, where Loch Eil ends, is the tip of Loch Shiel." The thing he drew was an even longer eel. "And where they meet"—his forefinger stabbed into the dirt—"is Glenfinnan."

"Is it far?" I was thinking of his poor leg.

"A week, nae more," he said. "If we move quickly."

I gave him a hand up. "Then we better be started."

He nodded. "Aye, lad."

Da had come over to check on us and heard the last of this. "I didna know this was to be a race," he grumbled.

"It's always a race when there are redcoats at our front door," Granda said, and winked at me.

I winked back, a kind of promise between us that we would keep up with the others, whatever it cost us. Stay up with them till we'd both seen the prince, and I had touched his hand.

There were a dozen pipers in our band and they set the pace as we marched westward. The Keppoch's womenfolk cheered and waved and some of them even blew kisses as we marched past. Granda chortled as if all the kisses were meant for him and waved back, but I stared straight ahead, trying to look older than my thirteen years. *I am a man among men,* I reminded myself firmly.

"Come on, Granda," I muttered to him. It was important not to fall behind at the start.

The Keppoch was out in front, riding on a glorious grey gelding. The braw, muscular chosen men who made up his personal guard walked beside him. Following close behind were the piper and the clan bard, whose job it was to turn the chief's brave deeds into song. The Keppoch's bonnet sat surely atop his white hair, sword and musket were shoved in his belt, knife in his stocking top; he looked the picture of a Highland chief. And though my best plaid was old and worn beside his, the Keppoch's grand bearing made me hold my own head higher. The MacDonalds were on the march.

Away to the south, beyond the Leanachan Forest, I could see the mountains rising up, the tallest with a cap of sparkling snow.

"Ben Nevis, lad," Granda told me, pointing at the snowcapped mountain. "Now ye've seen the biggest and the best Scotland has to offer."

"Och, Granda, I thought the MacDonalds were the biggest and the best."

Next to me, Jock, who worked on my uncle's farm, laughed. Then he slapped me on the back. "Good one, lad."

I beamed. Jock was no more than a humblie, like Granda and me. But his praise was worth a fortune. I grinned at him. Indeed, I grinned at the whole column of marching men. Here I was, far from home, seeing endless forests and mountains that nearly touched the sky. I was fairly bursting with pride. *What could be better,* I thought, *than marching with the men of my own name?* In the front or at the rear, I was a true MacDonald, the prince's man. I had the wind in my hair, the call of ravens from the trees, a belly full of bannocks, and a dirk in my belt.

At the start of the second day, though, things began to change. The Keppoch suddenly signaled his pipers to be silent. The word was passed back—no laughing, no singing, no talking.

"Granda," I whispered, "what's happening?"

He whispered back, "The Keppoch's scouts must have spotted something."

"What?" I asked quietly. "I thought we were still in MacDonald country."

A man in front of us turned around and put a finger to his lips, hissing a caution.

Then suddenly, beyond a small hill where the Keppoch and his bodyguards, the *luchd-tagh'*, had already passed out of sight, there came a loud crack, as if a tree had snapped in two.

Then more cracks—clearly shots from muskets—followed in quick succession. My heart began to beat so loudly, I felt it might leap from my breast. I tried to calm myself, fearful of a fit, but my heart kept up its awful pounding.

Quietly, all our men drew their weapons, as word quickly passed back, even to us humblies in the rear, *"Saighdearan dearg."* Redcoat soldiers. Government troops.

I drew my own blade, all at once aware of how small it was, how useless it would be against musket or sword. Yet I was swept up at the same moment by a hot passion. No longer worried about falling ill, I was a fighting man. We were on the high, solid ground Granda had spoken of. The wind was at our backs.

"MacDonald!" I whispered fervently, holding the dirk before me like a prayer.

The men in front of us began running and I followed, hurrying to catch up to the Keppoch, fearful that he might have fallen into an ambush. All those feet pounding on the ground made a rumble as great as any Highland waterfall and the rumble penetrated up through my *cuarans*, my shoes, all the way to my scalp. I felt strangely elated, as if I were running on air and not earth.

Cresting the hill, we were greeted by a great Highland cry, "MacDonald! MacDonald!" that bounced back and forth between the heathery hills.

Down below, we could see the Keppoch and his guards, less than a dozen in all. To my surprise they were rounding up at least two score of redcoats who had already tossed aside their muskets and had their arms raised in surrender. Two men lay dead, their red coats oozing dark blood that puddled around them. For a moment, I looked away. I'd never seen a man dead on the ground before.

And then I looked back, thinking: *A dozen against forty! That is how Highlanders fight!* I waved my dirk in the air and cried out, "MacDonald! MacDonald!" The men around me took up the call.

The Keppoch rode up to us, waving his pistol above his head. A thin ribbon of smoke still trailed from the barrel. His bonnet had fallen off and his white hair sprang about his head like a halo. He looked like a vengeful angel.

"They thought the dozen of us were an army," he said, laughing. "We've won our first victory, my boys, and we've barely left home!"

Then there was a wild cheer and the Keppoch's name was chanted like a war cry.

"Keppoch! Keppoch! Keppoch!"

And then the men cried out our MacDonald battle cry: "For God and St. Andrew!"

I sang along with the rest, my thudding heart keeping time to the shouts. *Courage,* I thought, *is a wonderful thing.*

By the time we swarmed down the hillside, rushing through the browning bracken, the English soldiers had all been disarmed and were cowering together, like sheep before wolves. Whenever a Highlander got close, the redcoats shrank back. You'd have thought they were surrounded by ravenous beasts instead of men like themselves.

"What are they so afraid of?" I asked Granda, who had come limping and panting down the hill after the rest of us.

He gave me a gap-toothed grin, though when he spoke he did it haltingly, as if the run had exhausted him. "They think . . . we Highlanders . . . are savages, capable of . . . anything. Even of eating them . . . if we've a mind to."

I laughed. "Maybe we are." Then I took a good long look at the redcoats. I had never actually seen an Englishman before, and was surprised that they were so clean shaven, which made them look like tall women. Their red coats seemed a lot cleaner than our plaids, with brightly polished buttons. Suddenly I wanted one of those buttons to give to Mairi to string around her neck.

"I'm going to talk to one," I said.

"To a redcoat?" He put a hand to his beard and scratched.

"Aye."

"Happy eating then," he said, and sat down on the ground.

When I got to the little band of soldiers, I saw that one was a lad, not that much older than me. He had cheeks as pink as roses. I opened my mouth to speak to him but nothing came out. Then I noticed that one of his buttons hung loose on his coat. I leaned forward, grabbed it, and pulled it off. Then, clutching it in my closed fist, I ran back to Granda, who was still sitting on the ground.

"Look!" I said, opening my hand to him.

"That's quite a prize," he said. "For yer sweetheart?" Though he knew I had none. His eyes twinkled and I could see he was proud of me.

"For Mairi," I said as I slipped the button through my plaid's pin to keep it safe.

"Aye, she'll like it. Probably think it's from her faerie prince, though." He shook his head.

There was a strange grumble about us, and I could hear some of our men complaining.

"We dinna need to march them with us," said redheaded Jock. He meant the soldiers. "They'll just slow us down."

"Aye," said another. "Let's just knock their heads in now."

And suddenly there was a rumble of calls for the redcoats to be put to the sword.

Stepping over to a large grey rock, the Keppoch climbed up on it till he towered over us all. He held up his hand for silence and, in an instant, we were all still.

"These redcoats will make a fine present for the bonnie prince," he declared. "I dinna want his gift spoiled by any of ye!"

This brought a roar of laughter from all of us, and then another cheer, but the English soldiers looked puzzled and unsettled, for they couldn't understand a word of our Gaelic speech.

"Go on, lad," Granda urged. He struggled to his feet. "Tell them what the Keppoch said." He knew Ma had taught me to speak the English tongue as it was spoken in the Lowlands. Her father had insisted she and her brothers learn it so they could never be swindled by a Lowlander.

I went back close to the redcoats again and said to one of them in English, "Dinna worry. We're no going to eat ye. Yet."

He was a fair-haired man with cold blue eyes, and a dirty bandage on his right arm. He seemed as startled to hear the words from my lips as he would have been if a dog had just spoken them. Then he pulled himself up stiffly, his eyes going even colder.

"Worry about yourself, youngster," he said. "Worry about what will happen to you when King George catches up with you." His accent was strange to me, though I understood his words well enough.

I was aware that Granda was watching me and suddenly I knew how to answer. "German George is no my king," I said boldly. "And he should start packing his bags now. It's a long road back to Germany."

At least I thought it was a long way. I had no idea where Germany lay. It hadn't been on Granda's dirt map.

The Englishman didn't reply to me. Instead he turned his back and began talking to his comrades in a low murmur.

"Come away," Da said, walking over and taking me by the arm. "Dinna shame me by blowing yerself up like a bladder. Yer granda has been filling ye with false ideas about war. I hope this is the last ye see of those redcoats and hope, too, that this war is quickly done."

8 ❧ GLENFINNAN

It took us another five days to reach Glen-finnan, through two days of sunshine and two of rain that fell as thick and hard as arrows. We marched in two columns, three abreast, the prisoners in the middle herded along like cattle.

"Och, why carry them along?" called out Uncle Dougal to the Keppoch when he came to inspect how the redcoats were doing. "Why no just kill them all and be done with it?"

The Keppoch shook his head. "Because we're no savages," he said, raising his voice so we could all hear, "nae matter what the English think. And I willna have these men mocked or mistreated."

In fact, he had them fed as well as us, which by this time was little enough. It had been days since the beef feast at the Keppoch's house and all our stomachs had shrunk to the size of dried peas. Feeding three hundred men on a couple of deer and a bevy of quails was hard enough, though Granda had given me his wee share, saying, "I have no the belly for this. I prefer porridge myself."

We passed by small huddles of villages along the loch, and large farms, where cattle and sheep grazed side by side in green fields. And though the farmers waved as we went by, and many even joined us in our march, they were all sparing with their food. We were too many for any one farm to feed and the Keppoch wouldn't let us just take a bullock for a roasting.

• • •

By the fifth day, walking from dawn to dusk, my legs were as soft and wobbly as curds of cream. Even some of the men looked grim and there was much grumbling.

"Are we still in Scotland?" I asked Granda. "Surely we've walked far enough to have reached London by now."

Granda laughed though I could see he was more tired than I. "The world's a good sight bigger than ye think, Duncan. There's room enough for a man to walk and walk and still find himself nae place at all."

"Nae place at all? I hope my feet are no bruised for nothing."

"Glenfinnan is close by," Granda assured me. "Just past yon hill." He pointed ahead. "I was there once as a boy."

There were doves—*cushie doos*—cooing in the trees, and a blank blue sky above us. The day seemed fair and promising. A small wind riffled the dark waters of Loch Eil, turning over little white-capped waves. It was hard to believe that all this marching was to end in war.

Suddenly our whole column came to a halt.

"What's going on?" Granda asked, though he seemed relieved to have stopped.

"Maybe another ambush," said Jock, speaking eagerly, as if such a thing would be welcome.

I stood on tiptoe trying to get a glimpse of what was happening to delay us, but there were too many men in the way.

Just then the white-maned Keppoch stood bolt upright in his stirrups and *that* we could all see.

"Even the Keppoch's stopped," I told Granda. Then I added, "Wait!"

A small bit of sound came threading back toward us.

"Listen," I said.

It resolved itself into the unmistakable skirl of pipes.

"I know that pibroch," said one of the men standing near us, a narrow-faced smith with forearms as big as small trees. "It's Lochiel's pipers. The Camerons of Lochiel are ahead of us. They are at Glenfinnan already."

Jock made a fist and shook it at the soldiers. "I knew it! I knew the British prisoners would slow us down and let Lochiel get there first."

"Pipers," the Keppoch yelled, still standing up in his stirrups, but turning his body halfway around to look at them, "give us a jig so we can join the dance!"

Our pipers filled their bags with air and started a low drone, like the buzzing of angry bees, drowning out the doves and the sound of our own cheers. The piping rose in pitch, then flowered into a warlike march that set us on our way, arms swinging, heads held high, as if this were the first hour of our journey, instead of the last.

We passed down a narrow glen lying between high craggy mountains and emerged into Glenfinnan, where the sun flashed off the surface of Loch Shiel like a shimmer of silver coins. The loch was a great, long finger of water pointing westward toward the sea, with green hills rearing up on both sides dotted with prosperous farms. The summer's wheat was golden in the fields.

Some boats had been dragged up onto the shore, where they'd been turned over, to keep any rain out of them. Men posted on the hilltops as lookouts waved and yelled when they saw us, and we shouted back cheerily.

Only the prisoners, huddled nervously together, took no part in the celebration.

To the north, rank upon rank of Camerons were marching down the hillside to form up in a great colorful mass along the shore. I thought they were more than twice our number, six or seven hundred at a guess. Beyond them, on the higher ground that overlooked the loch, another tartan-clad band of three hundred was assembled outside a small, stone chapel. I supposed that was where the prince would be, though I couldn't pick him out from the crowd.

The number of men overwhelmed me. We were a vast army of kilted Highlanders covering the hills. I saw the cold-eyed Englishman gape at the sight and that made me smile.

"Granda," I said, "is he here? Is the prince here?"

"Yer eyes are better than mine, Duncan," he answered. "Ye'll have to tell me."

Once all the clansmen had formed a rough crescent in front of the chapel, the Keppoch and his chief attendants joined those at the chapel door. As they arrived, the raucous cries stilled to a babble, the babble to a whisper, the whisper became a hush.

Once again I could hear birdsong, though this time the singers were gulls, white and wheeling over the loch, calling out in raucous voices.

Granda and I were stuck in the middle of a boil of men. How I wished I could run right up to the prince and present myself. Give him my hand. Maybe even beg him to let me stay and fight for his throne. But I knew that would only get Da in trouble, and me in worse. So I stayed where I was.

"What happens now?" I whispered to Granda.

The smith was the one who answered, his voice as quiet as mine. "We wait for the raising of the standard, lad." Then, seeing that I looked puzzled, added, "The king's banner."

"Aye," Granda added. "And it will be glorious to see King James' banner fly over Scotland once more."

"Wheesht . . ." cried another man, a small man with a beard down almost to his belly, "look who comes."

On my tiptoes again, I looked. "That's no the bonnie prince." In fact it was a man so ancient, so weak in the legs, he needed an attendant on each side to support him.

Granda smiled. "That's Duke William of Atholl, by tradition the royal standard-bearer."

"But Granda," I said, meaning to keep my voice small though it boomed out louder than I expected, "he's older than yerself."

"He was with us in the '15," Granda said, his finger to my lips to hush me. "A braw fighting man in his day."

"But where's the prince?"

"He's somewhere," Granda said. "They wouldna raise the standard without him. Duncan, lad, can ye see him now?"

I looked around again, but Prince Charlie still was nowhere in sight. Shaking my head, I turned back to watch old Atholl trying to unfurl the banner. It took him two tugs to get it loose and I was afraid he was going to fall over and go rolling down into the loch before it was freed. But at the second try, the banner whipped out into the breeze with a loud snap. It was red with a white square in the center surrounded by a thick blue border.

With a great cheer, the whole Highland host tossed our bonnets high into the air so that they looked like flocks of blue birds startled out of their nests.

"Long live King James!" we cried as the bonnets rained down among us. My voice was as loud as anyone's.

"And Prince Charlie!"

"Down with England. Down with the Union with England!"

When the shouting had faded away, Duke William unrolled a document and began to read from it. As it was in Scots-English, it meant nothing to most of the men, who spoke only Gaelic. Even I had trouble understanding, for his voice was so faint and the words were hardly simple. Besides, another brisk breeze—nearly a gale—had suddenly blown up off the loch, making it even harder to hear.

What he read seemed to be a letter from King James appointing his son as Regent of Scotland in his place until he could come over in person. The letter listed the king's various grievances, spoke of the justice of his cause, and went on so long, I—and everyone else—stopped listening. In fact, I spent much of the time looking around, trying to spot the prince, aching for a sight of him.

By the time Duke William came to a close, there were sighs and grumbles in place of cheers, as if all the men were as tired of the delay as I.

Standing by me, Jock put it best. "All talk, no action." And the men around us took up his complaint, sending it forward.

But then the bonnie prince stepped out from the huddle of men. All at once everything changed, as if the sun had suddenly burst through grey clouds. An excited buzz rippled through the Highland host.

"The prince!" Granda whispered.

But I already knew. He could have been no one else. Perhaps twenty years old, he was dressed in a dun-colored coat, with scarlet laces through his waistcoat, and a yellow bob on his bonnet. He held himself proudly, his head high, and in that moment I knew he was a man I would gladly follow into war.

The wind died as suddenly as it had begun, and the prince began to speak in the Lowlander's Scots-English. Although his voice was stronger than Atholl's, there was something queer in his accent.

Poor prince, I thought, *to have lived all his life among foreigners.*

"Duncan, tell us what he's saying," Granda urged.

"Aye, tell us," said Da, giving me a prod.

I did the best I could and from the buzz around me I could tell that others were doing the same favor for their own comrades.

"He says he's sure of our loyalty—and our courage," I translated. But immediately after that I became confused. As soon as I had started speaking, I missed the prince's next words and so quickly lost the thread of what he was saying.

"Er . . . his cause is righteous . . ." I stumbled on, sometimes just making things up when I missed the prince's meaning, sometimes guessing at what he'd just said. "And he says in the end . . . we'll all be . . . happy," I finished.

I was glad the speech was over, for the effort of concentrating had started a dull ache behind my eyes and my mouth was going dry. I worried that I might have a fit right there, right in front of the prince.

The prince waved, turning right and left to face all of his army. Then he waved, looking right at me. That single wave, that look, raised my spirits once more. And when the men let out another whoop and tossed their bonnets up so high, they filled the air like a vast blue cloud, I sent my bonnet flying up with the rest.

Had I gotten the speech right? Had he really promised to make us happy? Could his coming really mean an end to our failing crops, to our hunger, to the sicknesses that beset us? If so, this was surely the most wonderful day that Scotland had ever known.

9 ꝺ NIGHT

As usual, we set up camp in the open with only the sky to cover our heads and our plaids to keep us warm. But this night I fancied the stars were burning a wee bit brighter overhead. The air was clean, crisp, cool. Breathing it in was like drinking from a mountain stream.

The prince had seen to it that our prisoners were lodged in a byre where they were well guarded, though their officers were put up in a nearby cottage.

"I suppose it's because they're English and too soft to sleep in the open air," I said as I stared up at the stars.

For once Da had set himself down by my side, perhaps because he knew that Granda and I would be going home the next day. After all, we had seen the prince and that was all Da had promised.

Shaking his head, Da said, "Nae, lad, the prince wants to demonstrate his nobility by treating his enemies better than his own men."

On my other side, Granda chortled. "Yer da's putting a sour face on it as usual. But I think it's a fine ploy. If the prince's enemies know how kindly he treats his prisoners, they'll be better minded to surrender instead of fighting."

Sitting in front of us, Jock would have none of that. He banged his right fist into the cup of his left hand, declaring, "Better he should stake them out on the hillside and give the clans the byre."

All around us men grunted in agreement.

"We Highlanders who came out for him deserve better," Uncle Dougal added.

"Aye," John the Miller said. "Ye dinna see the Campbells here."

The MacDonalds all laughed, a rolling sound like distant thunder.

"Ye dinna see the bloody Campbells anywhere," someone called.

Granda patted my hand. "Not all the clans have declared for the prince yet, lad. But they will. They will. Even the bloody Campbells. Victory brings all rabbits out of their holes."

Just then we heard a rumbling noise and, turning, saw that some barrels were being rolled out from the chapel, where the prince evidently kept his stores.

"French brandy!" somebody called, and the two words passed through our company with surprising speed.

"There's nobility and *nobility*!" declared Jock, leaping to his feet. "But drink is the noblest gift of all."

The rest of us soon followed and we lined up in front of the barrels with our drinking cups held up, and a dram was poured out for every man.

When we returned to our campsite, Uncle Dougal raised his cup high. "To the Prince Across the Water!"

First all the MacDonalds, and then the rest of the men picked up the toast.

"To the Prince Across the Water!"

The sound of a thousand men or more rolled through the night air like a spring torrent down the hillside. It echoed in my bones.

Da allowed me a few sips. "Nae more, laddie. Yer too young for the whole cup." *And too weak,* his eyes said.

The brandy burned my throat like hot pitch, even more than the laird's whiskey had, and I coughed and coughed until Granda clapped me on the back. I was immediately light-headed and Da looked at me, shaking his head.

"Better to keep warm this way than in any byre," said the smith. "Do ye no agree, laddie?"

I hadn't breath to answer him and simply nodded. It was true. Once I'd gotten the few sips of brandy down, they left a warm glow in my belly.

All too soon the men lined up for refills.

"None for ye, Duncan," Da said. "I'll take nae chance of bringing on one of yer fits here in the prince's sight."

"Och, get the lad a cupful. I'll drink it down for him," said Granda, but Da looked right through him.

So, I thought, *I'm right about what I read in his eyes.* But it did not cast me down because what I really felt was that the prince's presence was keeping me hale and hearty.

Da went off with some of the other men to test their skill with the dirk, each taking turns flinging their daggers at a target set on a tree trunk. They laughed at each *thunk* against the bole of the tree. But Granda and I were excluded from their company.

I didn't mind. It was enough for me to be just sitting on the grass beside Granda, watching and listening as the night went dark around us.

Nearby, a small wiry man with thinning sandy hair played on a pennywhistle. The tunes he played may have been of his own making, for I knew none of them. But they were sharp and bright and made me tap my toes.

By his side, the twins from our village were engaged in a noisy game of dice, with a circle of men around them calling out bets. The sums they mentioned were so large, I suddenly realized that no one was taking them seriously.

Two other men—MacDonalds from the badges on their bonnets but from a different glen than ours—sat on a tussock close by, cleaning their swords. As they ran their whetstones along the blades, they talked of their wives and children.

The casual laughter of the knife throwers, the man playing his own tunes, the dicers, the small talk of men cleaning their swords, all made me feel—strangely—at home. There was a kind of trust here between the men. Clan next to clan, linked by our love for the Stuart and our goal to put his father back upon the throne.

I noticed then that the prince had begun strolling among the men, moving with an easy air.

Can I do it? Can I speak to him? Can I touch his hand? I wondered. Then I shook my head. Surely that would be a breaking of the trust. But if he just came close enough . . .

"Granda," I said, pointing to the prince, "he seems like a shepherd walking through his flock at the end of the day."

"Aye," Granda replied, "and counting heads to make sure none of them has strayed." Then he nodded at a tall, handsome man walking by the prince's side. "That's Lochiel, leader of the Camerons. See, he wears the prince's favor, that gold brooch at his neck. I heard the prince has given all the clan leaders such a token, with a bit of his own hair curled in it. Even the Keppoch has one, decorated with a figure of a lion."

"Lochiel's speaking at the same time as the prince . . ." I said. "Is he translating for him?"

"Likely he is. Our bonnie boy disna speak the Gaelic, but he'll learn when he has time."

I was sure of it. On the road with his men, his Highlanders, the prince would learn. I stared hard at him, willing him to come closer, wishing that I had one of the charms Ma used to summon the cows in for milking. But then he turned and headed the other way, waving vaguely in my direction.

I leaped up. "MacDonald!" I cried. "MacDonald!" Around me the dicers and the knife throwers and the others quit what they were doing and called out as well. The prince waved again, hesitated a moment, even smiled, but then moved on.

For a moment, disappointment washed over me and I almost drowned in it. But I realized suddenly that it mattered little if the prince actually *touched* me. I was already close enough to him for any of his magic to work. And indeed, I had never felt so well, so *whole*, in all my life.

"I could stay here forever," I told Granda. "Here with the prince, with the men."

He looked at me sharply, then closed his eyes as if suddenly weary.

"Granda, are ye all right?"

He opened his eyes and for the first time I was aware how faded they were, like the grey of weathered stone. "Aye, lad, I know the feeling. It comes before any battle, when the men are all around ye, with the singing and the drinking and the small games. When ye sit shoulder to shoulder at the campfire and talk of the things ye know—home and hearth and the working of the earth. That's when the important things sit on yer shoulders and hold ye close. Family, clan, tradition. Ye must hold faith with all three. It's bad luck to break with any of them."

"Yes. Yes," I said. I understood what he meant. I really did.

He shivered a bit as if with the cold, though it was a warm night and not a bit of wind. "It's a feeling of companionship, of being a tight weave with the other men."

I nodded without speaking.

"But soon enough there's the cries on the field and yer friends lying dead at yer feet. And the blood." He trembled all over. "The blood."

I was stunned. This didn't sound like Granda. "But, what about the glory? The honor?"

He looked up at me, and once more his voice changed. "Och, aye, the glory and honor. That's what it's about, of course. That's what it's *really* about." But his voice seemed empty, deflated.

Still, I kept at him. "Can we go with the clan? At least till the first battle? Just a few days, Granda. Da will listen if you put it that way. Not all the way to London, but a few more days." I was begging now, like a bairn at bedtime.

"Do ye care so little for yer own home glen?" Granda asked.

"Och, ye know . . ." I lowered my head. "There's nothing much at home but hard work, rainy springs, and cold winters."

Granda laughed, his head back, as if I had made a real joke. "Yer describing the whole of Scotland, lad." He took a long breath. "But ye should consider . . ." He stopped, as if trying to think what to say next. Then his face lit up. "Did I ever tell ye the story of the giants of Loch Shiel?"

"Nae; never," I answered, puzzled. *Why should he be telling me a story now?*

"Well," he said, "give the fire a wee poke and I'll begin."

I took a stick and stirred up our campfire till sparks flew up like bright birds into the dark. Granda's stories were always entertaining, but I wanted him to give me an answer, not a tale.

"Granda, about my going along with the men . . ."

"Sit still!" he said, as if I were a fidgeting child.

Everyone else was settling down around us. The dicers and knife throwers had quit, wrapping themselves in their plaids and lying down by their fires. The men sharpening their weapons were done and the swords put away. Only the man with the pennywhistle still played on. Its thin, bright sound accompanied Granda's story all the way to the end.

"When we came marching up this glen," Granda said, "ye surely saw there were farms, pastures, crops, and sheep."

I nodded.

"Well, it wasna always so. Once the land about this loch was filled with rocks so big, three grown men could scarcely shift one, working all together. It was a hard life for the people who lived here, as hard as the stones."

I settled into the story as comfortably as into a snug blanket. Granda's tales did that, sucked a person right out of whatever else he was doing, whatever else he wanted to know. Wrapped around him completely.

Granda went on. "Then one day the people of the village asked the old storyteller who lived on the hillside if they wouldna be better off going to live somewhere else."

"That's the right idea," I chimed in, thinking of our poor farm.

"Well, the storyteller told him there was nae trouble so bad it couldna be mended. 'Just give me a week,' he said, which they did. So, that very day he went to one of the neighboring mountains where two quarreling giants lived. Those giants squabbled all the time about which of them was the strongest."

"It sounds like the MacDonalds and the Campbells."

Granda grinned. "Very much like. Well, the old storyteller— sly as a fox, he was—told the giants that it was time to settle their quarrel once and for all. He invited them down to the loch, where each was told to pick up one of the great rocks and throw it as far as he could. The one who threw farthest would be the stronger."

"Is it a trick?" I asked eagerly, for I knew Granda loved tales of trickery.

"Wheesht! Let me get on with it."

I shut my mouth.

"Well, each of the giants picked up the biggest rock he could find and hurled it so far, it disappeared behind the hills. 'My stone went the furthest,' said one giant. 'Nae, mine did,' claimed the other. They turned to the old man to settle the matter. He rubbed his chin, saying, 'It looks to me like ye each threw the same. Ye'll have to try again.' "

Granda paused for a swallow of brandy then continued. "At the old man's urging, they threw again, and again he told them the same. 'I canna choose a winner.' Well, they hurled rock after rock over the hills until they were both so tired, they crawled back to their caves to sleep a hundred years. But by this time, of course, the whole of the land around Loch Shiel had been cleared. The people hurried to plow the rich ground and forever after they were blessed with large harvests."

I laughed and laughed at the old man's cleverness. "We need those giants in our own glen," I said. "There's enough rocks there for a hundred giants to throw about."

"That's the point, lad. There's enough work at home for a hundred *men* there," Granda said. "And ye, my lad, are one of them. Yer da and ma are right about that. Yer needed at home. As yer da is needed here." At that his story was over and he wrapped himself in his plaid, lay down, and promptly went to sleep.

10 ❧ PRINCE'S TOUCH

All around me, as the last light faded from the sky, the rest of the men curled up on the ground and began to snore. I seemed to be the only one of the Glen Roy MacDonalds who found it hard to sleep, probably because I had drunk only a few sips of the brandy.

Bedding down amid the heather was nothing new to me. I had done it many times before when we'd gone off to hunt hares and grouse for the pot. But no matter how much I shifted about, I couldn't find a comfortable spot. Besides, my mind was a-boil with thoughts about the prince and his promise, about the coming war, and about Granda's tale of the giants and the fact that even *he* now thought I was needed at home.

Or maybe Granda is just afraid to travel home by himself. I remembered the strange look on his face and how hard the last day had been, how much he had limped along. Maybe I wasn't so much needed at home as needed by his side.

At last, I realized that I was never going to fall asleep with my mind galloping like a runaway horse, so I got up and picked my way around the sleeping men. The snores arising from that hillside were monumental. Giants could hardly have made as much noise.

I decided that if I could get to the top of the hill and back, a brisk enough walk, I might tire myself out enough to sleep. So off I went at a good clip, a light wind burnishing my cheeks.

The hill was rocky—no giants had helped here—but the air was so fresh and clear, I drew in great draughts at each step. Above me the sky was a black bowl studded with stars that were reflected in the dark waters of the loch below.

I was nearing the hilltop and thinking once again about Granda's tale when I saw a figure silhouetted against the starry sky. He was sitting on the ground and hunched over, with his back to me.

Putting a hand to my mouth, I rubbed my knuckles across my lips. The man who sat there was Prince Charlie himself, alone and looking out over the darkened waters of the loch. His shoulders were slumped and he was rubbing his palms on the knees of his plaid britches. Even without seeing his face, I felt he was troubled.

Troubled? With all that glorious future ahead of him?

And then suddenly I thought I understood. The prince held the fate of these men, of a whole nation, in his hands. He had promised us a happier day, but he didn't look happy himself.

I remembered the first time my father had sent me alone to round up the cows and drive them into the byre for winter. I was so afraid I would lose count, that one of them would wander off and break her leg in a ditch, my stomach ached the whole time I did my work. When the task had been completed, I retched up my breakfast behind the byre and then had to go and lie down for an hour until my heart stopped racing.

How much harder it must be to be a herder of men. Granda wanted me to go home and take care of our wee family while Da was away. But the prince had so much more to worry about than that.

He sighed, never hearing me behind him.

And then I thought, *What has he to sigh about?* He was rich, after all. He didn't have to worry about the harvest or the rainfall. He didn't have to think about a daftie daughter or a son with the falling fits.

And, of course, that made *me* think about my fits and how wonderful it would be to be rid of them forever. If I left the prince's presence and went back home, would I still feel so well? Ma had said the prince could cure any illness with his touch. After all, he himself had promised us happiness. *If I feel well now,* I thought, *a touch from the prince will let me feel this way forever.* It would mean nothing to him, and everything to me and my family. So, step by step, I moved closer, the heather muffling my tread.

Just a wee touch.

I stretched out my arm, straining my fingers toward him. I was so close, I could brush his shoulder as lightly as a thistledown, and he wouldn't have to feel it. My whole vision narrowed down till all I could see was that one small patch of cloth, the part of his coat that covered his shoulder. It was now only a hairsbreadth away from my trembling fingertips.

I reached out a bit more and . . .

Without warning someone loomed out of the darkness and thumped me in the belly with the butt of his musket. I was thrown backward and thudded painfully to the ground.

"Back off there!" barked a voice. "Whatever mischief yer up to, we'll have none of it!"

The breath had been punched out of me and I was gasping so hard for air, I sounded as if I were choking. I looked up and saw a man in Lochiel's colors.

Behind him the prince stood, a quizzical look on his face. "I see no harm in him," he said mildly in his strange accent. "He's but a boy."

"King George would pay a pretty penny to see ye brought down, Highness," the guard warned. "And there's many in these parts poor enough to be tempted."

"Surely not," said the prince. "He's very small, even for this makeshift army. He was probably just curious."

I tried to sit up but my stomach hurt as though I had been stabbed. I slumped back, still panting.

"What's amiss here?" asked a new voice. From the corner of my eye I saw another man hurrying toward us, his hand clasping the basket hilt of his broadsword. He had a strange outline of light around him, from the campfires below.

"Do not worry yourself, gentle Lochiel," the prince assured him. "The guard you set to watch over me, he has just knocked down this boy."

"He was sneaking about," the soldier said gruffly. "He looked like he was up to nae good."

"I only wanted to . . ." I managed to say, but every word caused pain to lance through my stomach. I held up my hand, examining it for trembles.

The prince took a step toward me and extended a hand to help me up. I reached for it, my fingers trembling. *Just a touch,* I thought.

Then Lochiel moved between us, pushing my hand away.

"Come, Yer Highness," he said, "I've been going over the maps and I have some plans to discuss."

The prince drew back his hand. His right eyebrow raised in surprise. "Now? Do you not intend to sleep tonight at all?"

"We'll have all the time in the world for sleep if we dinna steal a march on General Cope and his men," said Lochiel.

The prince sighed, then spoke to the guard. "See the boy gets back to his people," he ordered. "It's the least you can do after treating him so brutally. If we had a hundred hundred more like him, young and strong and eager . . ."

"Dinna go," I tried to say. But I still had so little breath, the words came out as a feeble whisper and he did not hear me at all.

As soon as Lochiel and the prince had disappeared into the darkness, the soldier grabbed my arm and yanked me roughly to my feet. "Be off with ye, laddie," he commanded. "And dinna let me catch ye sneaking around again or it will go badly for ye."

I did not wait to find out what he meant but scrambled down the hillside to find Granda.

11 ❧ THE ROAD HOME

I must have made my way back all right, and fallen dead asleep, because when I woke in the morning, my plaid was still belted about me, and the August sun full in my face. My stomach no longer ached from the guard's blow, but my head was hammering as if the giants of Loch Lochy had been throwing it about all night long.

Granda was shaking me. "Get up, laddie. The men are leaving."

And, indeed, all around the clans had begun to gather into their marching groups and the low rumbling, wheezing drones of the pipes were just beginning. They made my heart leap and I scrambled to my feet. Adjusting my plaid, I started toward the MacDonalds' banner.

Granda's hand on my shoulder stopped me. "We're for home, Duncan," he said. "Remember—we've a crop to bring in and mouths to feed."

I said a foul word.

Granda gave me such a look then, I shut my mouth. But inside, my anger roiled. And my sorrow. I shrugged off his hand. "I have to say good-bye to Da."

"Ye just want to beg him to let you stay," Granda said. "But he willna do it."

I knew that. But I couldn't let him go without trying.

I found him in a bubble of Glenroy men, and burst through. He was talking about where they were going next, on to Fassefern and

Moy, then on down to Edinburgh, which he said was back the way we had come. So, for a little bit, I had hope that Granda and I might go with them. But when Da and I were face-to-face, I didn't ask. I just held out my hand. He took it in his, and then we looked deep into each other's eyes, his the color of slate slicked with rain.

"I know ye'll work hard, Duncan," he said, "and bring in our crops, what there is of them. Kiss yer ma for me." Then he turned back to his duty and I to mine.

Granda and I set out at once, but an army takes longer to get on the move than two humblies. We soon left them far behind, even though Granda's lame leg slowed us some.

"It's a harder journey back," he warned me, "without the promise of spying the prince."

So I spilled it all out, how I'd almost talked to the prince and how he said a hundred hundred more like me would win him back his throne.

Granda loved that, and said I was a storyteller for sure. But after that, we had little more to say for miles. And Granda had been right. It was harder going home than coming. Now there was nothing new to see, for we'd already been past the rich farms along the loch and seen the spread of the land between the hills, the cows and sheep on the green pastures.

And I had no hope of the prince to lure me on. No hope that Da would let me go along to the war. We had no pipers playing to stir the heart. It was just one foot after the other and only our small farm at the end.

Luckily, near nightfall, we fell in with a family of tinkers—a husband, wife, and two wee ones, twins just walking. They were traveling across the country, selling their pots, needles, and trinkets from a horse-drawn cart.

We greeted them pleasantly, which many folk don't do, and they shared their food with us. In exchange, for we had neither coin nor scrip to purchase anything, Granda told them some of his tales. Tinkers are great collectors of such stories, which they use to cozen housewives to buy their wares.

We took turns riding in the cart and walking by its side, and so outpaced the army behind us.

When night truly fell, we were well along the loch. It was the kind of black night without moon or stars, for dark clouds hid everything and promised rain. We drew tightly together around a big campfire, the little ones sleeping curled up in their mother's arms. That was when we began speaking of the Rising and what the bonnie prince looked like.

"The prince is strong," I said. "Scotland will no find him wanting, whatever lies ahead."

The tinker and Granda nodded, and I added, "And the one they call 'gentle Lochiel' seems hardly gentle at all. He's a fighting man for sure."

"Ye see well, lad," said the tinker.

Granda told him, "There were thousands of men to watch the prince land and thousands more promised. Frenchmen, too, it's said. They'll all rise up at his bidding."

Suddenly, the tinker man said in a strange, soft voice, as if he were dreaming, "There's nae good to come of it."

"Wheesht," his wife cautioned. "These be two strong Jacobite gentlemen."

"What's that?" I asked, never having heard the word before.

"Jacobite," the tinker said, "is the name given to those who support King James Over the Water. From the Latin tongue, where he is called King Jacobus."

His wife added, "A tinker knows many tongues. It is part of our trade."

I smiled at her then for calling me a gentleman.

Shaking his head, the tinker repeated, "There's nae good to come of it. War makes thieves and peace hangs 'em." It was something Ma had said often enough.

But Granda held up his hands. "Peace, man, we dinna mean ye harm." At that moment the fire sent out crackling sparks as if it were warring with us.

"Nobody ever means harm," the tinker said, "but wars harm the helpless nonetheless." He picked up one of the sleeping twins and carried him to the cart.

"My man means nae offense," said the tinker woman.

"None taken," said Granda, and I nodded.

A thin shred of cloud suddenly uncovered what was left of the moon, and then I could see the mountains far south of the loch. They were a dark, brooding presence. I began to shiver, and not from the cold, either. The tinker's hard words had been like a sword to the heart.

A while later, after we'd traded some more tales, we all got ready for sleep. The children were both bedded down in the cart, bundled together, but as Granda and I lay down on the ground next to the tinker and his wife, a sudden whooping noise made me sit up again.

"What was that?" I gasped. "A wolf?" The stories had made me uneasy, as had the tinker man's strange look into the future.

Granda patted me on the shoulder. "Rest easy, Duncan. It was just an owl hooting."

The tinker added, "There's nae wolves left in the Highlands, laddie. I saw the last one killed with my own eyes. There's only the foxes left, who some call their children, and they're nae threat to the likes of us."

Strangely, as soon as he had mentioned foxes, we heard the yipping cries of one on a hunt. So, without more of a beginning, the tinker told us a tale of a vixen fox who loved a man and what came of it, both good and bad.

After that I slept well and without dreams.

A small rain had begun to fall as we parted company with the tinkers at the head of the loch. They were going south to Fort William and its market, and we were headed north and east to our glen. There was a redcoat garrison at the fort, according to Granda, but as the tinker man said, "The redcoats' coin is just as good as yers."

Looking grim, Granda answered, "Only if ye dinna count the Scottish blood on it."

The tinker shook his head. "There's nae coin that doesna come with blood on it, but it all spends the same." He embraced us both, as did his wife, which made me blush.

Then the cart moved off down the road, its wheels splashing up puddles. Granda and I were left to contemplate the long and lonely way home.

Now the rain came down slantwise, churning the loch behind us into a lumpy grey mass. I hunched my shoulders against the wet, knowing it would be little help. Soon I would be soaked clear through.

Granda limped by my side, as soaked as I. To loft our spirits, he started a conversation. "I expect the prince will be marching on Fort

William soon enough. Our tinker friends might even sell him a pot or two."

I couldn't help laughing out loud at the thought.

Granda gave me a steely look. "If the English garrison at Fort William have a dram of sense among them, they'll be long gone by now."

I bent to pick up a rain-slicked stone and flung it from me, listening for the sound of it landing in the yellow gorse along the roadside. "It's a grand army the prince has," I said. "Surely our men will easily rout the English."

"Aye, surely," Granda replied slowly, "though it's no a patch on the one we had in '15."

"Oh?" The army at Glenfinnan had looked big enough to me. And we had already captured redcoats. "Bigger than all that?"

Granda said, "Much bigger." Then he saw my face, creased with worry, and quickly added, "But more and more clans will flock to the prince's banner once they see which way the wind is blowing." He grinned.

"Other Jacobite gentlemen?" I said, grinning back.

"Aye, though some will come for other reasons."

"What 'other' reasons? Not just for the prince? Not just to get back the throne?" We were walking slowly now, but the hardest of the rain had passed by and if we were lucky, there'd be sunshine soon. Scotland was like that, rain and then rainbows.

"That's enough for some," Granda said, nodding. "And for others the possibility that Scotland could be free of England forever brings them out. Some hate only the English government and want us to have our own parliament in Scotland again, as we did before the traitors in Edinburgh sold it for English gold. They want to get back what was so wickedly taken."

I remembered stories Granda had told about the Lowlanders. He had never a good word for any Edinburgh folk. "Weasels and vermin," he called them.

"Well, Granda, I hope we get our share of that stolen gold," I said. "Ma would like it."

"If we do, it will be honestly won," replied Granda. "And there's nae doubt many a poor man will follow the prince in the hopes of getting such gold. But there's others that will come along just for the love of a good fight."

"Like Jock," I said.

Granda gave me a sidelong smirk. "Just like Jock. Especially if we MacDonalds have a chance to crack a few Campbell skulls along the way."

"Crack! Crack!" I agreed, my fist in the air.

And suddenly we were striding up the road again, a road lined on both sides with bracken thick enough to hide a dozen men, if not an army of Campbells. The thought of the two of us fighting the Campbells seemed to shorten the road. Indeed, we fairly flew the rest of the way home.

12 ❧ THE FARM

By the time we got back, we were ready to be there. And we were full of stories—about the march, about the Keppoch, about the capture of the redcoats, and especially about the prince. I had rehearsed in my mind how I would tell it all.

Each step through the glen was a homecoming. The rocky ledges, the gurgling River Roy, even the banks of prickly gorse along the roadway cried a welcome.

As we made the last turning into the village, Ewan's sister, redheaded Maggie, saw us as she was out scattering corn for the chickens.

"They're here! They're here!" she called out. "Duncan and his granda."

Before we knew it, the whole village had come stumbling out of their doors and crowded around us.

"Did ye see him? Did ye see the bonnie prince?" Maggie cried.

Puffing out my chest, I nodded. "Aye. Saw him and talked to him."

"You never . . ."

"I did. He said he'd like a hundred hundred more like me."

She gazed at me with a kind of awe and I could feel my cheeks redden as if I'd stood staring up at the sun all day. Suddenly, every word about the journey I'd rehearsed on the road home dropped away from me. I might as well have been a mute.

No one seemed to notice. A buzz went around the villagers. "The prince spoke, spoke to him . . . to a lad from our village!"

Ma pushed through the crowd. "Give way," she said, "give way and let me see my Duncan." She pushed past John the Miller's fat wife and Ewan's old granny. Then she grabbed me by the shoulders and gave me such a hug, the red on my cheeks began to burn.

I mumbled something then, and turned away, looking for Mairi in the press of folk. Finally, I found her, standing on her tippy-toes behind Mistress MacKinnon, the farrier's fair wife. Mairi was waving her hand at me to get my attention. "Duncan, here! Here!"

I went over and handed her the button I had taken from the soldier. "I won this for ye, Mairi." Which was not really the truth but all I could manage.

She looked at the button I'd put in her palm, folded her hand over it carefully, and put her hand up to her breast. Then she spun around and about, and when she stopped spinning, she gave me a quick kiss on the cheek. "For courage," she said, though I couldn't tell if she meant for the courage I had used in getting the button or courage yet to come.

"Hurrah!" my brother Andrew shouted, and the others took up his cry.

"Och—it was nothing," I protested, meaning it.

But Granda basked in the attention, grinning like a man who's stumbled on a crock of gold.

"Sit down! Sit down," he cried, "and we'll tell ye all."

So everyone sat down around him, right there on the ground in front of Uncle Dougal's cottage. Ewan's ma brought out a dram of whiskey, which Granda began sipping the moment it was put in his hand.

"I have drunk the Keppoch's whiskey and the prince's brandy,"

he said, licking his lips. "But none can beat the taste of our own."
And then he was off, giving them every detail of our journey.

Now and then he encouraged me to add my piece, saying,
"Duncan was there, and perhaps he saw more." But I didn't have his
joy of words, and besides, the way he told the tale was so much better than the way I had rehearsed it. So much better than it had really
been. I couldn't compete and so I didn't even try. I just shook my
head each time he asked and, after a while, he stopped asking.

Granda spoke of the great Highland host gathered at Glenfinnan,
making it sound like ten times the number we'd seen. "A hundred
thousand," he said, "cheek by cheek and arm by arm from one side
of Glenfinnan to the other." And he called the great roll call of the
clans who'd been there. "Och, ye should have seen them," he said,
"all the lairds of the Stuarts, and the Camerons, led by gentle Lochiel.
The MacLeods were there in a mighty number. Clanranald, too."

"And the MacDonalds!" called out the farrier's wife.

"Of course the MacDonalds, and didna the Keppoch look
grand, Duncan?"

I nodded.

He went on. "And above them all, the golden St. Andrews cross
on a blue field flying. The king's own banner."

Mairi clapped and sang out, "The prince!" I guessed she was
speaking of that faerie prince of hers and not the Stuart, but no one
else seemed to mind, shouting out with her, "The prince!"

Then Granda took little Sarah in his lap, and continued with the
tale. He told of my translating from Scots-English into Gaelic, and
how well I had done, never mentioning how I'd stumbled nor that
I'd made up things. Of course, he might not have known, and I was
not about to say.

Everyone turned toward me and this time Sarah led the clapping. I blushed again, but now it was with shame. If anyone could have told the difference, no one said.

After that, Granda described the prince's fine clothes in such detail, ye'd have thought he had been the one that did the dressing. And when he was done, he started the whole tale over again, as a fiddler does, repeating a favorite tune.

Our brief time of fame was soon over, though. As Ma said, "It's God that feeds the crows that neither till, harrow, nor sow." She meant that we had work waiting to be done on the farm, work that had piled up while we were gone. And that we were not crows, to fly away from such work.

Andrew complained, saying, "Och, Ma . . ." and she fetched him a clout on the head.

"I would think," she said to him, "that ye'd be glad to go back to work, since there will be so much less of it to do now that Duncan's home." He brightened at that.

So first he and Granda and I went to the byre, the barn where the cows were bedded. We had to prepare it for the winter, a filthy job.

Then the cows needed tending in their summer pastures—the shielings—high up in the hills. While we'd been gone, Ewan had watched our cows as well as his own, but nobody had been happy with the arrangement, especially Ewan.

So I got myself ready to go up to our shieling hut alone. We had four good milkers—Bessie, Cana, Rona, and Flora Ann—and I was to keep them safe, and see to their milking till summer's end and they came back down to the winter pastures and the byre.

The hut was one my great-grandfather had built, a little stone thing with room for a wee fire, a mattress, and a small table shoved against the back wall, but nothing more. Still, it was enough.

• • •

It took half the day walking to Ewan's shieling, two hills over from our own.

Ewan greeted me with a little shrug, hardly interested in any word of what had happened.

"Yer a liar," he said, when I tried to tell him about talking to the prince. "It's like one of yer granda's tales, or yer sister's daft stories, full of clouds and nae sky showing."

I wondered if he was still angry with me, for I had gone and he had not. When I said so, he turned his back on me.

"It's all true, ye know," I shouted at him. But he treated me as if I were havering, so I had to gather up our cows by myself and drive them over the two hills to our own shieling.

The first full day up there alone was strange after so much time surrounded by other folk. Cows are not much for conversation, though they're not bad as company. I spent a lot of time twisting grass ropes and thinking now and again about Ewan's sister, Maggie. I replayed my brief moment with the prince more often than I should have. I worried over Ewan's calling me a liar. And I moaned a bit in my mind about not being with Da and the men.

But otherwise I settled into the hills. I watched a golden eagle catching the hard wind in its wings. A flock of peewits flew in one day and were gone the next. I kept an eye on the hundreds of hares playing by their burrows, for holes that large could break a cow's leg.

A great stag and his harem of hinds crossed at dawn and at dusk every day and we greeted one another solemnly. *He is king here and I a lowly subject,* I thought. *But even a lowly subject can know a bit about the hills.*

• • •

Every few days Ma or Mairi or Granda would come up to lend me a hand with churning the milk into butter or wrapping it up to be made into cheese. But most of the time I was simply alone, with too much time to think.

Ma always worried when she had to be up in the shielings, thinking about all that was left at home to do, so she rarely visited. And it was a long, hard walk uphill and down for Granda after his march to see the prince. But Mairi loved it. She said she felt closer to her faerie folk than when she was up in the hills.

"The Folk are there," she would say, pointing to a wee puddle or a stream. "And there." Though I could see nothing but the water and the little ripples as the wind passed over.

Of course we didn't dare let Mairi come up to the shieling on her own. Too daft to care for the cows by herself, she'd go running after any butterfly or strange light she saw, leaving the cows unmilked. This time Ma had left her with me for a couple of days and I made sure to keep her close and give her plenty to do.

"The prince is watching," Mairi told me in confidence, and I knew from the faraway look in her eye that once again she did not mean Prince Charlie. "Soon he'll take me away from all this hard work." Her hand was on the butter churn as she spoke.

"And I suppose he'll give ye wings while he's at it," I said, and she hit my shoulder with her fist for saying so.

I suppose I deserved that for being so unkind, but for a moment I had wanted to shake some sense into her. After all, I had seen a real prince and here she was still havering on about the prince of faerie. But then, I reminded myself, Mairi believed every word of her own faerie tales, and if it brought her comfort, who was I to destroy her dream? "I'm sorry, Mairi."

"That's all right, Duncan." She stroked the spot where she had just hit me, as if trying to soothe away the hurt. "How are ye to know? Was Prince Charlie real to ye before ye saw him? Did ye believe in him before he spoke to ye?"

"Of course I did," I muttered, but she chose not to hear me.

"My prince told me once, when I was sleeping, that I'll soon go live in his palace, and have pretty winged maids to serve me." She began to rub at her fingers, which were rough and red from all the churning. "When I am in the Fair Country, my hands will turn soft and white. I'll wear a dress of the finest silk . . . " She smoothed down her homespun plaid skirt. "And I'll sleep in a huge bed with pillows and silk sheets. It will be like sleeping in warm snow."

"Warm snow? Hah!" I cried. "That's havers, Mairi. Who would want to sleep in warm snow?"

"I would," she said, her thin face wreathed in smiles.

"Well, we can hope for something better now without expecting the Fair Folk to help us," I told her, and I grabbed up her hands and held them tight. "There's a *real* prince in Scotland now. And he's going to bring health and wealth and happiness to our poor land."

"My prince is as real as yers," she said, pulling her hands away and hiding them behind her back. "Yers comes from across the water but mine comes from under it, where the Fair Folk dwell."

I stomped away from her to go and bring back the cows for milking. Honestly, she was such a daftie.

A day later, as we watched the great stag and his hinds come up over the hill and dawn, Mairi forgave me.

"Tell me again," she urged. "Tell me all about the prince. *Yer* prince." It was a peace offering of sorts but I was too tired to take it as offered. I had already told her the story of my meeting with Prince

Charlie many times. And while the story had gotten better with each telling, by now I was thoroughly tired of it.

"Mairi, I've said everything a hundred times already." I started to stand, but she put her hand on my arm and pulled me back. The sudden movement startled the stag and he stamped his feet and raced away, the females right behind him.

I was sorry to see him go, afraid he would never return, for a deer startled once may be gone forever. But Mairi only shrugged. "Ye'll see him again, just like yer prince."

I had to smile at her. It was hard to hold a bit of anger against her.

"Tell me, Duncan, please." The wind puzzled through her straw-colored hair. "Ye make the prince sound so wonderful," she said. "With his scarlet laces and the yellow bob on his bonnet. I wish I had seen that." She raised a hand to her hair as if straightening a bonnet of her own. "And when he spoke to ye, yer heart near bursting."

"Well, he didn't say all that much." I was suddenly embarrassed at having exaggerated my telling of it. "He only said he wished he had a hundred hundred other strong young men like me."

"A kind thing to say," said Mairi. "He must see truly indeed, to know the brave, strong heart in yer small body."

"I'm no so small!" I told her indignantly, my voice rising at the end.

Mairi lowered her eyes, and I turned and left her, going into the shieling house, where I poured new milk into the churn and worked at it all the morning, till sweat beaded my brow and rolled down my back.

After a bit, she came in to watch. Neither of us spoke a word.

Suddenly, we heard a haloo and went outside, where we saw several figures struggling up the hill, each carrying a basket. It was Granda and Ma and the little ones all waving at us.

"There's news!" Granda called. "Grand news!"

I stood and waited while they labored up the rest of the hill, red-faced and puffing, for this was one of the few cloudless autumn days, with a sun shining full down on us.

"News of Da?" I asked.

Granda sat down on my stool and wiped his forehead with the back of his sleeve. "I'm sure yer da's well enough."

Ma added, "More than well. He's probably been drinking and feasting for days."

Mairi was up now and bouncing on her heels. "Feasting for what?"

"The prince has taken Edinburgh!" Andrew and Sarah cried out together.

I let out a cheer, but Granda waved me to be quiet. He had caught his breath and was ready to tell the rest.

But first Andrew and Sarah had to be hushed. Only then did Granda continue. "Ye recall when we left them, they were off toward Edinburgh. Well, they got into the city with hardly any trouble at all, and made their way up to the castle itself."

"Is it a strong castle, Granda?" Mairi asked.

"It is a *very* strong castle, my lass," he said, "perched high up like an eagle on its rocky nest. Well our brave men knew that anyone trying to get in at the West Port gate, the nearest at hand, would be shot to pieces by the castle guns."

"So . . . " I said, eager to have him get on with it. "So . . . "

"So, it was just at dark, which can seem blacker in the midst of a battle than up here amid the hills, that Lochiel made a wise decision. And a lucky one, too. He brought his men away from the West

Port and to one of the lesser gates, the Netherbow. And just as the Camerons had concealed themselves, the gate was thrown open to let a coach get out and Lochiel and his men raced in."

"God on our side," Andrew and Sarah cried together.

Granda leaned back and grinned.

"The castle taken?" I whispered.

"Taken!" Granda said. "And all before the redcoats had eaten their evening meal."

I laughed at the thought of the redcoats fleeing, spilling bowls of porridge and cups of ale, as the Highlanders chased them out of the castle and along Edinburgh's twisty streets.

Granda added, "They proclaimed James the Eighth king at the market cross the next morning, and the prince entered the next day in triumph, so old Hamish told me, and he heard it from a messenger up the valley."

"The war's won then?" Mairi asked, wide-eyed. "Da can come home now?"

"It was but a single battle, child," said Ma.

"And it was over before ye could clap yer hands." Granda grinned, ruffling her yellow hair.

"I'll wager Da was in the thick of it." I swung my arms about, pretending to chop off English heads with a sword while guarding myself with my shield.

Andrew copied my every motion until he fell over, and waved his bare feet in the air, which made us all laugh. All except Ma.

"This is nae game." She clucked her tongue. She looked angry and frightened at the same time.

I turned to her. "Da will be fine, I know he will. If ye had seen him on the march, with the men, ye'd have faith in him."

"I have faith in yer da. It's the English guns I dinna trust."

"Now, Catriona," Granda said, "we silenced those guns at Edinburgh and we can do it elsewhere. Besides, yer frightening the little ones." Indeed, Sarah had gotten a wide-eyed look about her.

"Aye, what was I thinking," Ma said. "I've not come up here to call in the bogies, but to get both of ye to leave off yer work for a while. I've a nice dinner—cheese plus some honey to spread on fresh-baked barley bannocks. We'll make a right feast of it and drink a cup of fresh milk to Bonnie Prince Charlie's health. And to yer da's."

"Milk, pah!" said Granda, but he said it smiling.

We all crowded into the hut and Mairi and Sarah helped Ma take the food from the baskets and put it all out on the little table. I got a pail of milk from the shed and poured some carefully into each of the wooden mugs.

Then we gathered around the table and Ma was about to say the grace when Mairi clapped her hands together. "Oh, what a land this will be from now on! I wager the faerie folk willna be frightened to come out anymore. And yer prince and my prince will bring a long peace to us all."

Granda smiled at her fondly and raised his cup. "That's as good a grace as any, my lass. Here's to a long peace, indeed."

But Ma had the last word, as she often did. "There's a big difference, Granda, between a single battle and a war."

13 ❧ THE GLOAMING POOL

We sat eating bannocks for a long while, using the fact that our mouths were full to keep from talking. But at last we were done, and I feared that the talk would turn again to the war, with Ma and Granda taking different sides. All I wanted was for the celebration to continue. I tried to think how to put that into words.

That's when Mairi jumped up and, without a word, skipped out the door.

"Duncan, ye hurry after and keep an eye on her," Ma ordered me. "There's danger all around."

"Aye, ye know how flighty she is," said Granda.

I dropped a half-eaten bannock, licking the honey from my fingers as I dashed out after her. Once outside I saw that she'd stopped to wait for me.

"I knew Ma would make ye chase me and I didna want ye to have to run too far." Her face was lit with an impish grin.

"That's good of ye, I'm sure," I said as she took my still-sticky hand and pulled me after her.

We walked along the hills where the cows chewed contentedly on the remains of the summer grass. September can be a mean time of year, and October worse, but the cows seemed content enough.

Goodness knows there had been lean times the last few years, when I had often wished I could fill my belly as easily as they. But the prince had promised to put things aright, and I knew he was a man of his word, for wasn't he already winning our country back from the English?

"Where are ye taking me?" I asked, for we were already quite a ways from the shieling hut.

"Och, ye know where we're going," she replied, slapping my arm. "We're going to tell the Fair Folk the news that good times lie ahead for their people and ours."

She started down a small, rocky path; and I did, indeed, know all too well where it led.

"We're no going down to the Gloaming Pool. Ye know Ma says to stay away from there. There are slippery rocks and dangerous reeds and—"

"Wheesht!" Mairi said, wagging her finger at me. "I'm in nae danger. The prince is always looking out for me."

"Stay here!" I told her, not a plea but a command. The pool was a dangerous place. Last year one of our cows had gone down the path and broken its leg.

Mairi looked at me, her eyes suddenly moist. "Oh, Duncan, would ye no like to come away to the Fair Country, where it's always summer and they drink fresh dew from crystal cups and fly on the backs of swans?"

She was getting that faraway look again and I needed to humor her or she would get agitated and run off.

"I suppose."

Brightening, she took my hand again. "Good. When I go, I'll take ye with me."

"I dinna think so," I said firmly. "Somebody will have to stay here and do the work."

"Aye, I see that," she said, nodding soberly. "But dinna think I will ever forget ye, Duncan MacDonald, my own dear brother."

My fingers slid from her grasp and she darted off, laughing.

I ran after her and that made her laugh harder. "Mairi, ye know what Ma said!"

"Och, I'm going anyway and yer too slow to catch me," she teased.

Though I was stronger than she, with a longer stride, she seemed to fly along on her bare feet like a swooping swallow skimming over the grass. By the time I caught up with her, she was kneeling on the rocky ledge overlooking the pond, her skirts petaled around her.

Flopping down beside her, I laid a weary hand on her arm, like a bailiff making an arrest. I was breathing hard and the blood was pounding in my head. My fingers were tingling strangely, the way they sometimes do before a fit begins.

"There," she declared, pointing down.

The Gloaming Pool lay thirty feet below us, with lilies on the surface and a patch of hollow reeds at the far end. Sunlight glancing off the water made my eyes blur and I had to shake my head twice to clear them.

"Mairi, the Fair Folk dinna live there," I said. "There's only rocks and reed beds and a boggy bottom. Now come away before Ma gets upset." The tingling in my hands was worse now. I knew I had to get her away quickly.

She shrugged my hand off as I slumped onto my back, drawing in deep breaths to try to settle the throbbing in my temples.

"Yer wrong, Duncan. See the ripples they make in the pool sailing their wee boats back and forth." She jumped up.

"Och, that'll just be a trout under the water," I said, not looking but concentrating on trying to stop the ache in my head.

"There's nae fish in this pool, Duncan."

"Then it's the wind—or the midges."

Mairi spat on her finger and held it in the air. "There's nae wind." She set her hands on her hips. "And I canna see any midges."

"They're too small to see," I said, sitting up carefully. "But ye can still feel them when they bite!" I gave her a nip on the arm and she squealed and wriggled away.

"Och, yer a beast!" she cried, ripping up a clump of grass and flinging it at me.

But I was tiring of the game. Besides, I was suddenly sweating. The tips of my fingers had gone numb. *Oh, God,* I thought, *no here, no now.* Not when I had been sent to fetch Mairi back.

"The prince . . ." I must have said it aloud, meaning that the prince was supposed to have cured me.

Mairi grinned, turned, and started off down the hill, waving her arms over her head. "The prince!" she cried.

"No, Mairi!" I called after her and tried to stand. I was brought back to my knees as if an invisible hand had caught hold of me. A blinding light stabbed my eyes. My knees buckled under me and I toppled to the ground, choking in agony. I rolled onto my side, my arms and legs twitching uncontrollably. In my head was the buzz of a thousand tiny voices. My eyes rolled up in my head, and then there was nothing I could do but give way and fall into the darkness.

14 ⁊ LOST

When the darkness cleared, there were lights dancing before my eyes, like flies with wings of flame. A buzzing filled the air. I knew what it was and was fair used to it. It didn't scare me as it had once.

There were voices in my ears, too, but I could hardly understand what they were saying. They were like the piping of birds in a far-off forest.

"Laddie. Laddie. We're here. Dinna fash . . . here."

One of the voices grew louder and louder until I could tell it was Granda's. He was talking to me but the words were all jumbled up. He put an arm under my shoulder to help me up, and set my bonnet back on my head. I only managed to get to my knees before my stomach clenched like a fist and I heaved up all over the grass. The stink of it made me dizzy.

There was another voice now, further away but getting closer. It was Ma's.

"Mairi!" she was calling. "Where's Mairi?"

Where was Mairi? Why hadn't she been the one to help me up, as she had done so many times before?

"She'll be about," said Granda. "Dinna fret yersel'."

Gripping Granda's arm with both hands, I hauled myself upright, swaying giddily. I felt Ma's steadying hand on my shoulder.

"Duncan, where's yer sister?"

And then I remembered. "The Gloaming Pool." At least I tried to say it, but the words came out as a wheeze.

The sun was just starting to sink, the night drawing in. Fear clutched at my heart. "Ma," I cried, "the pool!" There, the words out at last.

But before I even finished, Ma had gathered up her skirts and was hurrying down the slope toward the pool while the rest of us could only watch her go. At the bottom, she fell to her knees, then crawled the last few yards to the edge of the water, wailing and keening.

I pulled from Granda's grasp though he cried after me, "Ye've barely the strength to stand, lad."

Lurching down the hillside after Ma, I could see what it was she was seeing, even through the dim light of the gloaming. There was a dark, humped shape in the water, small and unmoving, caught up in the reeds.

Granda edged sideways down the slope after me as best he could, with Andrew and Sarah calling out, "Wait, wait!" and "Dinna leave us behind!"

Even as I stumbled downhill, I saw that Ma was already in the water up to her knees, tentative about the footing because she couldn't swim. She was weeping loudly, crying Mairi's name.

And there floating before her was Mairi, her face turned downward in the water, yellow hair streaming about like strands of golden seaweed, dark plaid skirts as lovely as a scallop shell about her legs. She seemed to be reaching for something, something just beyond her grasp.

Ma got to her before I was quite down. Wrapping her arms around Mairi's shoulders, she turned her over, crying, "Och, my lassie, my poor wee lassie." Mairi's face was a strange grey in the light, mushroom grey, and for a moment I barely knew her.

I waded into the pool, Granda beside me. Then he was in front of me, looking back.

"Give me a hand, Duncan," he said as he eased Ma aside. He picked up Mairi in his arms, the water pouring off her.

Suddenly, I couldn't move a step closer, almost afraid to go near, as if death were a disease and I might catch it.

"Take her legs, Duncan," Granda ordered.

His voice cut through me like a soldier's sword. I took one step, then another; I felt I was wading through mud, not water. At last I grabbed her legs, choking on a sob as I did so. How could this cold, limp body be my dear daft sister, my sweet companion of so many years?

We lifted her up between us, grunting as we did so. She was unbearably heavy for one so small, as though the Sidhe were clinging to her skirts and wouldn't let her be taken. But in truth it was all the water soaked into her clothing that was weighting her down.

We set her on the grass and made her modest, her skirts pulled down over her legs, her hands crossed on her breast. Then Ma knelt over her, tears dripping onto Mairi's face, mingling there with the water.

Granda's face went as grey as ashes round a campfire then, and for the first time I thought he looked truly old. Which was odd, seeing that he'd seen many dead men in the '15, but maybe this was different, for there was no glory in it, none at all.

"I'm sorry," I began, ready to haul it all onto my own shoulders. "If the fit hadna taken me . . . " I tried to say more, but my voice caught in my throat, like a rag on a nail.

"It couldna be helped," Granda whispered. "It couldna be helped." He said it over and over, as if repetition could make it true.

"Och, my poor wee lassie," Ma said, weeping. "What did ye think ye were doing?"

But I knew. And knowing just made it worse. Mairi had been reaching out for her prince. And he had taken her.

II. CHOPPING NETTLES

> ☙ *March–April 1746*

Fie, now Johnnie, get up and run!

The Highland bagpipes mak' a din!

It's better tae sleep in a hale skin,

For it will be a bluidy mornin'!

—Scottish folksong

15 ☙ PRACTICE

The months after Mairi's death dragged out slowly, like a bad dream that wouldn't end. We healed as best we could, but it was not easy.

I tried hard to remember everything about her, the way her hair had looked like summer wheat with the fringe almost covering up her eyes. The way she leaped about, clapping her hands, and singing tunelessly. But the only thing I could recall was her face grey with death, and her hair floating like seaweed in the peaty waters of the Gloaming Pool. It was a sight I could not forget.

Ma leaned more on Scripture and old mottoes in her grief. She scrubbed the cottage till her hands were red and raw. Granda threw himself into work on the farm as though the cows, which we brought down early from the shieling, were better companions than us. Ma and Granda hadn't exactly forgotten Mairi, but they seemed bent on trying.

On the other hand, Andrew and Sarah hardly noticed Mairi had gone, and that griped me even more. Surely they were old enough to understand. Yet Sarah, especially, kept talking about Mairi as if she'd just run off for an hour and would be back soon, with a handful of flowers to strew about the cottage door.

I had many an argument with Andrew and Sarah both, furious that they acted so childishly. I turned my back on them at the end of such fights. And all the while, I felt guilty, for fighting with them, for being alive instead of Mairi.

Only Ewan would talk to me about it, saying, "She was the best part of ye, Duncan, for all that she was daft."

I think the whole family felt torn, a banner ripped in two. Nothing but Da's return could mend us, or so I believed.

But Da didn't come home.

The sparse harvest turned into a wicked and painful fall. Everyone in Glenroy went to bed hungry and arose weeping. We worried about what winter would bring. Granda grew too thin and too old over the harsh winter to help.

And still Da didn't come home.

Word arrived back that—while the Highland folk suffered— our armies were doing well enough, chasing the redcoats from Scotland and following them right down into the heart of England. That, at least, gave me hope. I looked forward to hearing more.

Word of those successes was carried by travelers, tradesmen, and tinkers. I waylaid every one of them, bringing them home to share our little food. Granda and I questioned them well into the night and they told us everything they knew.

But nothing came from Da.

Of course I knew he couldn't write, but he could have gotten someone to write for him. Or someone to carry a message. That he didn't made me angry with him, furious.

Ma worried he was dead. But I never once believed he had died. I didn't feel the ache for him under my breastbone that I did for Mairi.

"If Da is to die before I can tell him of my anger, I will give God my back as well," I told Ewan as we met to practice our swords.

His eyes opened wide and I could see the fear in them. "Dinna say that, Duncan," he warned "For yer sake and ours."

"Och, God knows I dinna mean it," I said. But, just in case, I whispered under my breath, "Just let him stay away for all I care. I'm doing the work of a man now." Which didn't make sense, of course, as I had wanted to be on the march with him.

Around that time, I began to think: *If I am a man doing a man's work, then surely I can go with the army on my own, and my cousin Ewan, too.* Ewan had done his own da's farming on their plot of land. Like me, he was tending to his da's chores.

We talked of it ceaselessly, Ewan and I.

"Look at my arm," I would say, showing him the new muscles got from the harvesting, got from being a year older.

He showed me his own muscles, bunching up when he clenched his fist. Then he punched that fist into my arm.

We grinned at each other, man-to-man.

Now that the winter chores were done, Ewan and I figured we would head out after the troops.

"It will be one less mouth to feed." That would please Ma.

"We'll earn a white cockade for our bonnets," he added, "sewn by the ladies of Glasgow and Edinburgh, just like the other men."

And, I thought, *I'll find Da and tell him how he'd hurt Ma by not sending word. How he hurt us all.*

"Brothers?" I said, holding out my hand to Ewan.

He spit in his hand and grabbed mine. "Brothers."

To this end, we practiced our sword and knife fights daily whenever we could get loose of our chores, but told no one of our plans. We didn't want our mothers to talk us out of going. As they were certain to try.

But though we'd sworn we'd be off at once, it was weeks later, winter still shaking its rough head at us, and still we hadn't gone.

Once again Ewan and I were practicing with our wooden swords. It was one evening after the cows had been milked and their muck carted away. We were on a patch of weedy ground on the far side of a copse to the east of the village, where nobody would see what we were about.

"Ha! Caught ye again!" Ewan announced. "That's three times!" He sliced at the empty air with his sword. Unlike a real sword, it didn't whistle as it came down, but made a whuffling sound, like an old dog.

I stepped back and laid my hand over the spot where he'd bruised my ribs with the edge of his sword. I bit my lip to keep the pain inside.

"If we were in battle, ye'd surely be dead by now!" Ewan laughed.

"Nae, I wouldna," I told him, a red flush coming to my cheeks.

"Would!"

"I'm too angry to lie at peace!"

"Angry? What for? Prince Charlie's army is heading toward London and then fat Georgie on the throne will have to pick up his skirts and run. What's to be angry for?" Ewan looked at me oddly.

"Because we're not there, ye ninny!" I raised my sword and jumped at him, swinging wildly.

Ducking aside, he smacked me across the back with his wooden blade. I stumbled forward, fell, and this time hadn't the spirit to get up. Instead I sat on my haunches, my head hanging low. Ewan was definitely quicker than me. And older. And stronger. As many of the redcoats would be. As most of them would be. The very thought made me shiver.

"This is nonsense," I said, angry more at myself than Ewan. "Redcoats dinna fight with swords and targes. They use muskets. Why are we practicing with these?" I could not find pleasure in anything. *My anger is like a fox caught in a lure, chewing at its own foot,* I thought.

"Dinna be daft, Duncan. A musket shoots once and needs re-loading." Ewan sounded like his father, for over the winter his voice had deepened. Down the wooden blade came again. "Besides, once ye've learned how to use the sword well, killing King George's men will be as easy as chopping nettles." He grinned.

"There willna be any redcoats left for us at all if we dinna get moving soon," I reminded him. "And none of the MacDonalds will welcome us then." I stood slowly and put my hands on my hips and said like an angry clansman, "Och, ye've come for the whiskey and the cheering, laddies, but what fight have *ye* fought?"

"So we miss out on the redcoats, there will still be raids against the Campbells and such," he chided.

"Who's the daftie now?" I said. "Prince Charlie will bring peace to the Highlands and the clans will leave off their quarreling. They'll be no glory left for us at all, Ewan MacDonald."

"Aye, and cats will leave off chasing mice." Ewan laughed. "That's a dream, Duncan. If ye carry on like that, ye'll end up as silly as . . . " His voice trailed off and he looked abashed.

He couldn't have hurt me more if he'd jabbed the point of his sword right into my heart, though it was almost a year since Mairi had died.

"I only meant . . . " he began lamely.

"Aye, I know what ye *meant.*" My voice was stone, but my in-sides had turned to soured milk. "Yer a hard, mean lad and ye'll make a hard, mean man." I gave him the kind of look my da often gave me. "My sister's gone and yer making a joke of it. I thought better of ye, my cousin and brother-in-arms."

He turned a pale color, tried to say something to make amends, but I gave him my back.

And the worst of it was, Mairi wasn't really gone. Not completely. I had seen her the last time I'd had a falling fit. But I couldn't tell Ewan that. I couldn't tell *anyone*. They'd have thought me mad.

16 ❧ RETREAT

Ewan and I made up, fought again over small things, and made up once more. We were cousins and sworn brothers. Who else would we talk to?

We were persuaded to stay by small things: His ma had a rough cough, my granda was slower, older. Who would tend the cows? Bring in the peats for the fire? The water from the stream? We were our families' men, now. How could we desert them?

Ewan and I still practiced with our wooden swords, a feeble hope now, no more than a game. One of these times I came back home over the brae with the setting sun spilling light as red as blood across the hills.

Granda was standing by the cottage door, looking south and west, his color better than I'd seen in months.

"Is everything all right?" I called out.

He pointed down the road where I could see the back of a stranger heading out of the village. "Better than all right. A tinker's just been by with news. Our men are not far from London now."

"London!" I was both excited and worried. If the prince's men made it all the way to London, what use would they have for Ewan and me? "Would the traveler not stop for something to eat?" I wanted to talk to him myself.

"Nae, lad, he was just passing through. But he told us that our men have swept through a dozen English towns on their way to the capital, like a river gushing down the mountainside. They've sent the redcoats running for cover and old Georgie packing his crown."

I clapped my hands, just as Mairi would have done. This was great news. "Oh, Granda, we should be with them!"

"Aye, lad, we should be there."

For a moment we were both silent, staring at the darkening hills. We were full of wishing, though wishing and knowing are two sides of a great glen, with a lot of land lying between.

"Da will be with them, won't he?" I thought a minute. "He's never been so far from home."

Granda looked thoughtful. "Aye . . . " he said slowly, leaving unspoken: *If he's still alive.* "Aye." Then he smiled, which caused crinkles around his eyes. Clapping me on the arm, he said, "Duncan, my lad, think on it. How different this is from the '15, when we Highlanders were forced home with our tails between our legs."

"Ye were still brave, Granda. No dishonor to ye. Retreating in the face of overwhelming odds . . . "

"Aye, but this time our men will catch King George by the collar and pitch him off his throne."

"Aye, and Charlie will sit in fat George's place."

Granda frowned at me the way he did once when I'd made a rude noise in church. "Nae, nae," he corrected. "He'll dust the throne off and keep it for his father, King James, when he comes across the water."

"Aye," I said, though who was King James to me, who'd been just a handsbreadth from the prince? "And then everything will be put right."

Granda grinned once more. "Everything will be put right," he said, smacking his lips as though looking forward to a dram of whiskey in celebration.

Everything will be put right, I suddenly thought, *except Mairi will not be here when a real prince reclaims his throne.*

Ma was hunched over the grate, scraping out the ashes when we went inside. By the bunching of her shoulders, I could see that the news the tinker had brought had not made her happy.

"How will they ever get home?" she fretted as she worked. "London's so far from here. Hundreds and hundreds of miles. What are they thinking, going all the way down there, leaving the safety of Scotland for England's dangerous roads? The Stuart has his Scottish throne now. What does he need more?" She gathered up the ashes, still talking to the hearth and not to us. "Och, I sometimes think men are like bairns off into the woods without a care as to what they'll find there."

For a moment I had no notion what she was nattering about.

"They're going to London to claim the *united* throne, woman," Granda said, one hand on his hip. He glared at her bent back. "Scotland and England together. As it has been these hundred and forty years. The men will come back when they've done what they've set out to do. And no before."

Standing to glare back at him, Ma went on speaking, her anger running deep, "By that time, we'll be well into another winter and then into spring again. They could lose their way coming home, and then where would we be?"

"We'd be with a Stuart on the united throne," Granda said with exasperation.

"What's a Stuart to me with a family to feed, and only an old dodderer and a lad to do the farming?"

She must have seen my face then, fallen in like a poorly-made pudding. "Oh, Duncan, I didna mean to shame ye. Ye've done a man's work, for all yer only fourteen years old. It's been yer hand at the harvest and yer shovel in the byre and of course I know it."

"I'm near fifteen," I said sharply, though I still actually had a season and more to go.

"We couldna have gotten the crops in without ye, what little there was." She looked again at Granda, wiping her sooty hands on her skirts without being aware of what she was doing. "Without ye, Duncan, we'd all be dead as Mairi on our own doorstoop. Without ye, yer da would have nothing to come home to, nothing at all."

Her anger turned to tears and with each falling drop I was undone. How could Ewan and I even think about going off to London and leave our poor mothers to work the farms alone? There was much to do still to get things ready for wintering over.

When I told Ewan this the next day, he reluctantly agreed.

"It's a long way down to London," he said. Then he looked at me slyly. "Besides, there'll still be fighting, closer to home. Pockets of redcoats to bring into line." He sounded as if he knew more than I did. After all, he'd been on raids and I had not.

So we agreed to stay home for a time more.

The next news we had was at midwinter. It was brought by a runner sent by Lady Keppoch to all the MacDonald villages in the glen.

He gathered us outside our cottages, though inside by the fire would have suited us better. Snow lay on the ground, a dusting of it, like faerie lace.

With a grim face, he told us that our men had turned back from the very borders of London, within reach of the king's throne. The prince was persuaded by the likes of Lord Murray and the other chiefs that London would be a death trap for them all.

"Turned *back?*" Granda said, his jaw dropping. "Running like whipped dogs?" He was trembling with anger, and I with him. "I dinna believe it."

Lady Keppoch's man shrugged. "I but report what I have been told."

"That's nae good enough," Granda said, shaking his fist. "And what of the Keppoch? What of himself?"

I waited to hear his answer, remembering the Keppoch as I'd first seen him, that strong-willed old man.

"The Keppoch wasna consulted till after the decision was made, and by all accounts showed himself unhappy with it," the messenger said, his long face made longer by this exchange with Granda. He turned as if to go, having said his piece.

"And where are they now?" Ewan's ma asked.

John the Miller's wife leaned forward, holding her young babe in her arms. "Are they on their way home?"

Lady Keppoch's man turned back, saying, "By the time the reports of the retreat reached us, other reports had come as well. As far as we know, Prince Charles' army is already back inside Scotland, resting."

"Resting!" Granda spit to one side.

"Resting where?" asked Ewan.

"That I dinna know," the man said.

"Resting *why?*" I asked.

Granda put his hand on my shoulder. "Aye, that's the real question, laddie." But we both knew we'd get no answer from the man.

He'd only given us this last bit of information reluctantly and now looked to be gone before giving us anything more.

That night we talked well into the darkest hours. Ewan and his sister and ma and others came to our cottage, settling themselves in front of the fire.

Granda talked of the retreat in the '15, and we listened with grim faces, the hearth fire putting shadows under our eyes. "There was nae singing, nae joking, just the shuffling of feet," Granda said. "Nothing worse than the silence of a retreating army."

Ewan glanced over at me and our eyes locked. We made a silent promise. We would meet the retreating army wherever it was and join up. *Now!* New blood might put iron into their spirit and turn them around again.

"Will Da be coming home soon?" Andrew asked as we sat at breakfast the next morning. Silent, Ma ladled out a half-bowl of thin porridge and put a bit of bannock by each bowl.

Sarah repeated the question as if she'd just thought of it herself. Wide-eyed, she asked, "Will Da be coming home soon?"

Ma still said nothing, but the look on her face spoke for her. She was afraid for Da and didn't want to frighten the rest of us with her fears.

I gave them both a shake of my head. "We dinna know."

But Granda boomed, his voice over-hearty, "Of course he'll be home soon. And with him an English musket for Andrew and the silver buttons off a red coat for Sarah."

I shivered, remembering the button I had given to Mairi. And then I remembered word-for-word Granda's description of an army in retreat, how silent and how downcast they were. The sooner Ewan and I got there, the better.

"And what will Da bring for Duncan?" asked Sarah. Then before Granda could answer, she began singing in her wispy, high-pitched way a song she and Andrew had made up:

> Prince Charlie's been tae London toon,
> He disnae want tae roam.
> Prince Charlie's been tae London toon,
> And now he's coming home.

After that dismal meal, Granda took me by the arm and walked me to the byre, our feet leaving soft prints in the snow. When they heard us coming, the cows began lowing, but more like a conversation than a cry.

"I didna want to say this in front of the bairns," Granda told me, "but I've been turning this retreat over and over in my head and it makes nae sense." I knew what was coming, for I had been worrying about the same thing. "Ye dinna track a fox to his den then turn for home without setting the hounds on him."

"Maybe . . ." I said slowly, "maybe King James made a bargain with King George." It was all I'd come up with in a night of worrying. "Maybe they've agreed that one could have Scotland while the other kept England."

"Aye—I wondered about that, too," Granda said, "but it doesna seem likely. Kings dinna give away their jewels without a fight."

"Then what *do* ye think?"

"I think . . . " He paused. "I think the little prince has a cunning plan."

"What kind of plan?"

"To bring the English troops where we can more carefully take them apart."

"Destroy them?"

An eagle circled high over the snowy fields. It was waiting for something. Maybe the clans were waiting for something, too.

"Aye. Destroy them *completely*. It's nae good to have an army at yer back still able to fight. The prince has the right of it. Make the redcoats come back to Scotland, where we have our souls, and then cut them to ribbons." His voice was soft as he said this. *Soft and hard at the same time,* I thought. "Besides, we marched down to London once," he added slowly, "and could do it again. When the redcoats are no more."

Granda's explanation made a lot of sense to me. "And, Granda," I said, "if the prince's plan is to lead the English soldiers up to Scotland, then . . ." I smiled. *Wait till I tell this to Ewan.* "It means we're still at war."

"Yer a smart lad," Granda said, patting me on the head. "Dinna let yer mother know what we've talked about, though. It would only fret her more."

I went right down to Ewan's farm and whistled outside the byre. He came out wiping his hands free of muck and stared at me, for we rarely met during the day. Daylight was for chores.

"My granda's got the right of it," I said. "Come with me to the copse and I'll explain."

As we walked, leaving a trail a child could follow in the snow, I told him what Granda had said, adding, "And having been down to London once, the Highland army knows the way!"

"So they'll need us now more than ever."

"That's right." I clapped him on the back.

"Pick up yer sword, then, and let's go at it again." He went over to the ancient oak where we'd hidden our swords under the fallen snow. "We're no nearly ready enough."

I smiled. "But we *will* be. Aye, we will be. And there's nothing stronger than a Scot on his own land."

Ewan grinned at me. "And I know something ye dinna know."

"How can that be?"

"John the Miller's wife is my ma's friend and she got a letter from her man. A runner came yesterday."

"I saw no runner."

"Yer too much in yer own head, Duncan. Dinna ye want to know what I know?"

I sighed. What if the letter was about Da? What if he had died? And then I gave myself a shake. John the Miller's wife would certainly have been right over to talk to Ma if that had been so. And Ewan would not have been grinning like a simpleton before me. "Tell me." *Better to know the worst than to guess at it.*

"He wrote that the prince is going to camp near Inverness, only a few days' walk from here."

"Just a few days?" My heart seemed to stutter in my chest, then start again.

"A straight line from here, my da used to say."

"And are we right, Ewan . . . we're sure they'll want boys like us?" I had never doubted it, but now that the time was here . . .

"With Cumberland on their tail, they'll take babies if any can crawl that far," Ewan joked.

Our time had finally come, then. It was now. *This moment.* Our mas couldn't hold us back this time. My fits wouldn't keep me from battle. I could smell honor in the air. And glory.

Excited, I grabbed up my wooden sword from the ground, feinted twice, then slapped it down hard on Ewan's sword arm.

He pulled back. "Ow!" he cried. "That's no fair. I wasna ready."

"Do ye think the redcoats will know—or care?" I said, making a face at him. "Find the high ground and charge, that's what Granda taught me." I gave a whoop and ran at him, and this time the shafts of wood clashed together, beat after beat. Then I fetched him a heavy blow on the shoulder and he made a sound like a cow in labor.

"Hah!" I cried, and then, "Ooof," for he'd gotten me right back, on the muscle of my sword arm. It almost made me drop the sword, but I held on and after a while the stinging subsided to a low, tingling ache that ran from my shoulder to my hand.

We swatted at each other for another few minutes, neither landing any real blows after that. But the noise of the swords pounding together began to get inside my skull, until my temples were throbbing.

"We're good," Ewan cried out. "We're *very* good. The clan will be glad of us, ye'll see. Side by side in the battle."

His voice was like an iron band being tightened about my head. The air around me began to turn watery. I looked up and there was Mairi coming toward me, a crown of gillyflowers in her golden hair. I reached out to her.

"Nae, yer no allowed to touch me, Duncan," she said. "No yet."

Go away! Did I say it aloud? I meant to. I knew I couldn't be seeing her. She was dead. We'd buried her, her wheaty hair bound up in ribbons. But the throbbing in my head, the tingling of my arm, the iron band at my temples, the watery air—they all began to take their toll. And then I knew what was really happening.

Taking a mighty breath, I cried out, "Enough!"

Ewan just stared as I threw my sword away and fell into the dark, thinking: *Who would want me by their side in battle now?*

17 ❧ APPARITION

The cold and snowy winter turned into a cold and rainy spring. I worried about the plowing and the planting, I worried about the seeds rotting in the ground. These were a farmer's worries and not a soldier's.

Ewan's concerns were the same. And while we still played at fighting, we spoke often about the farms we tended, the need to strengthen a *cas-chrom,* or foot plow, or how best to sharpen a scythe.

More than once, Ewan had to get me up from a fit. Our small battles, wood against wood, seemed to bring them on. One particular time, I was wet and cold from rolling in the snow. Ewan walked me to the door of my cottage, his hand under my elbow. It hadn't been a particularly bad fit, but I'd banged my hand when I fell.

"Dinna say a word to my ma," I cautioned him. Not that he would.

He nodded.

Then my stomach growled. "Do ye think we've missed dinner?" He hadn't, of course. Since his ma had only Ewan and Maggie to feed, meals always waited on his return. But my family often ate without me.

"Good luck," he said, and left me at the door.

I hadn't actually missed the evening meal this time, and I understood why the minute I got in. A stranger sat on a stool by the fire and Ma was busy cooking up a big dinner for once.

I took a moment to dry off by the fire, then Granda called out, "Sit down, lad."

No one spoke about where I'd been or why I'd come home so wet.

We had cheese, turnips, barley bread, and some salted beef. Ma poured out drams of whiskey for Granda and the stranger, a Highlander named John McLean.

McLean was a thin, grey, wiry sort. His clothes were worn and dirty from long days on the road, the colors all drained out of them. He had a handkerchief with two knots tied about his neck, and a cap stuffed into his belt. Cap and belt were as grey as the rest of him.

He ate like a man starved, and only after eating his fill did he tell us the news. It was news, of course, that Ma was feeding him for. But the news wasn't good.

Leaning back and smiling a thin, grey smile that had no warmth or humor in it, he said, "The English have been getting back Scotland town by town, fort by fort."

"I'm sorry to hear that," said Granda, as Ma and Sarah busied themselves clearing the table. "Ye'd have thought the redcoats had learned their lesson."

"That they have," McLean said, picking his teeth. "But no the one we'd have them learn."

Granda leaned forward. "And what do ye mean by that?"

"They learned in the '15 that we would run home. And that they could run after us."

"Och, man, I was in the '15. With the MacDonalds, in our place of pride, the right wing of the battle line. The place given to us by Robert the Bruce himself, after our bravery at the battle of Bannockburn. Dinna talk of what ye dinna know."

McLean's grey eyes became slits. "I was there myself, old man. Fighting alongside my father and my brothers and my cousins."

Granda paused, considered a moment, then put out his hand. "Peace then. Highlander to Highlander." He turned to Ma. "Another whiskey, Catriona, for my brother-in-arms."

So now I knew it all. The clans had come home, but with the English right after them, taking back again all that we had won on the way down to London. Ewan was right. There would still be much fighting left.

"The man who's leading the redcoats," said the traveler, sipping his second dram, "is King George's own son, Cumberland."

Granda spat on the floor. "Pah! Cumberland's just a fat, pink-faced daddy's boy."

I started to laugh at that but McLean raised his hand. "He may be young and as fat as a Christmas boar, but he's already made a name for himself on the battlefields of Europe. Dinna dismiss Cumberland, friend. His bite is much worse than his growl."

"He's an Englishman," I put in. "And they always run away from a *good* fight."

McLean leaned over the table and glared at me, his eyes no longer pure grey but struck through with red lines, like lightning against a stark sky. "He's no called the Butcher for nothing, *laddie*. But yer too young and untested to understand what that means."

"Aye, he is," Granda agreed.

Ma's hand went to her cheek and for a moment she was as pale as a ghost. "Butcher?" she whispered.

It suddenly felt too close in the cottage. My cheeks burned, and not just from the heat of the fire. I needed to get out into the air. I could feel the tightness around my temples starting, and the beginnings of the firefly flickerings.

If I stayed much longer inside, I might have a fit right there in front of the traveler. So I went outside, and I was not exactly walking slow, either.

It was a cold evening, which the wind made colder, and me outside without my bonnet.

The moon and winter stars shone icily overhead. As soon as I was out of sight of the cottage, I leaned against a lichen-covered tree trunk, hoping to shelter from the wind. Taking three deep breaths, I thought that if I could calm my breathing, let my head clear, I would be fine.

Still, I kept straining my eyes to probe every shadow beneath the trees, looking for a sign of Mairi coming toward me. Thankfully, she was not there, and I knew then that the sickness was passing.

I waited a few minutes more to be sure. It was dark now and the trees had taken on the shapes of giants, their limbs stretching out like gnarled arms. Just then I saw something come drifting through the greenery, a human figure, but thin and faint in the fading light, like a wraith out of one of Granda's tales. Yet my head was no longer throbbing, and I felt clear through and through.

"Mairi?" Her name slipped out, as soft as a sigh.

But it was a man. Not Mairi, not an apparition after all.

As he came closer, I could see that he was *scawt*, scruffy, his clothes hanging loose about him, torn and dirty, greyer even than McLean's had been. His plaid was threadbare. He wore mismatched cuarans on his feet. Only his sword in its sheath was still whole. What he looked like was a corpse that had dug its way out of the grave.

I was rooted to the spot in sheer terror, unable to decide whether to run or—even more shameful—shout for help.

The spectral figure lurched closer until I could see eyes like dying embers under the shadow of his tattered bonnet. The cockade on the bonnet was grey, the badge muddied. His plaid was a dark brown in most places, though a bit of the red showed through.

With a shock I recognized him, even with the pale skin pulled so tight over the bones. Even with the eyes sunken in and the nose now so prominent. Even with the streaks of grey in his hair.

"Da?"

He looked even deader than Mairi when we'd set her in her grave. The tinkers told of such apparitions, how the dead sometimes come home to tell the living how they died.

"Da?"

Did I dare let him follow me home? How would Ma react, seeing him this way, wound in his grave cloth, his eyes like shining coals? Such a sight would kill her on the spot. And Sarah and Andrew would have screaming nightmares for the rest of their lives.

I knew I would have to challenge him here, now. I raised a hand, made a fist.

And then the ghost spoke, its voice creaking like an old wagon wheel. "This is a poor homecoming, Duncan. Have ye nae words of welcome for a weary man?"

His voice broke me, and I ran into his arms like a wee bairn. The arms tightened around me and they were a live man's arms, not a dead man's, though they were so much thinner than I remembered.

"Da," I said. "Da." I could barely keep from weeping.

18 ❧ THE HOMECOMING

Da hardly spoke on the way home. I started out asking a lot of questions, but quickly realized he wasn't going to answer, or hadn't the breath to answer, so I stopped.

I was angry with him and glad he was safe. I was curious and cautious. I was ready to cry and wanting to laugh all at the same time. It was the strangest sensation, as if I were treading on a boggy moor. One wrong step and I'd sink forever.

We walked back to the cottage in silence. Smoke was billowing out of the chimney and stretching south, like a long, accusing finger. Da let me enter the house first, as though he were a stranger who had to be led inside.

The warmth from the fire hit me like a fist in the face. "Look!" I said brightly. "Look who's come home."

Ma was at the hearthside, bent over her darning. She glanced up quickly, scowling at me for staying out so late. And, I suppose, for bringing another stranger home. McLean was long gone, but Granda still sat at the table, where he'd been drinking drams with the visitor.

Ma looked past my shoulder and her whole face changed, like candle wax melting. With a whimper, she dropped her needle and thread, stood up shakily, then dashed toward Da. She threw her arms around his neck and sobbed on his shoulder, soaking his grubby plaid.

"Nae, nae," he said, patting her softly on the back, a gesture of affection I had never seen him use before. "Nae, nae, my darling, hush ye, dinna fret."

Sarah and Andrew didn't recognize Da at all. They squeezed into a corner, cringing away from this gaunt stranger until he softly called them out by name.

"It's Da," Andrew whispered.

"But he's got so old," Sarah whispered back.

They crept forward slowly and let Da pat them gently on the head. "Ye two have grown," he said, his voice rough and dry.

"Ye have shrunk," said Sarah, and Andrew elbowed her. Then they both threw themselves at him and he covered their heads with kisses.

I wanted to be young again and kissed that way. But I wasn't. I'd been a man for half a year.

In all this time Granda hadn't shifted from his spot, but now he sat up straight. "Yer a long way from yer proper post, Alisdair," he said. "Is the battle over and won?"

"Many battles are over and won," Da said carefully.

"And the final battle? To end the war," Granda said. "To bring the Stuart what he's come here for."

"There's been nae such," Da answered bitterly. "And well ye know it. And there'll be none if good sense prevails."

"Those are queer words coming from a Glenroy MacDonald," said Granda. Silently I agreed.

"These are queer times," answered Da, "when a man returns from a long journey and nobody offers him a scrap of food or a dram." He took off the belt with the sword and slammed it on the table.

I went to the table, poured a dram of whiskey in a cup for him, then pulled out a stool. He sat down on it heavily and groaned.

At the same time, Ma went to the cupboard and brought out some cheese and oatcakes, setting them on the table. "We had some beef, but . . . " She looked around as if not sure where the meat had gone, McLean, the hungry stranger, already forgotten.

Da started to eat without taking off his bonnet, stuffing the cheese into his mouth like a starveling, and following the cheese with the oatcakes. It didn't take him long to clear his plate. He washed everything down with a long draught of water taken straight from the pitcher, and a sip of the dram right after.

"Surely there was food at Prince Charlie's camp," said Granda.

"Do ye think so?" Da challenged him. He poked himself in the ribs. "Do ye no see the state of me? I can count my bones as easy as my fingers these days."

"An empty belly's nae excuse for failing in yer duty."

How can he answer that? I wondered.

Da's voice got dangerously low. "Old man, I was as ready as any to follow the Keppoch and fight for his cause," he said. "I owe my land and my honor to him. But I owe a duty to my family as well."

Granda all but growled at him. "It wasna us that took ye away from the prince."

Da slammed a fist on the table. "We fought hard and marched far, only to be turned around with victory at hand. Led back we were, like sheep, back to the very place we started from, tired and misused." He took a deep sip of his whiskey. "The prince's gamble has failed, old man, and his cause is finished, and there's not a Highlander come home who'll tell ye otherwise."

"Finished?" Granda picked out the one word. "Ye beat the red-coats and marched to London just a few short weeks ago."

I leaned forward, wondering what Da could say to *that*. Just then, one of the logs on the fire made a popping sound and Da looked up, startled, something almost like fear in his eyes. Then, realizing it was only wood in the hearth making that noise, he said, "More cheese, Catriona. Please."

She brought over another slab and put it carefully on his plate. He picked it up and tore at it with his teeth. Then he followed this with another sip of whiskey before going on. "Aye, we beat the redcoats in some battles and we beat them to the gates of their own capital city. But dinna fool yerself, old man, they were still an army. And every day they got stronger while every day away from Scotland we got weaker."

"It's still at the Keppoch's side ye belong," said Granda, "and at Prince Charlie's. No here."

Granda was right. The prince needed *all* of his men.

Da's face went white and angry. Two spots of red, like fire, stood on his cheeks. "So ye'd rather see me dead and picked apart by the crows than here caring for my family?"

"I never said that," said Granda.

He never did, I thought.

"Aye, ye did," said Da. "Ye just didna find the right words."

Ma made a small sound, almost a whimper. I felt like doing the same. Sarah and Andrew each took a handful of Ma's skirts and Sarah put her handful up to her mouth.

"I stood by my chief," Granda insisted stubbornly. "I didna run off when swords were drawn."

"And we've heard that story as often as we're minded to," Ma interrupted, wiping tears from her cheeks with the flat of her hand.

Granda gripped the tabletop and stood up sharply. I could see

Ma's words had shocked him, but before he could rebuke her, she spoke again, in a firmer voice this time.

"Old man, ye and yers fought one battle, then ye went home to yer farms. Ye were only away for weeks; Alisdair has been gone half a year. He's been all the way into England, right into the wolf's lair. And God's seen fit to bring him home to tell us about it. What more do ye want? He's yer son. Can ye no be proud of him?" She put her hand on Sarah and Andrew's heads as if to emphasize her point.

Granda's lip quivered, but he couldn't seem to find any words to answer her. Instead he sank back onto his stool and gazed into the fire.

We were all silent after that. Minutes passed, long minutes. The fire began to sink into embers. Da sipped his whiskey and Ma took his plate away. Sarah and Andrew sat down by the fire and rolled a ball of yarn back and forth between them. I just looked at them all, wondering what had just happened and who—if anyone—had been in the right.

At last Da cleared his throat.

"Duncan, go and fetch Mairi in," he said, starting to sound like himself again. "It's over dark for her to be running about on her own. Ye know how she is."

The silence that followed was deep as a grave.

I swallowed and looked over to Ma, who turned pale as whey.

"She's . . . no here, Alisdair." Ma looked at the floor, suddenly unable to meet Da's eyes.

Da stiffened, but he didn't ask why. He just waited and the silence came again, deep and dark.

It was Granda who told him, with great pity in his voice. "She's been dead these five months, son," he said. I had never before heard him talk to Da like that, as if he were a boy.

Da looked at Ma, then stared about him as if he'd stumbled into the wrong house. "Could ye no have sent word?"

"All the way to England?" said Granda.

Da shook his head, but I think he suddenly remembered that he'd sent no word to us, either.

Ma put her hand on his arm. "That's news that travels badly at the best of times. We didna want to add our troubles to yers."

Da seized her hand so hard, she winced. "What happened? Did she fall sick?"

"She drowned," Ma managed to say, almost choking on the words.

"In the Gloaming Pool," said Granda. "She slipped and went under and was caught by the reeds. She didna suffer."

"How?" Da asked. There was an edge of anger to the word. "Was there nobody to watch her?"

My heart seized on me then. I could scarcely breathe.

"She ran off," said Granda, beating out each word like a blacksmith pounding on an anvil. "There was nae helping it and nae blame to be parceled out."

Da slumped back down into his chair and laid his head in his hands. He made a moaning noise that might have been Mairi's name.

"Ye can only chase a butterfly so far," said Granda, consoling now. "In the end it slips through yer fingers and is gone."

Fresh tears sprang from Ma's eyes, but she wiped them away quickly with the hem of her apron. She fetched the whiskey jar down again from its shelf and poured more into Da's cup. He downed it in one swallow.

"I thought I was done with death," he groaned.

Granda beckoned to her to refill the cup quickly and Da gulped that down as well.

"I should never have left," Da said, sounding hollow.

"Aye, ye had to," said Granda. "Ye couldna see into the future."

"That's sure," Da agreed. "If I had, I wouldna have been half the fool I've been."

"Ye havena been a fool, Da," I suddenly put in. "Fighting for the prince—"

"Maybe no a complete fool," Da interrupted. "Och, well, I suppose it must be told once at least. Then we need speak of it nae more." He drew himself up and his eyes took on a distant gaze, as if he were staring down a long tunnel into the past.

I had seen other storytellers start that way. But I knew this telling was going to be different. There'd be little to cheer about and less to laugh at. One look at Da's face told me that.

So we all came back to the table and listened to Da, and the tale of the clans marching down to London and back was as black as the Highlander McLean had said, and blacker. For what had been promised the Stuart all along the way—men and weapons and support from France—had never come. The rising up of the English for our king had never happened.

And the long march homeward, Da said, seemed twice as far as the road down south.

"I held to the Keppoch as long as I had a heart to," he told us, "though others of our clan had already melted away like spring snows. Then in February came the orders to march on to Aberdeen, through weather that was the worst in years. By the time we got there, most of us had icicles . . ." and his right hand described them as he spoke, "hanging down from our eyebrows and beards. We couldna see more than ten yards ahead."

Ma put a hand out to touch his. "But you were close to home."

And, I thought, *close to Inverness. Where Ewan says the prince is now quartered.*

"Da, did you go on with the army to . . ."

He interrupted. "There is no army now." His voice was rough, as if the dust and dirt and ice had corroded it. "Just bands of clansmen scouring the hills for food, and making their ways home. The two weeks before I left, all we were given was a weekly allowance of oatmeal. Ye canna expect to keep an army on that."

How can he say there's no army? I wondered. *If I know about Inverness, he must know, too. The prince needs the MacDonalds around him more than ever. And if Da willna go, I'm more than ready to take his place.* But I didn't say this aloud.

"I did hear that Alan's son, Struan, had come home," Granda admitted, turning to look at Da. "And two more in the next glen." As if he were finally agreeing.

But I was not ready to give up so easily. *The army,* I thought. *Inverness,* I thought.

"The ones who've come home are the ones with some sense," said Ma, unable to keep still on the matter. "They know they're needed here to feed their families and keep their children safe."

"What about Ewan's da?" I asked. "He's not home yet."

Da lowered his head and it was a long moment before he spoke. "It's the worst news I have to bring that poor family." His voice quavered. "Dougal's dead. Cut down by an English dragoon at Falkirk. It's his cuaran I wear on my right foot. I asked his forgiveness when I took it. If the dead can give permission, I had his."

Uncle Dougal dead? I blurted out before thinking, "Do they know? Have ye told them?"

"I'll tell them in the morning. Let them have one more good night of sleep," Da said. "God knows they'll not have another."

"Godspeed, Dougal," Ma said.

"Godspeed," we all echoed.

19 ❧ BREAKING THE NEWS

The next morning, I went with Da and Ma to break the news to Ewan's family. His ma took it well, only sitting heavily on the hearth bench, asking, "Did ye give him a decent burial at least?"

Da nodded and Ma went over and held her hand.

Maggie put her head in her ma's lap and cried aloud. But Ewan said nothing, slamming out of the cottage.

"Go to him," my aunt told me. "He's like a bull that's been stung by a burr. There's nae telling which way his pain will make him charge."

So I went out after him and found him down by the stream where the women do their washing. He was all alone, staring into the rippling water, looking where the April ice had made a rippling white skin against the shore. For a moment I wondered if he could see his father there as I could see Mairi when the world went watery.

He didn't answer when I spoke his name, but when I got closer, he knelt and dashed a handful of icy water over his face to disguise his tears. When he stood up again and faced me, I could see that his ma had been right. It wasn't grief that burned in his eyes now. It was a terrible anger, like lightning seeking to blast a tree. If I didn't take care, I'd be that tree.

"Yer da died as he would have wanted," I said. How stupid the words sounded, but I couldn't stop myself. "He was in the front line, fighting bravely, Da said."

"Aye, and yer da's alive and here to tell ye all about it," Ewan answered sharply.

I ignored the barb in his words. "I wish yer da was home and safe as well."

"I'll wager ye do, but they're different men, it turns out."

"This is nae time for us to quarrel."

"Is that what ye think in yer craven's heart?"

All I felt in my heart at that moment was anger, but I kept myself in check.

Then he added, "Have ye given up on yer prince?"

"How can ye say such a thing?"

"How could yer da do such a thing?" he countered. "Come home when the prince needs him most?"

And for that I had no answer.

"What do ye want to do, then?" I asked.

"Go."

His answer didn't surprise me. "But surely yer ma will never let ye go now."

He shrugged.

A cold wind puzzled through the trees. I shivered with it. "Maybe ye should wait a bit for yer ma's sake," I said.

"My ma has her grief, and I have mine," Ewan said. "A woman doesna understand these things. I'm going to take my da's place. I'm set on it, Duncan, as sure as stone. And ye must take yers."

"Yer speaking through pain," I said. "Ye need to think longer."

He shook his head. "I've done all the thinking I mean to," he said. "My father died in battle, Duncan, like a true MacDonald. At least there's glory in that. And honor. I'll no bide here while there's fighting yet to be done." If anything was stone, it was his face.

"Ye'll never find the way, Ewan," I told him. "Yer as likely to walk into Butcher Cumberland's camp as into Prince Charlie's."

"I'll have my dirk drawn if I do. I'm no afraid. Ye can bide here if ye like—with yer *da*."

He didn't call my father by a shameful name, though it was all there in his voice and in the curl of his lip. My fist clenched all by itself and I swung at him then, but it was a clean miss.

Like gunpowder that's felt the touch of a taper, Ewan exploded. His fists pummeled me—my arms, my ribs, my jaw—until I lost balance and toppled to the icy ground.

"None of yer family are fighters," Ewan crowed. "Why dinna ye crawl off home like ye've been taught!"

Sucking in a deep breath, so cold it made my throat sting, I grabbed his right leg and pulled it out from under him. He fell backward with an angry yell and splashed into the burn. The water did nothing to cool him off and he was on his feet again before I could blink. But this time I was ready, and my own rage was up. I'd not let him speak ill of my father, not without making him pay.

I fended off his first blow and drove him back with a jab of my own.

"When we practiced with yon wooden swords," Ewan said through gritted teeth, "I thought we were making ourselves ready."

"So did I, Ewan." Not the whole truth, I knew.

Suddenly he lunged forward and grabbed me by the front of my sark. With a shift of his weight he threw me to the ground and landed heavily on top of me. I smacked the flat of my hand into his chin and we rolled over and over, grabbing and punching.

"If ye'll no come, then I'll go without ye," Ewan gasped. "Ye can lie abed and think of me at the prince's side."

The prince's side. "Ewan . . . " I began.

He rammed his elbow into my cheekbone, which ended my sentence, and my head rang like a chapel bell. I grabbed his hair and pulled him over so that we rolled together into the burn, kicking and splashing. The shock of the cold water brought us both up straight.

"Ewan . . . " I tried again, but his hands were on my throat.

"Two lads can turn the tide of a battle," he said.

I struggled to prize his hands away but when I did, I found I had no voice with which to agree.

"You know, a grown man will fall from his horse when he tries to skelp a wasp that's buzzing in his face. So we can be wasps, Duncan," he said. "And sting the redcoats." Then he thumped me in the belly so hard, we fell free of each other and I retched into the stream.

Ewan stood and glared down at me. "Maybe another man will die for want of somebody to guard his back if our fathers' places go unfilled."

I clambered to my feet and saw Ewan's fist coming at me. I ducked under it and charged headfirst into his midriff. He staggered back, the wind knocked out of him.

With all the strength I had left, I smacked him hard in the jaw and he reeled back, twisting, about to fall face first into the burn.

"I *agree* with ye, Ewan," I said to his back, my voice hoarse as a crow's. "So, stop thumping me for a minute and let me agree."

Ewan neither spoke nor moved and for a moment I was amazed at my triumph. Then an awful thought occurred to me. *Ewan might drown, just like Mairi.*

And again it would be my fault.

"Ewan!" I screamed, grabbing him under the arms and hauling him up onto the bank. He coughed up water, then lay gasping, his legs twitching like the tail of a fish caught in a net. Relieved that he was alive, I flopped down beside him.

"I'm coming with ye," I heard myself saying. "We swore it—remember?" Besides, if Ewan went to war and never returned, I would always wonder if he died for want of my guarding his back.

Without getting up, Ewan stretched his arm toward me, offering me his hand. I clasped it for a moment, then let it drop. Eventually we recovered our breath and sat side by side, dripping wet, shivering with cold, grinning like fools.

"We'll go right after noon then," said Ewan. "Put on some dry clothes and then go off as if to do yer chores. Ye can slip away then. Meet me at the copse as soon as ye can."

"I will."

"By the time anybody marks that we've gone, it will be too dark to follow. Before they can catch up, we'll be gone for soldiers."

"Gone for soldiers," I repeated. The words gave me a queer feeling inside.

I went quickly back to our cottage, half-excited, half-fearful to be caught out. When I got in the door, ready with explanations, I had to offer none. Ma was still off comforting Ewan's ma. Sarah and Andrew were away somewhere doing chores. Granda was probably grousing at Da in the byre. I had the place to myself. I was glad of that, yet oddly I missed the to-do when the room was filled with family.

First, I knew, I had to get warm. I dried off in front of the fire, peeling off my plaid and sark once they were dry. Then I opened the big chest in the corner, pulling out my other plaid, the plaid stockings, my good sark, and the wool jacket. Then I rooted around until I found my bonnet. If I was going to be a Highland warrior, I wanted to look like one.

Dressing quickly, I turned my attention to food. I packed bread, cheese, oats, and a flask of water, but took only enough to last me a few days, for I wouldn't steal from my family.

Besides, I thought, *soldiers on their own land should be able to eat well enough.* I'd already forgotten Da's experiences in the snow and the cold.

I thought about taking down my da's sword. He'd hidden it again behind the lintel stone. But I doubted I could get the stone out and onto the ground and back again by myself. Besides, it was *his* sword, not mine.

So I went over to my pallet and, reaching under, pulled out the dagger Granda had given me on the march to Glenfinnan. Thrusting it in my belt, I stood and ran my hands down my chest, finally feeling like a soldier.

Then I looked around our little cottage, so warm and familiar. I knew every stone, every beam, every stick of furniture. Would I miss it? I hadn't given it a thought when we went to Glenfinnan. But this time was different.

Dinna be a daftie, Duncan, I told myself. *If ye keep this up, ye'll soon be weeping like a bairn.*

A noise at the door startled me and I turned around. Granda pushed the door open and was just coming into the room.

"There's a chill tightening my chest," he said, beating his fist against the front of his sark. "I need a wee dram to loosen things up." He reached up to the shelf where the whiskey jug sat, and poured himself a cup.

"I'd best be off about my chores," I said, backing toward the door.

"Yer chores, aye," said Granda. "Ye'll be needing that old dirk of mine to keep the wolves and bears off the cows, I suppose." He pointed at the knife in my belt.

"Ye . . . ye told me I could keep it," I said, nervously fingering the handle.

"Aye, I did," Granda agreed, sipping his whiskey, "and I'll no take back what was freely given. But ye should have a care for where such a gift might lead ye."

"What do ye mean?" I had a sinking feeling Granda was about to tell one of his tales. I'd have to stop and hear him out lest he grow more suspicious.

Granda sat himself down on his stool. "I've told ye many stories in yer time," he said. "Some of them happy and some of them sad."

"Aye, Granda." I kept my voice free of the hurry I felt.

"Dinna let *yer* own tale be a sad one," he said, looking down into his whiskey. "We've had enough of that. Stand proudly on the MacDonald line, to the right hand of the prince. Our rightful place since bloody Bannockburn." He smiled into his cup. "That's tradition as ye know. Come back safe bringing yer story with ye."

"How did ye guess . . . " I began. Then I had to laugh. Here I was standing in front of him in my plaid and stockings, the bonnet on my head and the dirk in my belt. Even a village simpleton would know what I was about.

"Haste away," he said, "before yer da and ma have ye tell a different story." Then he turned from me, but not before I saw that his eyes had grown watery.

I raced out of the cottage, feeling blessed. Granda would surely stall them and give me extra time to get away.

I climbed the northernmost hill overlooking the village to meet Ewan as we'd agreed. He was dressed in his best clothes as well, and was crouching low in the dark bracken that was brittle with cold. I saw he'd armed himself with a pitchfork and a hunting knife.

"So here we are," I said.

He hissed, "Get down, ye ass, or we'll be seen."

I sank down beside him and looked back at the rough little cottages that comprised our village. "No one's looking for us yet, Ewan."

"Ye canna know that."

"I can."

"Nae, ye canna." Then he laughed. "Squabbling like bairns when we're soldiers?"

I laughed, too, and held out my hand. "Peace?"

"Aye," he said. "Then let's swear again to be brothers-in-arms, Duncan, until this thing is done and honor satisfied."

"We've done that already with spit."

"When we were boys," he said. "We're men now, and they do it with blood."

Nodding, I took out my dirk and held it between us. Ewan drew his thumb down the edge until it drew blood, then showed me the cut. I did likewise. A sudden wind bent the trees. I shivered, and not with the cold.

"Till this thing is done," I said.

"Till this thing is done," he agreed.

We looked at each other, suddenly too awed to grin. Blood is a great binder.

"Well," Ewan asked at last, "are ye ready to march?" It sounded like a challenge.

"Of course," I answered. I think I meant it. "We'd best shift or Prince Charlie will have to hold up his big battle for us."

That made him grin.

Then side by side, we marched like soldiers through trees already topped with the growing dark. Down the far side we went, heading north and east toward Inverness, toward the place where the prince waited.

21 ✌ THE ROAD TO CULLODEN

Before nightfall Ewan managed to sneak up on a rabbit and bring it down with a throw of his knife. I couldn't hide the fact that I was impressed.

"That way we can save the food we brought with us," he said, for he'd taken the same cheese, bread, and oats that I had.

"For emergencies," I agreed.

We made camp at the edge of a field, under a canopy of pine. I put together a wee hearth of stones and we piled branches and bark in the middle. But though Ewan struck the flints a dozen times, he couldn't get our little heap of kindling to burn.

"I've a knack for this," I said, taking the flints from him, and making a spark on the first strike.

"So, Duncan, we're a good match," he said. "Only I'll play Da and ye'll be the wife, tending the fire!"

"Och, soldiers need to know how to make a fire, too, ye ninny," I said, heatedly.

"Peace, peace." He held up his hands. "Can ye no take a joke?"

To show him I could, I let the argument go, and instead set about finding more kindling. I even came upon a well-aged log that I put on the flames. Soon we had a fire going that was as cheery as any in the hearth at home.

"Do ye think they'll come looking for us?" I asked, as Ewan roasted the rabbit over our makeshift spit.

"If they've any wit at all, they'll know where we're bound. As many as wish can meet us at the prince's camp," he said.

Two days later, in a rain that bucketed down, we found a road running north, around the shore of a great dark-water loch. We guessed it would lead right to Inverness but were wary about being seen.

"We dinna want to run into a troop of redcoats," I said. "Just the two of us."

Ewan agreed. "A pitchfork willna help us much then."

We stayed in sight of the road but never set foot directly on it. We saw carts pulled by oxen, horse-drawn carriages, even men and women on foot carrying baskets, but we didn't see a single soldier. Still, we were wary of being on the road ourselves, so it took us longer than the five days Ewan had predicted. In fact, it took double that. But not one of those days was I sick with a fit, as if heading toward the prince had brought back the healing magic.

When we lay down to sleep that final night, deep in the last year's bracken, we could see lights far off in the distance. Our supper that night was a cold one. This close to our goal, we were afraid the wrong folks might spot our fire. We ate what was left of the cheese and were glad of it.

"What do ye think?" I asked, pointing to the far-off lights. "Might that be Prince Charlie's camp — or is it Cumberland's? Will the army still be there?"

"I reckon those are the lights of Inverness," said Ewan. He pulled out his knife and made a great show of sharpening it on a nearby rock. "And of course they're still there. We'd have heard otherwise."

"Inverness." I'd never been to a city. The thought of the place, bustling with city folk, markets everywhere, made my breath momentarily feel solid in my throat. I didn't question Ewan's certainty. I wanted it to be true.

All at once, the lights grew dim, then disappeared completely. For the first time, a nameless fear gripped me, as if I were about to have a fit. I knew a soldier shouldn't be afraid, but I was trembling all over.

"What's happened?" I managed.

For a moment Ewan looked as confused as I, then he sniffed the air and laughed. "It's only a mist, Duncan. We're going to have a damp night. We'd better get to sleep while we can."

Now I could feel the mist myself, and was embarrassed to have let myself be so frightened, like a bairn frightened by a bad dream. But at least Ewan, too, had been uneasy.

And why shouldn't I be a wee bit afraid? I asked myself. *There's certainly much out there to be afraid of. An entire redcoat army somewhere ahead of us. Or behind.*

This did nothing to make me feel better. So I decided to tell myself one of Granda's stories to put myself to sleep. The only one I could remember was about a piper lad who walked deep into a dark cave in search of a magic chanter for his bagpipe. It wasn't a comforting story, for it ends badly for the boy. He disappears and his family never sees him again, but at last I fell asleep. I suppose I dreamed of victory. Soldiers always do.

We woke very early. The line of light was hardly on the horizon and the mist was slow to clear, as if the day were loath to begin. The middle of April can sometimes be cold and sometimes promising. This day stood somewhere in-between. More hopeful were the bluebells already poking out their brave little heads all around us, and the damp curls of ferns pushing up through the black ground.

We stood up and shook out our plaids to get the damp out of them.

"What's left to eat?" Ewan asked.

"Only an oatcake," I said, taking it out of the pouch at my belt. It was mostly crumbles. We were lucky to have it, though. Ewan had killed our last hare two days earlier, and the bread had gone then, too.

"That will have to do us," said Ewan, taking half from my hand. "Until we feed on the Duke of Cumberland's best beef," he added with a grin.

I tried to grin back but I was too cold. I shivered visibly and Ewan stared at me. "Now mind ye have none of those fits, Duncan," he said. "I canna be waiting on ye. Besides, Prince Charlie needs hale men in his army, no sick ones."

His words smarted, but I knew he had a right to say them.

"Dinna ye worry about me," I said. "I'll see the road through, and fight at the end of it. I'm feeling fine. Only a wee bit cold." To prove this, I belted my kilt and did a few deep-knee bends.

Ewan nodded approvingly, then gave me a friendly clap on the shoulder. "Ye've the making of a soldier, sure enough, Duncan. Just stay on yer feet and follow my lead." He strode off.

The hair on the back of my neck bristled and this time I shook with anger, not the cold. He was treating me like a bairn, a child, who knew nothing about war.

Have ye forgotten which of us went to Glenfinnan and which stayed home? I thought. *Or which of us won the fight in the burn and which needed to be rescued?*

For a minute I thought about calling Ewan back. But I didn't want to start another fight. Soon enough we'd have all the fighting we wanted.

After an hour of slogging through the wet bracken, neither of us had said a word. A thin drizzle began and the ground under our feet grew slippery. The drizzle quickly turned into a shower. In a short while, our plaids were as wet as if we'd fallen into a burn.

I could just about make out the huddled buildings of Inverness in the distance, and beyond them the grey shimmer of a large body of water.

"Is our army quartered in the town itself?" I asked, breaking our long silence. In fact I was hoping we might find the MacDonalds set up in a building in the town and get out of the rain for a while.

He shrugged.

"Ye mean ye dinna know?"

He shrugged again.

"Och, Ewan, ye stupid . . . " I suddenly stopped. Calling him names would only lead to a fight. "We'll ask when we get there then." That seemed straightforward enough.

Ewan wrinkled his nose. "Inverness is full of townsfolk, and there's none of them can be trusted," he said. "We'll find our way just fine without asking."

"So," I said, "we're to wander around like sheep without a dog until we go over a cliff."

"We're soldiers," he answered, pushing a wet bit of hair out of his eyes. "Of course we'll find our way."

"That's nae answer, Ewan," I said, and strode down to the road, heedless now of possible redcoats.

Just then I heard a clatter of hooves and saw an open carriage heading toward me, coming from Inverness.

"Duncan!" Ewan shouted and all but tumbled down to the road to stand by my side. "What are ye doing?"

"It wouldna do any harm to ask these folk, would it?"

The carriage coming toward us was pulled by a single horse straining with the weight of its passengers and not making any great speed.

"Och, maybe no," Ewan conceded. Then, seeing there wasn't risk of being trampled, he stepped directly into its path and raised a hand.

The driver reined the horse in and glowered at us. He was a stout, ruddy-faced gentleman in a frock coat with a three-cornered hat perched on top of his white wig. At his side sat a younger, slimmer version, likely his son. Behind them, safe from the mud kicked up by the horse's hooves, was a small, sharp-faced woman, who craned around the driver's shoulder for a look at us.

"Bandits!" she exclaimed shrilly. "They've come down from the mountains to rob us!" She had a basket full of cakes, pastries, and wine bottles in her lap.

"Hold yer peace, woman!" the stout man told her. "It's only a couple of vagabonds. Mere boys. Probably MacDonalds by the red of their plaids."

"That's no red, Da," said the son. "That's brown, like barnyard muck."

"We're Glenroy MacDonalds. And *soldiers*," Ewan declared, planting his feet wide apart and grabbing onto the horse's reins. Then he added recklessly, "Come to join Prince Charlie."

"That seems likely enough," said the son with a smirk.

Ignoring his remark, I asked as politely as I could, "Can ye tell us where we'll find him?" Though what I would have liked even more was to beg some of their food.

"He's camped up at Culloden House," the stout man answered, waving his hand vaguely to the northeast of Inverness, as if we knew exactly where he meant. "His men are scattered about Drummossie Moor."

"I told ye they were still here," Ewan whispered to me.

"Cumberland's no far off, they say," the son piped up keenly. "Nae more than a couple of hours."

"A couple of hours!" Ewan sounded delighted. He turned and looked over his shoulder at me. "I wager there will be a battle this very day."

"This very day?" My voice suddenly sounded high, unsure.

"Aye, and if ye dinna stop blocking the way, we're going to miss it," the gentleman complained.

"Have ye come to join the fight, then?" Ewan asked, his hand still on the horse's reins.

"Fight? Are ye mad?" The gentleman laughed and his son joined in. "We've come to watch."

"There's no been a show like this since the last summer's cattle market," said the son. "There were jugglers and dancers and even a performing bear. Faith, but it was a braw day!"

Ewan almost turned purple with rage. "These are no jugglers, laddie! These are yer own people fighting for their freedom. Have ye nae thought for the honor of yer family and yer home?"

Well said, Ewan, I thought.

"My family and I have more pressing concerns," said the stout man, leaning forward and peering at us over his piggy nose. "Peace and good trade's what we care for and what this poor land needs most. No some foreign prince come to strut and caw about the countryside."

"Hughie, let's go!" the woman demanded. "There's a hill over by Mackie's farm. We'll have a fine view from there."

The driver raised his whip and made to lash out at us. "Out of the way, ye ruffians! Go fight yer battle if that's what ye want."

Ewan dropped the horse reins and clenched his fists, looking determined to block their way. But I moved next to him and put a hand on his arm.

"I'll fight with ye here if that's what ye want, Ewan," I said, "but there's no honor in fighting these cravens. Save it for the red-coats."

"Aye," he said, moving to the side of the road. "There's more than a bit of sense in what ye say, Duncan." But his arm was trembling under my hand, and I swear, he was ready to draw his knife and fling it at the merchant's heart.

The merchant touched the whip against the horse's sweaty back, and they took off down the road.

"Townsfolk!" Ewan spat in the dirt. "I warned ye they couldna be trusted."

"Surely *some* of them must support the prince," I said. "They're Scots after all."

"If any do support him, they'll be turned as easily as bannocks on a griddle if they see the advantage swing Cumberland's way."

I didn't say it, but in my heart I feared he was right.

We trudged northeast, leaving the road again and going over fields muddied by the footprints of many men. The wind began to gust rain into our faces, cold and hard as little stones.

Ewan kept muttering, "Hurry, Duncan, hurry." He didn't want to miss the battle, sure it had already started. I was shivering again. Who knew that honor could be so cold? Or glory.

• • •

Occasionally, we saw small bands of figures in the distance, scrambling over the hills. They could have been farmers—or soldiers—for all we knew. None of them was ever close enough to hail.

"Damn them!" Ewan cried.

I wasn't sure if he meant the bands of figures, the redcoats, or the merchant and his family.

After several hours in the pouring rain, it was difficult to tell which way to go. Without the sun to give us a clue, we simply followed after the men we occasionally glimpsed through the grey rain.

"Watch out!" Ewan warned me. "There's a ditch here. We'll have to jump it."

We approached the ditch's edge and looked down. What we saw there made my blood run cold. My legs started to shake so much, I was afraid I would fall in. Ewan looked as shocked as I.

More than a score of muddy bodies wrapped in worn, filthy plaids were spread out the length of the ditch, some curled up like bairns in their cots, other stretched out full-length in puddles. Not a one of them was moving; a chill like death hung over the place.

"This is nae ditch!" I gasped. "It's a grave!"

22 &~ DRUMMOSSIE MOOR

"Wheesht!" said Ewan. He was staring hard into the ditch. "There's something queer here, Duncan. Look close." He grabbed my arm.

I didn't want to look any closer, but I also didn't want Ewan to think I was afraid. So I peered down and saw what he meant.

"There's nae blood on them," I whispered.

"Look closer," he demanded. "Ye can see them breathing."

I looked closer. Now the rise and fall of their chests under their plaids was clear. And there was a strange sound, too.

"They're snoring!" I was so relieved, I almost began to laugh. But then I had another thought: *What if they're enchanted?* I'd never really believed Mairi's tales of the faerie prince. She was daft after all. But hadn't I seen her apparition each time I had a fit? Hadn't I felt the prince's healing power? Maybe there weren't faeries, but surely there was magic. I made a quick blessing sign over myself, spitting three times as protection against enchantment.

"What's up with ye?" Ewan asked.

"I'm warding off any witchcraft. Can ye no see they're under a spell? How else can they sleep on when they're being called out to war?"

As if to lend power to my argument, the skirl of pipes began off in the distance, calling all Highlanders to battle. The rain had slackened, there was a sliver of morning light, more grey than blue, and the sound of the pipes carried clearly, all the tunes of glory blending into one keening summons.

Ewan frowned, unsure whether to believe me. He looked down at the sleeping men and chewed his lip. "What should we do?"

"We'll have to try and wake them for the bonnie prince's sake," I said.

"How *do* ye break an enchantment?"

How indeed? I thought of Granda's stories. *Kisses. Good deeds. An innocent heart.* It was something different in every tale.

"I dinna know for sure," I told Ewan, "but I know we have to try." I slid one foot over the edge of the ditch and began to climb down.

"If ye go down there, ye could fall under the spell yerself," Ewan warned.

"If I do, pull me out."

Ewan nodded and hunched over, one hand poised to grab me if I should fall asleep.

When I reached the bottom of the ditch, I skirted several puddles and stooped over one of the men, a redheaded giant. I looked for the telltale signs of enchantment, the ones from Granda's stories: spiderwebs over his face, elflocks knotted in his hair, or an unnatural color to his skin. Suddenly he groaned and his eyes opened a crack. They were the green of gooseberries.

"What's this?" He grabbed the hilt of his sword and bared his teeth.

I jumped away, pressing my back against the side of the ditch. Then he saw my bonnet, with its identifying badge, and his haggard face relaxed.

"A MacDonald lad," he said, then yawned greatly, taking his

hand from his sword. "Away with ye then and leave me to sleep in peace. I've nothing here for ye to steal."

"The MacDonalds are no thieves," I answered indignantly. "I'm here to help ye."

"Help me do what?"

"To answer the pipes, man. Can ye no hear them?"

He yawned again. "I answered those same pipes yesterday and stood for hours in the cold to nobody's good. And the day before that, and many other days, going back a full nine months." He turned over and tried to make himself comfortable.

"There must be a way to break the spell that's holding ye here," I said desperately.

"Yer daft, boy," he said, twisting back again and looking at me with those gooseberry eyes. "It's nae witchcraft that's brought us to this. It was a night of stumbling through bog and over hillock till we were close enough to smell the redcoats' cook fires. Do ye know what rations we got yester eve? One biscuit for each man. One biscuit! For a whole night's march without a stop or a charge."

"We've come to fight," Ewan called out. "Not to lie about like pagans on a Sunday."

The man glanced up and saw Ewan crouched on the edge of the ditch. "Then go and do it, and leave us in peace."

"We thought ye were dead," I told him.

"Dead *tired*, laddie, and our bellies as empty as a pauper's purse. I'm happy never to wake again if it means an end to all this marching and starving." He shoved me away roughly and laid his head down in the crook of his arm. In an instant he was fast asleep again.

"Come away, Duncan," Ewan urged, stretching his arm down

toward me. "There's nothing we can do here." I took hold and he hauled me up beside him.

"It's nae enchantment," I said. "It's exhaustion. Da looked like that when he got home. These men might as well be corpses for all the life that's left in them." I started toward the sound of the pipes, but Ewan had another thought and motioned me to wait.

"They might be of some use yet," he said, laying his pitchfork on the ground. Before I could stop him, he was sliding down into the ditch which was still as a grave.

As soon as I realized what he was up to, I shook my head and hissed at him. "Stop it, Ewan."

He ignored me and crawled within an arm's length of the nearest Highlander, a large grey-bearded man wrapped in a green-and-yellow plaid. Stretching out a hand, Ewan eased the man's sword from his side. All at once the sleeper snorted. His fingers twitched, as if seeking the missing weapon. Ewan froze and I held my breath.

After a long, anxious pause, Ewan took his prize and clambered back up beside me.

We looked at each other and Ewan broke into a toothy grin. "Now I'm a real soldier," he said. Then he stood and started off and I followed.

As soon as we were out of sight of the ditch, Ewan stopped to admire the fine broadsword he'd taken, with its intricate basket handle for protecting the fighter's hand. He took a couple of swings with it, and to tell the truth, he had trouble wielding such a sword. It was a man's weapon, and heavy. But that didn't put a dent in his pride.

"Now *this* is a proper weapon to fight with," he declared. And resting the blade of his new sword on his shoulder, he marched off at a jaunty pace.

Once again rain pelted us, almost muffling the sound of the pipes. Still, there was enough of a thread of sound to follow. As I strode behind Ewan, I was both jealous of his sword and worried that a blade gotten by theft might prove his undoing. I thought to say something, guessed what he would answer, and never said a word.

Now we could hear drums as well as the pipes. And then the murmur of distant voices. It stirred us more than a thousand songs or tales of bravery.

"MacDonald!" I cried out, taking my dirk from my belt. Ewan turned and winked at me. We were here. Here in time for the battle. And onward to glory.

A hundred yards ahead of us was a walled enclosure of rain-slicked stone. Past that we could see a great body of men, their ranks stretching off into the distance. I smiled. Here were many more than had been at Glenfinnan. I tried counting them, and got lost in the numbers. The men were mostly Highlanders, their tartans smeared into a dull blur by the rain. They were huddled together, moving their feet restlessly.

As we got closer, I could make out some of their badges and the dull colors of their plaids. "MacLachlan and Clan Chattan," I told Ewan. The sight of them gave us fresh strength.

Then Ewan halted and pointed. "Look there," he said. "That line of red."

I peered through the drizzle and finally could make out a packed crimson formation far off on the opposite side of the moor. There must have been thousands there. At least double the number of Highlanders I could see. Flags and banners waved soddenly over their heads and their drums beat out *rat-a-tat-tat, rat-a-tat-tat*. The men were steady and unmoving, but as full of menace as a leashed hound.

"Butcher Cumberland's army!" I could hardly breathe.

"Are ye still in such a hurry to meet them now ye've seen them?" asked a voice.

I held my dagger steady and Ewan hoisted up his sword with both hands.

"Easy," said the voice. "I'm on yer side, lads. There'll be plenty of fighting soon enough. No need to do it among ourselves."

The speaker was a young man seated on the ground with his knees pulled up almost to his chin. He was partly concealed by a gorse bush but had leaned forward to have a sight of us. We moved around to have a better view of him and as we did, I saw he wore a black-and-red plaid. There was a sprig of heather in his bonnet and the badge of a MacDonald. I was sure I had seen him before.

"I was hurrying to answer the pipes myself," he went on, "when I got a cramp in my leg and dropped to the ground like an old woman. Here, give me a hand up, lads. I think it's gone now."

He stretched both hands to us and we pulled him to his feet. He loomed over Ewan by a good head.

Suddenly I recognized his plain, craggy face. "Yer the Keppoch's son."

"That I am," he answered proudly. "Angus Ban MacDonald of Keppoch."

"Duncan MacDonald of the village of Glenroy," I said.

"Ewan MacDonald, also of Glenroy," Ewan said, punching his thumb into his chest.

"I was at Glenfinnan," I added.

"That was a long time ago," Angus Ban said ruefully. "When hearts were lighter and the cause a clear road unmuddied by blood." He eyed Ewan's sword. "That's surely a man's blade yer carrying there, laddie."

"It was a man that gave it to me," said Ewan, keeping his voice even, though his fingers tightened around the sword's hilt.

"Be worthy of it, then," said Angus Ban, "and ye'll do yer chieftain proud." He turned as a huge cry went up behind him and I saw bonnets being tossed in the air.

"What's happening?" Ewan asked, a tremor in his voice. That was the first I knew that his nerves were on edge.

"Dinna take on so!" Angus Ban told him. "That's just the prince riding before our men to fire their mettle. He wants to make them ready for the charge."

"The charge!" Ewan said. "Then why are we waiting? Let's find the MacDonalds now."

The prince! It was all I could think of and I squinted through the rain. And there, past the cheering men, I saw him. He was wearing a tartan coat and a buff-colored vest, riding a gray gelding, and waving to his men. The wind was behind him, blowing his hair about his ears. As he rode past, the men cheered, shaking their swords over their heads. At that very moment, the sun broke through a gap in the clouds and light poured over him like God's own blessing. The skirl of the pipes, the beating of the drums, the loud cheers all lifted me up like a surging tide. I turned to tell Ewan.

He had an excited gleam in his eyes, and he clutched the hilt of his sword with both hands. I knew he was feeling the same thrill.

I snatched my bonnet from my head, waved it, and cried out, "MacDonald! MacDonald!" and Ewan did the same.

"That's it, lads," said Angus Ban. "Now, both of you, follow me. If ye want to serve the prince and join the charge, here's yer chance." Then he strode away, saying over his shoulder, "Our reckoning's come at last, here at Culloden."

23 ❧ BATTLE LINES

We're away!" Ewan cried, speeding after Angus Ban. I had to practically run to keep up.

As suddenly as it had come, the sun was gone, and cold rain once again spit at us, this time slowly turning to sleet. A horseman galloped by, splattering us with mud. Six men, with badges proclaiming them to be Camerons, raced past, nudging us to one side. "Out the way! Out the way!" one cried and Ewan gave him a look as sharp as a dagger.

Still we kept up our pace and Angus Ban said, pointing, "My father argued against this ground, saying it's too flat and open."

Flat? Open? As we ran by, I looked with horror at where he was pointing. We were on the side of a large, featureless moor. Sleet sheeted down into our faces, obscuring the other side. But I knew from my previous glimpse that the redcoats were lined up facing us, patiently waiting for a signal to advance. I could still hear their drums beating: *rat-a-tat-tat*.

We dodged around a huddle of men standing quietly in thin tufts of yellow grass.

"There's a bog in the middle," Angus Ban was saying. "That suits the English horse and cannon too well. A Highland man wants cover, and high—"

"High, solid ground and the wind at his back to charge from," I finished for him, remembering Granda's lesson. And suddenly I worried if this battle was an awful mistake, being here on the low, boggy ground, the wind spitting sleet in our faces. *Oh, Granda, I* thought, *ye should be here to give them all advice.*

"We'll charge home whatever the ground," said Ewan, raising his sword as high as he could manage and slicing through the sleety air. "We're MacDonalds!"

We hurried briskly past an enclosure, beyond which a line of Atholl Highlanders stood, their faces grimly fixed on the enemy. I looked where they looked and shuddered. The English still stood as imposing as a stone wall. They would take some beating.

"The MacDonalds are further on," Angus Ban said.

Beyond the Highlanders and to their rear, I spotted a small group of horsemen trying to steady their mounts. In the middle, I caught sight of a tartan coat.

The prince!

I wanted to run to him, to tell him how we had spoken at Glenfinnan, wanted to touch the hem of his coat. But Angus Ban kept pushing us on.

"A wee bit further, lads," he said, heading us past the first group of men.

I had expected to find our clan assembled there, in the place of honor by the prince's right, but as we passed by, I quickly realized by their banners and badges that a different clan mustered here.

"Where *are* the MacDonalds?" I asked, looking about. "I thought we always battled at the prince's right hand."

Angus Ban made a grimace. "Away over there, on the left." He spat the words out. "Robbed of our place of honor by the men of Atholl."

I was appalled and thought: *The other side of an honor is an insult*. I felt the insult like a knife to the heart.

"That canna be right," Ewan blurted out. "The prince wouldna treat us so."

"He did it as a sop to his generals," Angus Ban explained, not letting us catch breath. "Murray, the laird of Atholl and the prince's chief general, insisted his own men deserved to be on the army's right, along with Lochiel's Camerons."

Putting a hand up to shade my eyes from the sleety rain, I tried to see where our MacDonald men were gathered. "It's bad luck to break with tradition, my granda says."

Angus Ban stopped us and said grimly, "Good luck or bad, it's all that we have. We'll do our duty still, lads, even if there's a sour taste to it. And make our own luck this day."

"Aye," Ewan agreed, equally grim.

I thought about Granda and what he would say—us battling from the left side, on low and boggy ground. The wind spitting into our faces. "Aye," I said at last, thinking that honor was in the fight, though I could still wish for a better position.

We made our way eastward between the front line of Highlanders and the second line, where men stood in clusters a hundred feet behind. Ewan hailed the first band of men we passed, but they made no response. From their garb, I could see they were Lowlanders, and unhappy ones, too, their stooped shoulders and long faces telling their story all too well. They were pressed together in a tight huddle against the cold rain, wearing breeks and not the belted plaid.

"Da said there were *no* Lowlanders fighting for the prince's cause," I said.

"There's always some join up for the promise of silver," Ewan remarked. "But they look none too happy now." He grinned. "Well, let them moan. We'll bring our honor home without them."

"Are we near the MacDonalds yet?" I asked Angus Ban.

"Not far. Not far."

More horsemen galloped by, this time going toward the spot where the prince's small band waited. I turned to watch them go and got a face full of mud. Wiping it off with the sleeve of my jacket, I hurried after Ewan and Angus Ban.

We passed a line of Stuarts, in their green-and-red tartans, a banner of yellow and blue flying bravely above them. Then the Frasers, with badges of yew in their bonnets.

"Go, young MacDonald!" someone called out to Angus Ban, who waved in greeting but never stopped. Ewan turned and raised his sword with both hands, grinning and trotting backward.

"They're no cheering for ye, ye daftie," I said as I passed him by, but I was smiling, too. Yes, there was wind and sleet and a boggy moor. Yes, the men were tired from being up all night, and they were hungry. But we were Highlanders, the Keppoch MacDonald's troops, the prince's men. There would be a victory this day. The Stuart was God's own.

Ahead, I saw three McLean men pushing four small cannon into position. They were arguing with one another over how the things should be loaded. From what they were saying, I guessed the proper gunners were either dead or had long since deserted. I had once caught Andrew trying to use Ma's spinning wheel. He'd been as much at a loss trying to work it as these men looked to be with their big guns.

But I was not worried. God's sun had wrapped the prince with its warmth. We could not fail.

• • •

At last, well beyond the cannon, we found the MacDonalds under our clan banner: the white cross on its bloodred background.

I took a deep breath. "Ewan," I called, then couldn't say more. I felt tears pooling in my eyes. I bit my lip till the pain made the tears go away. A MacDonald doesn't cry.

Ewan never noticed. He'd let the sword fall to his side. "We're here." He sounded relieved, excited, ready.

Looking around, I thought I recognized a few of the men from Glenfinnan. I hoped to see someone from our village, and then I spotted John the Miller on the far side of our line. I raised my hand to wave, and was pushed aside.

"Here, lad, out of the way." It was redheaded Jock, Uncle Dougal's farmhand. He seemed not to know us as he dashed down the line. He'd either slept through the morning or gone foraging for supplies. He wasn't the only one late. There were scores of men just now running to find their places.

"Get . . . in . . . place. Firm . . . up . . . the . . . line . . . ye verminous layabouts." An officer on horseback pushed the men into position, cursing them for their tardiness, and using his horse's rump as a battering ram. "Get a move on there, ye bloody laggards."

"Where now?" I called to Angus Ban, but he never turned to tell us. Probably hadn't even heard me over the constant drum of rain, the shouting of the officers. "Where should we go?" I tried again.

Now the pipers were playing in earnest, each with his own clan's rant. Drummers, too, pounded out a beat, trying to forge the disordered lines into shape, like a blacksmith fashioning a straight blade from molten steel.

"Get in *line*!" one of the captains was screaming, his voice overriding the noise. "Ye canna fight like that! Form a proper rank!"

"Och, we'll look like the English laddies that way," someone cried back at him.

"Ye've nae red coat," someone else shouted.

The men near me laughed uproariously and pointed to the other side of the moor.

This time I could barely see them through the curtain of sleet. Just a blur of red, like a wall. I stopped and stared. "Ewan, look!"

He stopped as well.

Then one dark-bearded giant of a MacDonald called over toward the English side, "Did ye remember to shine yer buttons before battle, little mannie?" He turned and lifted his kilt at them, showing them his bare bottom.

Soon the MacDonalds were all hurling taunts toward the silent redcoats, questioning their manhood and insulting their wives and mothers.

The English made no reply.

There seemed to be thousands of men on both sides of the moor. I'd never seen so many assembled in one place. Glenfinnan had been a small gathering compared to this. Surely this would be the battle to end all others. I would have a story, indeed, to tell Granda and the family when I got home.

Angus Ban had been ahead, and came back to collect us. "Come on, come on, lads. Our line is just over there." But now he, too, stopped to look over at the English. Then he glanced to our side as well. "Look at the way our line's been drawn. It's all aslant. We've twice as much ground between us and the redcoats as Murray and his men have."

I tried to see what he meant, wiping the rain from my face to do so. The clan that had taken our place of honor was, indeed, a good deal closer to the redcoat line than we MacDonalds were. The line running from us to them looked like ripples in a river.

"It's still no enough to keep the English safe from our swords," I said to him, speaking more boldly than I felt.

"Aye!" Ewan said, lifting his sword.

"Good lads," said a man with a bloodstained sark standing next to me. "There's glory in that."

But my mind had begun to turn a different way. It wasn't glory I was thinking about. The longer I looked at our slanting line, I understood what Angus Ban meant. We had almost twice the ground to cover than the Atholl Highlanders. We would be twice as long under the English guns when we charged. Then I grimaced, cursing myself for such unmanly thoughts. Surely we would win twice the glory this way, twice the honor. We would do what we must, and victory would be ours.

It *had* to be.

ngus Ban grabbed my arm and hauled me on through great splashes of muddy bog and trampled heather. Ewan trotted after us. At last we reached the band of Keppoch MacDonalds, where Angus Ban left us, saying to a bony man with a blind left eye, "Look after them, Sandy." Then he pressed on to the front ranks to join his father.

When we tried to follow, Sandy blocked our path with his bill-hook. "Ye lads best bide here," he said, "as Angus Ban wishes. The front of the line is for them as has muskets or pistols. I canna look after ye there."

Our new neighbors were all humblies, too poor to afford swords and firearms, or boys like Ewan and me. Our arms were scythes, hatchets, billhooks, knives. But at least we knew we were all MacDonalds.

"We're going on to the front," Ewan insisted, dodging around Sandy. "I've got a sword."

Before he could take another step, one of the Keppoch's captains shoved him back with the butt of a musket.

"Ye belong back here, laddie," he said curtly, "sword or nae sword. And that one's mighty big for a boy to wield. It'll give you a sore arm before dark. But mind yer place here and ye'll get yer fair share of the fighting and the glory, I promise ye that."

Ewan bit his lip and lowered his head while the captain passed by. Then he whispered hoarsely, "They canna do that to us."

"A soldier has to follow orders," I reminded him. "We're at the battle, and that's what counts."

The humblies around us stank of wet plaids, long days of walking, and longer nights without proper food or washing. They were as ragged and thin as Da had been. But I was certain that when the time came, these tattered troops would fight as bravely as the Keppoch himself.

So we waited.

And waited.

And waited some more.

By my side, Ewan muttered, "When does this thing start?"

"Aye," a man with a raised hatchet said, "and it's always the same. Get ready and wait. Och, Highlanders dinna wait well."

And still we waited.

A sudden sharp *bang* off to our right made me to turn. My heart stuttered in my chest. I saw a plume of white smoke curling backward on the wind.

The MacDonald front line let out a cheer.

"What is it?" I cried, for we couldn't see anything but towering men in front of us.

Sandy smiled back at me. "First shot to us!" he called. "See how the smoke curls." He raised a filthy hand and pointed.

The cheer washed over us, and Ewan and I joined in as well, shouting at the top of our lungs.

As our yells died away we heard something new. It was a muted "Hurrah!" from the scarlet ranks on the other side of the moor, the first sound they'd made.

Something sour spurted up suddenly from my throat into my mouth. I wondered what the redcoats had to cheer about since I couldn't see more than the backs of the men in front of me.

And then it came. The English cannon belched out a billow of flame and smoke in one mighty roll and the sound was like a pair of huge church bells being slammed together. The air around us shook with the din and an iron ball arced overhead.

"Missed," came a voice. "They've not sighted well."

"Och, ye nearsighted bullies," cried another.

The men laughed, a rippling sound like the River Roy in full flood.

Then another clanging rang out, and a shot plowed into the lines to our right.

Again, I couldn't see what had happened but this time I heard the cries of injured men and the startled curses of those about them.

"Damned ball got Lewis!"

"Bloody redcoats."

"Look out! Look out!"

Is it bad? I wondered. And then: *Does it get worse?*

"Hold steady, lads!" called the chiefs and their captains. "Hold steady!"

Time seemed to slow down. Our own gunners returned fire, and the small cannon burped out a few balls. But the English were so skilled at their brutal craft, they reloaded swiftly, answering every musket shot of ours with twenty of their own.

Then the cries around us began to multiply. Names were called out like a devil's roll call.

"William's hit!"

"It's Johnnie. Johnnie."

"Ronald Mackie, where are ye?"

"To me, lads, to me! Captain Andrews has had it. To me."

The crash of Cumberland's cannon—so many to our few—was like an iron door slamming shut over and over again.

Back and forth through the slow time. Yet my heart was hammering to a faster pace.

Ewan placed his sword point-first on the ground and leaned on it to brace himself. "It sounds like the gates of Hell crashing shut!"

Just then, past his shoulder I saw a cannonball smash a man into the ground, bounce up, and flatten two others. It was the first I'd actually seen such a thing, and everything suddenly began moving fast again. The clang of cannon, then the crack of bone. Blood spraying everywhere.

"My arm, they got my bloody arm . . . " the man on the ground cried. Someone else knelt by him, holding a cloth to the spurting wound.

My stomach heaved mightily at the sight and I had to turn away or throw up.

"Why dinna we charge?" I heard a voice beside me grumble. "Let us loose, man."

Ewan shuffled his feet and poked at the ground with his sword. "This is nae sort of a battle," he said loudly, "to stand here and be shot at, like grouse on a moor. Without doing something back. We canna even see the redcoats from here."

"Aye," said a boy about Ewan's age, his blue eyes squinting. "How can ye fight someone if ye canna even see him face-to-face?"

"Let us go, forward or back," came from someone behind me. I turned to look. There were at least thirty humblies it could have been.

"My bloody arm," the man on the ground called again, but his voice was beginning to fade. "My arm . . . oh God, oh God, oh God."

"The prince is biding his time," Sandy told us.

"The prince knows what he's doing," I added.

Sandy nodded. "That he does," he said, raising his voice. "As he proved at Edinburgh and Falkirk and Carlisle. Take it easy, lads. He wants the redcoats to come closer before we charge."

"We'll be dead long before that," the grumbler said.

Suddenly, I realized I agreed with him. It shamed me to think so, but I couldn't help it. *Why should Cumberland's troops come any closer,* I thought, *when they can kill us from the safety of the other side of the moor?*

"I have to get to the Keppoch!" I cried. "I have to tell him . . . "

But before I could take a step forward, before I could dodge blind-eyed Sandy, and push through the boil of men, there was another cannon blast from the redcoats.

And another.

And another.

And I found I couldn't move at all.

The blasts of the English cannon kept hammering at us and men kept falling—in front of us and then well to the right of us, and to the left, while our own guns fired fewer and fewer shots in return.

I felt the whole body of MacDonalds around me shiver every time a cannonball ripped a bloody path through our ranks. That shiver was like the moment before I fall into one of my fits. I had to bite my lower lip hard to keep from crying out.

"Close up!" the captains shouted after each round.

Close up? I thought. *And make a better target for the cannon? Surely that is madness.* Besides, my feet didn't want to move.

"Close up, damn ye," the captains cried, "and hold yer ground!"

The ranks in front of us had been thinned out like barley at harvest. Now I could see across the rain-drenched moor to the other side; could see the British guns, with grey smoke curling above them like the wings of the angel of death.

"Close up yer bloody ranks or I'll shoot ye myself," our captain called.

"Listen to the man," Sandy ordered, and grabbed at two boys with his enormous hands, moving them closer together.

So we closed up ranks, stepping over the maimed, the whimpering, the dead. I forced myself to move. I had no choice. I closed my eyes against the sleet.

And then we waited some more.

Time once again dragged on painfully, measured by the ceaseless booming of artillery, punctuated by the cries of the wounded. Granda had been right. Dying men called for their mothers. Their mothers and God.

I kept opening my eyes wide as if I could pull myself out of this particular nightmare. Then the sleet and the sound of the guns made me squint again.

And still we stood, not charging, not running, just standing, like men in a bare-knuckle fight terribly outfought, but still unwilling to fall.

A dark-haired lad next to me glanced back over his shoulder, as if checking for a clear route of escape. I longed to look back as well.

But Ewan grabbed me by the arm, whispering, "Let's get on with it." As if there were something he and I could do.

"Let loose, damn ye," I said to him and he looked at me, startled, and let go.

Sandy suddenly muttered, "It's no like the Keppoch to stand still for a bloody nose. What's holding him?"

"I thought ye said the prince—" I began.

And next to him a red-bearded man added, "Bloody nose or bloody head, give us the bloody signal, man. Let us charge!"

Then a cannonball ripped through a line only ten yards from where I stood. A shattered leg spun through the air toward me in a shower of blood, landing at Ewan's feet.

I couldn't look; but, glancing away, I saw Ewan's face. It was as grey as a dead man's, and spattered with red. Where he gripped his sword, his knuckles showed white.

"Ewan, are ye hurt?" I cried.

He looked down at the severed leg and then suddenly leaned over and spewed his last meal onto the ground. Wiping his mouth hastily with the back of his hand, he croaked, "Not I."

"Close ranks, ye slackers," the captain called.

I stepped over the severed leg, moving up into the next line of men, on the end, Ewan beside me. The ranks ahead of us were thin and, for a moment, I could see the whole muddy field. It stretched like a black sea before us. Humped with bodies, trampled heather, broken patches of gorse, it looked like a road to Hell.

Then the ranks closed together again and all I had before me were the backs of MacDonald men.

I thought about telling Ewan that we could leave now, that honor had been served. But suddenly there was a fresh skirl of pipes from the center of the Highland army. The drums started a new beat and the Mackintoshes of Clan Chattan moved across the field. And it was too late to say anything at all.

"The charge!" Sandy cried behind me. "The Mackintoshes have gone!"

Beside me everyone tensed like dogs held on a leash, ready to leap at the throat of a bear.

"Do we go?" Ewan asked. "Is it time?"

"Almost, lad, almost," Sandy told him.

Yet still we were held.

Then a minute or two later, another cry came rolling down the line of men in front of us.

"Atholl! Atholl!"

The Atholl Highlanders were the ones at the far end of the field—our place of honor, and much too far for me to see. But I could tell by the cries that they must have surged forward.

"The charge! The charge!" called someone behind me. And we were all shouting, a hearty cheer that—for an instant—drowned out the thunder of Cumberland's guns.

25 ❧ THE CHARGE

Now we'll have them!" Ewan shouted, his voice shrill.

I tried to cheer with him, but my throat was suddenly parched and nothing came out but a croak. It took a while before I could even work up some spit.

"What about us?" a red-bearded man cried out. He was standing ahead of us. "Are we to charge or no? Has nae order come?"

To our right, the Camerons suddenly broke into a run toward the English, shouting their battle cry: "Sons of the hounds, come here and get flesh!"

By leaning sideways, I could see part of their charge. They went flat out, their swords above their heads, their targets before them, screaming at the redcoats. Suddenly there was a round of English fire, simultaneous stabs of light that brought a dozen men tumbling to the ground.

"Will nobody help them?" I cried out loud, but who could hear me in all that noise? Not the Camerons, surely. Those who were still alive kept up the charge, screaming wildly at the redcoats, knees pumping as they raced forward. It was glorious and awful at the same time.

"The Stuarts and the Gordons are away, too!" came a cry ahead of me. Now I could see those clans charging across the soggy moor toward the English guns.

But for some reason, we MacDonalds were still leashed.

"Let's go! Let's go!" The mutter was all around me now, and then the mutter turned to a shout. I found myself shouting along with them, my heart beating so loudly, I feared it would burst through my sark. Raising my dirk above my head, I cried out, "Let's go! Let's go!"

There was a great crash, like trees falling, as the English musketeers fired off yet another volley. A second followed close on the first, the wind carrying plumes of smoke across the sodden field. I took in a big breath of it and started to cough.

Ewan clapped me on the back. "Ye'll need breath for our charge, Duncan."

I nodded, and ran my tongue over parched lips. "I'll . . . have . . . it"—cough—"when . . . I . . . need . . . "

But Ewan had already started edging his way forward, ahead of me, displaying his sword as if it entitled him to a place on the front line. I moved to catch up with him, though carefully, in case his blade came too close to my head. Men pressed against us from behind, until the ranks were so tightly packed, we couldn't advance any further.

"We're in the thick of it now," Ewan said, a feverish gleam in his eyes.

"Aye," I agreed, my heart now beating like one of the drums.

"Claymore!" came a yell from the front, our ancient MacDonald call for attack.

I tucked up my kilts as the men around me did, and pulled my bonnet down tight over my brow. Some of the brawnier men even cast aside their heavy plaids entirely, leaving themselves only in their sarks, but freer to wield their weapons. I couldn't bring myself to do that.

Then the pipers filled their bags with air and started to play a rousing march. The drummers set up a rapid beat. Our front line fired off their muskets and pistols, a noise so close, I thought the English were upon us until I realized it was a ragged sound, and not the measured volley of the redcoats.

"Now, we're away!" cried someone a row ahead of me and then we were finally moving forward, six ranks deep, across the muddy moor. Not a charge but a muddle.

"MacDonald! MacDonald!"

"Och, give me room," I implored, elbowing the dark-haired boy who'd somehow slipped over to my right. He elbowed me back in the ribs, hard enough to raise a bruise. We jostled this way for a half-dozen steps, though we'd barely space to move, much less fight.

I wondered, as we pushed at each other, where Angus Ban might be. And the Keppoch. Right in the front, I supposed, and exposed to the English guns. And where were John the Miller and Jock and the rest of the Glenroy men? Somewhere close, I knew. There were only a few lines ahead of me now. But so tightly packed, all I could see was Ewan to my left, the boy to my right, and the backs of a hundred or so MacDonald men.

If this is a charge, I thought dismally . . .

"MacDonald!" someone called again, as we waded shoulder to shoulder across the moor. My feet kept making sucking noises in the boggy ground, and the springy heather made walking even harder. *The Keppoch was right,* I thought. *And Granda, too. This ground is a poor choice for us.*

"Shift!" Ewan said suddenly to me. "Duncan, move to my left so ye dinna block my sword arm." Though we both knew he needed two hands to wield the bloody thing.

Nevertheless, I let him shove me over to his left, and was glad of

it, for there was more room on that side and I could leave the jostling
lad behind.

I raised my dirk. Only yesterday it had seemed such a grown-up
weapon, yet now, after a morning of muskets and cannon, I knew it
wasn't much. But if I could be Ewan's wasp . . . *Well,* I thought, *my
dirk might do some duty yet.*

"Claymore! Claymore!"

The MacDonald call came again, this time erupting from hundreds of throats at once.

Clanranald's men rattled their swords and shouted: "*Dh'
aindeoin co theireadh e! Gainsay who dare!*"

Then the MacDonalds of Glengarry roared back at them,
"*Creaghan-an-Fhithich!* The Raven's Rock!"

Not to be outdone, Ewan and I joined in the Keppoch's yell
along with the rest of our men. "*Dia 's Naomh Aindrea!* God and St.
Andrew!"

The yell seemed to give me the strength I needed. *Once we
charge, no one can stand against us,* my heart told me, as I thought
of what Da had said about Edinburgh, about Falkirk. *The English
always run before Highland swords.*

The men in front of me suddenly charged, and I ran after them.
Behind me the pipes screamed out for blood. They sang of glory.
And suddenly all I could think of was killing the redcoats, the
sassanachs, the invaders.

"God and St. Andrew!" I screamed.

But half a dozen steps later, my feet began sinking into muddy
pools. The lingering smoke in the air caught again in my throat.

"This . . . is . . . hard . . . going," I cried out. The boggy ground
had grabbed off my right cuaran and I had to kneel to free it.

"I'm caught, too." That was Ewan right behind me. Then I

heard him laugh. "That's it, then. I'll go shoeless. Come on, Duncan, we're almost to the English line." He shook his sword. "Let them taste our steel."

"Wait for me," I begged. I didn't want to face the English alone, with only my dirk. A wasp has the right to be a little afraid.

"But we're so close, Duncan."

"Och, we're not that close. Look, will ye, Ewan? Ye can barely make them out. They're a hundred yards away. There'll be plenty left for us." I got the stupid shoe back on and stood.

The crash of English musket fire and the iron boom of their cannon came again. Huge clouds of smoke rolled across the moor, plunging Ewan and me into a choking darkness. Then a rush of hot air whipped past my ear and I flinched from it with a sharp intake of breath.

Cannonball!

I clutched my dagger so hard, the pommel left an imprint on my palm. Sighing in relief when the ball flew past me, I looked for Ewan to make a joke of my fright.

"Did ye see me shake, Ewan?"

He didn't answer.

"I was like a tree in the wind, Ewan."

He was silent.

"Ewan?"

Then some of the smoke cleared and I saw him, off to my right. He had been slammed to the ground by the cannonball so suddenly, he'd not even had a chance to cry out. His face was white, his head was covered with bright-red blood. Shards of white breastbone showed through his open chest. His right hand—the sword hand— was gone completely.

Oh, God, Ewan. If I hadn't asked you to wait . . .

I looked around, desperate for help, then saw his severed hand a couple of yards past a gorse bush, its lifeless fingers still fastened around the hilt of the stolen sword.

Oh, God, Ewan.

I knew then with crushing certainty that I'd killed him as surely as I'd killed Mairi. Suddenly, I remembered Mairi telling him: "There's blood on yer head, Ewan, as if ye were wearing a scarlet bonnet." An uncontrollable tremor began to run down my arms and legs, and I sank to my knees, one hand stretching out helplessly toward his body.

"Ewan!" I cried, for an instant unable to summon grief, only a strange kind of relief that it wasn't me there on the ground.

"I'm sorry. I'm sorry," I cried, relief turning to shame.

Someone grabbed me by the arm and hauled me roughly to my feet.

"Up, lad!" a gruff voice ordered. "The best service ye can do the dead is to avenge them."

An abrupt shove propelled me forward. I struggled onward, my dirk held before me, through more smoke and muck and sleet. I was so dazed, I didn't notice the face of the man who had grabbed me. I hardly noticed anything. Even the din and roar of the battle faded to a distant buzz. I felt as if I had been plunged into an icy pool and would never be warm again.

As I moved forward, I tripped over something, a man, a Cameron, knee-down in the muck. Blood dripped from jagged wounds in his neck and chest, mingling with the mud. I touched his shoulder. It was cold as ice and as hard.

"Is there nae end to this blasted moor!" someone exclaimed behind us. I could hear the sucking sound of his feet in the bog.

"Go on! Go on!" cried someone else.

I left the kneeling man and struggled on. Another man lay face-down in the bog in front of me. I stepped over him. Still another lay faceup, sleet melting into his eyes. More, then more, faceless, arm-less, legless, headless men. I didn't know their names. I couldn't see their faces for the mud and blood and smoke and sleet.

What could I do for them?

Take revenge.

But revenge sounded like poor comfort in the midst of all this horror. How could more bloodshed wash away what had already soaked into me? I was covered in it, head to toe. I remembered Ma saying, "Hope is sowing while death is mowing." Mowing indeed. Death had mown us down like a scythe through corn.

Directly ahead, the crash of muskets grew. The calm voices of English officers barking out their orders seemed distant, uncaring. As if we Scots really were only a crop to be cut down in the field, not flesh, not blood.

Blood—dear God—so much blood!

The image of Ewan's hand by the gorse bush suddenly came back to me. Not his blanched, dead face, but his severed hand. I fell to my knees and began to cry.

"Fire!" commanded the calm English voices. And immediately after came the awful boom of cannon. The mass of standing men ahead of me quivered.

The cannon boomed again.

And again.

The pipes behind me fell silent as if they had nothing more to say. The beat of our drums faltered.

"Grapeshot!" someone cried in warning.

Granda had told me about grapeshot. *Awful stuff,* he'd said. *The worst.* The cannonball replaced with bundles of musket balls, nails, scraps of metal. At close range, it could kill or maim half a dozen men at a go.

Oh, God, I thought, *not grapeshot.*

A huge groan went up around me as if the very earth protested.

I stood. I don't know why. Staying down made more sense. Staying down meant staying safe. But I stood.

Not for honor.

Not for glory.

For revenge.

"On!" cried our chiefs. "It's no far now, brave lads!"

Once again swords were brandished in the air, banners waved. I lifted my knife. Now it seemed as heavy as a sword.

I found a group of Highlanders. I couldn't tell which clan. Just men, muddy, bloody, nameless men. Men who were still standing. For this moment.

The pipes—were there fewer now?—resumed their labored tunes. We started forward.

The sleet lessened. The smoke lifted. Ahead I saw someone I knew: a mane of white hair; a tall, handsome, mud-spattered old man. So, I was near the front line.

If only I can get to his side, I thought. *The Keppoch will see me through.*

There was another volley of musket fire, then a further round of grapeshot. Beside me, three men staggered backward, falling on the boggy ground, their sarks just crimsoned tatters.

By now the men in front of me were crouching low or flinging themselves full-length on the heather to avoid the next English volley. Before I could do the same, a giant of a man stumbled backward, colliding with me, knocking me flat on my back. He dropped his sword as he fell, pinning me to the ground beneath him.

Winded, I lay gasping until I could summon the strength to wriggle out from under. I pushed myself up onto one knee and stared at him. His lifeless eyes—one blue, one a blind white—gazed up at the leaden sky. A jagged fragment of iron was embedded in his forehead like a dagger.

Stupidly, I wondered what his name was.

And then I thought: *Sandy. Sandy MacDonald, of course.*

Somehow I managed to get to my feet. I could have turned then and run. God knows, others were racing away. Ma would have told me to run. Da, too. I looked down at my hand, the one that still held the dirk. It was covered with poor Sandy's blood. MacDonald blood.

"To me!" Suddenly I heard a familiar old voice up ahead yelling. "To me, sons of Donald! Will ye no charge, for the sake of yer honor!"

I knew then that I couldn't retreat. I owed Sandy something. I owed Ewan something. I owed the Keppoch something. Not a throne for a king. Not vengeance. I understood that now. What I owed them was my honor. It's all a man has, all a MacDonald has, after all.

"For God and St. Andrew!" I cried, and started forward again.

26 ❧ FLEEING

"To me, sons of Donald!" the Keppoch called again.

Peering through the billowing smoke and the sleety rain, I caught a glimpse of him. He stood as boldly as a young warrior, sword in one hand, pistol in the other, his guards gathered around him. A young man with flame-colored hair was just now lifting a flag from the fingers of a fallen standard-bearer, then raising it overhead where it flew bravely in the sullen wind.

I moved closer.

The Keppoch looked around, at men skulking away, not like wolves, but like their sons, the little foxes. "My God, has it come to this?" he exclaimed, staring right at me, right through me. "That I am abandoned by my own children."

"Not I," I croaked, holding up my dirk.

He didn't seem to hear me, though, for he turned and started toward the English lines, his guards following in his wake. As he strode along, scattered groups of fighters, men who had been lying prone on the ground, men who'd been scurrying away, men who were behind me and around me, took heart and ran to join him in one last desperate charge.

"God and St. Andrew!" they called, before disappearing into the smoke.

I meant to go with them. God and St. Andrew knew I wanted to.

But suddenly my legs wouldn't obey me any longer. I couldn't take a single step. It was as if I had been turned to stone.

"Fire!" came the calm command from the English line, so close now, I could see the buttons on their uniforms.

This time the noise was deafening. Smoke spouted from red-coat muskets, gouts of fire, and scorching wind.

"No!" I gasped, thinking that no one charging into that storm could survive. Not the Keppoch nor any of the MacDonalds. And all at once I was running forward and weeping; sobbing for Ewan, and for big Sandy, and for the boy who'd lost his leg in the first round of cannon shot, and for all the maimed I had stepped over to get to this place.

And weeping, too, because for some reason, I was still alive on bloody Drummossie Moor at a place called Culloden. I—who should never have come to this muddy hell in the *first* place. And weeping because it was to be the very *last* place in the world I would ever know.

Suddenly, a wounded MacDonald came rushing out of the murk, his plaid trailing behind. He elbowed me aside, knocking me face-first into a large puddle in the bog.

As I splashed about in the cold water, a dreadful torpor seized hold of me. The noise of battle faded away and a voice whispered in my ear: "Stay here. That will be an end to yer troubles. Here ye can know peace."

Peace. That was what I wanted. *The peace between musket fire. The peace between battles. The peace between wars.* And then I had one last thought: *The peace of the grave.* It sounded so wonderful.

For a moment, I felt I was standing between two worlds, one where I could surrender to that blessed final sleep, the other where I was wide-awake in the midst of fire and smoke and noise.

"Stay here," the voice whispered again.

And I almost listened.

But honor wouldn't let me. I pushed up hard, my fingers seeking some hold in the mud. Spitting out brackish water, I struggled to my feet, using the back of my hand to wipe the muck from my face. All I could see now were billows of smoke and the tartan of broken Highlanders who were stumbling around as if lost in a winter fog.

"Get up!" I told myself. "Move, ye slacker, move!" So I got up slowly and began to move, finding my way only by instinct and trudging toward what I thought was our front.

An agonized groan made me stop. Before me, sunk to his knees, hands clutching his belly, was a man, a MacDonald. From the quality of his weapons, I knew he was one of the captains. Beside him, on a tussock of muddy grass, lay his sword.

"Here, sir," I said, offering my hand, "let me help ye."

He waved me away, a trickle of blood spilling over his lips, bright red until the sleet turned it pale. "There's nae helping me," he croaked. "I'm done, lad. Go to the aid of the chief. That's yer duty now. Nae use trying to help a dead man." He pointed off to one side, in a different direction that I'd been heading. "Go to him."

"Who, sir?"

"The Keppoch, lad." Then he started coughing up more blood.

For a minute I thought about taking his sword. He had no more use for it. But it was a heavy thing by the look, too heavy for me. And a man's sword is his own. Taking it could bring me the same bad luck as Ewan. I hurried away.

The field was covered with bodies. Apologizing over and over to the dead men I stepped on, I made my way forward till I came upon a group of nine Highlanders crazed with battle madness. Even though it was clear that they could make no headway against another hail of bullets, they clashed their swords against their targes and bellowed out their defiance, saying "Come for us, ye sassanachs, or we'll be coming for ye!" One yelled the loudest. He was broad in the shoulder and wild-eyed, a bloodied fist wrapped around his sword hilt. "Sassanachs!" he cried again.

"Ye canna kill the Highland spirit!" called his companion, half a head shorter.

Next to him was a wiry old man, his beard more white than grey. He was hurling rocks at the enemy and screaming, "We'll show ye how to fight like men."

But the English just stood, calmly reloading their guns, preparing to fire again.

"For God and St. Andrew," I shouted, ready to join in one last, mad charge. There was a bloodred haze over the field. I took a deep breath.

27 ✌ THE KEPPOCH

Close to my right, I suddenly heard someone cry out, "Get him up! Take a leg there, Iain!"

It was a familiar voice, like a lifeline, and me about to drown in a river of blood. The haze before my eyes lifted and I turned toward the voice. Running to him, my legs were suddenly as spry as they'd been in the early morning. The rain parted like a curtain, and there was Angus Ban standing over his father's body.

The Keppoch fallen? It was as if the earth had cracked wide.

Angus Ban had the chief by the head and shoulders while an old, grizzled clansman—Iain at a guess—was trying to take hold of his legs, which were slippery with rain and mud.

"Let me help, sir," I called, rushing to their aid. Sliding my dirk back into my belt, I took a grip of the Keppoch's left leg, leaving Iain to the other.

"Yer a fine sight to see, lad," Angus Ban told me. "Where's yer young friend?"

A droop of my head answered him. Then I really looked at the Keppoch. He had a bloody wound in one arm and another—much worse—gaping in his chest. I couldn't tell if he were breathing or not. "Is he alive?"

"Barely," Angus Ban said grimly. "But we'll no leave him here for the sassanach to finish."

"No if I have to carry him myself, sir." Though the one leg was slippery with mud and rain, I swore I would not let it go.

"It willna come to that, lad."

With Angus Ban walking backward and Iain and me going forward, we carried the Keppoch like so much butchered meat. He was not a light burden, with his sodden plaid and jacket, his great sword and brace of pistols. But just as I hadn't taken the dying captain's sword, I knew we couldn't dishonor the Keppoch by removing his weapons just to make things easier for ourselves. Not while he was still alive.

"Hurry! Hurry!" Angus Ban said, trying to keep us moving. "Before those damned guns start up again."

We were certainly going as fast as we could, but the boggy ground kept grabbing at our feet, the dead bodies strewn over the field kept getting in the way. We had to warn Angus Ban each time where to step and which way to go or he would have fallen backward over them.

"Hurry, both of ye," Angus Ban said again, before glancing down at the Keppoch, whose lips were moving, though no sound came out. Then he added, "Not far, Father, not far."

Not far to where? I wondered, but didn't dare ask. I needed all my breath.

There was another crash of muskets and a ball smacked the water between my feet. I jumped and let out a frightened sound. The Keppoch's body tensed.

"Leave me!" he croaked. "Save yer own lives!"

"Wheesht, Father!" Angus Ban told him. "I'm no bairn that ye can tell me what to do." Then he said to Iain and me, "Keep moving. Hurry. Hurry. *That* way." He tilted his head toward the edge of the moor where there was a stand of trees.

When other retreating clansmen saw who it was we were bearing to safety, they formed a ring of swords around us to keep off any redcoats who might give chase. I didn't recognize a one of them, except by their badges.

"It looks bad," a bald man told Iain.

"Shut yer mouth," Iain replied. "He's not deaf, ye know."

"Hurry," I said, picking up Angus Ban's cry. "Hurry." Because it *was* bad. Anyone could see that. And because the Keppoch's leg was a dead weight about to slip out of my hands.

We hurried, if a snail's pace could be called hurrying.

"There's cavalry coming up on our flank to the left there, Angus," Iain said. As soon as he spoke, I heard the ominous drumming of hoofbeats.

"Pay nae mind," Angus Ban ordered. "The prince has men in reserve who'll keep them at bay." Then he said down to the Keppoch, "Almost there, Father."

My arms felt on fire. My back was aching. *Not far,* I told myself. *Not far.*

Now the smoke was clearing, and by turning my head to the left, I could see the Highland line.

Line! What had been full of glorious warriors such a short time before was now a huddle of frightened men. Few Highlanders still stood upright, and those who did clumped in ragged groups. Several of them were falling back into defensive formations. But the greater number were simply running toward us, toward safety, as fast as their weary legs could carry them. And who could blame them? Surely not I.

Suddenly, directly ahead of us, I saw a well-ordered body of soldiers in blue uniforms, their muskets primed and at the ready.

"Angus Ban," I whispered, "we're done for. Look behind ye."

He turned his head, then gave a short, sharp snort of laughter.

"Dinna fear, laddie," Iain said for him, "those are the Royals, loyal Scots like ye and me. Only they've fought in the king of France's army so they're wearing his uniforms. They've come home to stand by the prince."

The French? Have they arrived at last? The prince will like that, I thought.

"Stand," growled one of our guardians. "And that's all the Frenchies have done—stand. While the rest of us charged and died." He spat to one side.

Even as the man spoke, a squad of red-jacketed English dragoons came galloping across the moor in pursuit of the fleeing Highlanders, heading straight toward us. I saw them raise their sabers, glinting wickedly in the feeble sun.

I was so terrified, I almost let the Keppoch slip from me. But in one efficient motion, the Royals swung their muskets about and unleashed a booming volley at the redcoats. The English dragoons swerved sharply aside and pulled back out of range, their horses kicking angrily at the air.

"Did ye see that!" I cried, hope returning. "The English horsemen fled. They *fled!*" I held tightly to the Keppoch's leg, suddenly full of strength again. "My da says . . ."

Angus Ban shook his head. "They have time and territory on their side, lad. They dinna need to put themselves in danger. Och—didna the Keppoch warn about this ground." His voice broke as he spoke his father's name.

The Royals opened their ranks, allowing us and other fleeing Highlanders to pass through. Then they closed ranks behind us.

"Are we safe now?" I asked Iain, hope flaring in my heart.

He looked grimly toward some redcoats who had suddenly

surged around our flank, trying to engulf us. Our own Scots cavalry galloped off to meet them, but they were badly outmatched, like a handful of straw hurled into the face of a flood.

"At least we're no longer on boggy ground," I said. Instead it was hummocky and covered with scratchy gorse. *But much better,* I thought, *than muck and mire.* "Are we close yet?"

"There!" Angus Ban replied, tilting his head toward a flimsy hut about two hundred feet further along, partly hidden in the trees.

We staggered toward it, conscious that a battle still raged around us, but determined to find safety for the Keppoch. When we got there at last, Iain kicked open the door and we managed to get the chief inside.

28 ⚘ THE OLD BOTHY

The hut was low, dim, and damp, the walls green with mold and the thatched roof half fallen in. The smell was awful, like a byre that hadn't been cleaned for months. There were a few bits of furniture—several broken chairs, and a battered oak table in the one room. A half-dozen wounded men were already sheltering inside, sitting on the floor, their backs to the leftmost wall, all so badly off, none could lift a hand to help us.

Gently we lowered the Keppoch onto the table, which looked almost too rickety to support his weight, yet—amazingly—it held, as if borrowing some of his own strength.

"There, Father," Angus Ban said, "we'll be fine here."

Though how anyone could be fine in this low, damp place, I couldn't even begin to guess.

The Keppoch lay still, his arms and legs hanging loose over the table ends. Exhausted, I stared at him while trying to rub some life back into my aching arms.

"Father?" Angus Ban bent over his father, then laid a hand on his cheek. The old man's mouth hung open; there seemed to be no breath passing between his lips. Drawing his hand slowly down over his father's brow, Angus Ban lovingly closed the Keppoch's eyes for the last time. He whispered, "Good-bye, Father."

"Godspeed," I said.

Angus Ban looked up, nodding. "Godspeed, indeed."

Only then did I notice that the MacDonald men who had guarded us on our retreat were now crowding in the doorway. One stepped forward and said softly, "Angus Ban, our duty is done here."

"Aye," Angus Ban agreed wearily. "Ye've served yer chief well, all of ye. Good luck to ye now."

The men turned and rushed away.

"Ye, too, Iain," Angus Ban said quietly, so that no one else in the dim, smelly hut could hear but the three of us. "Go now, quickly. Go back and tell my stepmother what has befallen. Bring her my father's sword." He unbelted belt, sheath, and sword from his father's body. "Tell her I'll come when I can and if it is God's will."

Iain nodded.

I moved away so they wouldn't think I was eavesdropping on purpose, though I heard it all anyway.

"Tell her that if things go hard with her—as I fear they will—to shelter in the cave at Loch Trieg. She knows the place. Tell her to rely on my brother Ranald in all things. He's only twelve, but has a canny old head on those young shoulders."

"I should stay," Iain began. "For yer father's sake. For the chieftain."

I turned to look at them, wondering what the answer to that would be.

"My father is dead," Angus Ban said brutally. Then, as if to soften what he'd just said, he added, "Nae, man. I am yer chieftain now, so ye must obey *me*. I want ye to live for Scotland and for the Keppoch MacDonalds. We need men of yer strength for the tasks ahead." He clasped Iain's arm.

Iain nodded again and drew away. Then he stood a moment looking out the open door. Just before he went through, he turned and said, "For God and St. Andrew." Then he was gone.

I was surprised at how quickly he'd left. But Angus Ban himself surprised me even more. Pulling the two pistols out of his father's belt, he set about loading them with powder and bullets.

"Sir," I asked, "do ye mean to continue the fight?" For if he was going back to the lines, I would, too. "I'll go with ye."

He looked up as if finally remembering I was still there. "What's yer name, lad?" he asked me.

"Duncan MacDonald," I replied. "Of Glenroy."

"Well, Duncan of Glenroy, if this sorry day hasna made a man of ye, nothing ever will."

"I dinna feel much like a man," I said slowly.

Angus Ban rammed the loaded pistols into his belt, then looked at me again. "Aye, I know what ye mean, Duncan. But feeling sick at a slaughter means ye have a good brain in yer head, and there's nothing unmanly in weeping for the dead." He nodded as if agreeing with himself. "But this is nae time for philosophy. When the redcoats get here, they'll put a torch to this place, and to everything else for miles."

"But yer father . . ."

"Gone to his rest," said Angus Ban. "And honorable it is. Nothing can disturb him now."

"What about these brave men?" I gestured to the wounded lying against the walls.

He leaned forward till his mouth was near my ear and whispered, "There's none here who can be moved without great pain, Duncan. Look at them. Chest wounds and gut wounds. The worst. This is nae hospital but a mortuary. They'll all be dead before nightfall."

I gazed around the hut, squinting in the dim light. He was right, and I knew it. Indeed, half of those who had been alive when we arrived were already dead, slumped over or fallen to the floor. The others were scarcely moving. But to just go without them . . .

"Cumberland doesna mean to leave a Highlander standing. It's madness to stay here with the dead and the dying, lad. They'd tell ye that themselves, if they had the breath." He looked around slowly at the men in the hut. "To stay would only add two more to Cumberland's count. A grand gesture signifying nothing."

I tried to take in what he was saying, and failed. He put his hand on my shoulder and the weight of it made me tremble.

He looked deep into my eyes. "In France they say *sauve qui peut*, every man for himself. That's what we've come to now. It's all that stands between Scotland and complete ruin: the saving of a few good men from this debacle. We must choose to live, lad. Go home and help rebuild our poor ruined land. Ye must do it. And so must I."

I nodded. How strange that leaving felt even harder than staying. "What about the prince, sir?" I asked. "And the throne?" I gulped and gestured to the men. "Has all this been for nothing?"

"We will get the prince safely away," he said. "I am going to him now. And there's always another day for our fight. But first we must survive this one."

"Right, sir." I took small hope from that. Ewan and his da would not have another day.

He took what I said for agreement, though I wasn't sure how I'd meant it. "So, good luck to ye, Duncan MacDonald of Glenroy. I hope ye wish me the same."

I tried to smile and couldn't. "Good luck, Angus Ban MacDonald of Keppoch," I said, and saluted him.

He turned and slipped out the door and—as I watched— sprinted for the cover of the nearest trees.

29 ❧ THE DEVIL SET LOOSE

Standing for a minute by the open door, I let the cold, damp air clear my head. It was still light, the sleet had stopped, and a slight drizzle was now falling. What Angus Ban said made sense: that we should all go home and work our farms, knowing there would be another day to fight for the Stuart. But who would work Ewan's farm now? And who would be alive and willing when the prince next called us out?

I had no answers, only questions, striking my tired head like grapeshot. So all that was left for me to do was to leave the dim, awful hut with its dead men. I had just checked the dirk in my belt and started out the door when I heard a loud clink behind me. Turning, I saw something glinting on the floor, picking up the bit of light from the open door. Whatever it was lay just below the Keppoch's dangling hand.

I went back inside and picked the thing up—a gold brooch with a painted lion on the top of the arch. The lion had red stone eyes. I knew at once the brooch was the one the Keppoch had been given at Glenfinnan, the brooch with the prince's hair locked inside. It must have shaken loose from the Keppoch's plaid and fallen to the floor.

Should I take the time to pin it back on?

I hesitated, considering. Why had the thing fallen off now and not when we were hurrying away from the battlefield? Why now and not when Angus Ban was in the hut? Why now and not after I had left?

And then suddenly I knew that the reason the brooch had fallen here and now was that God didn't want it taken as plunder by the redcoats. He didn't want Angus Ban to own it. God wanted *me* to have it.

But why?

If I sold the brooch, it would bring enough money to buy my father's farm twenty times over. I could give some of the money to Ewan's ma to help with their farm. I could do what Angus Ban wanted—help out Glenroy. But then wouldn't I be as much a plunderer as the redcoats? Worse even, since I'd be stealing from my own.

The golden brooch lay heavy in my palm. So I would not sell the thing.

And still the question was why. *Why should I have it? Why now?*

Then I thought about the prince's hair, set in the brooch behind stone. It might cure me of my fits. I could break the glass easily. But again, I'd be taking the brooch as plunder. I doubted magic would work that way, not healing magic.

I closed my fingers over the thing, and that's when I knew what to do. *I'll take the brooch to the Keppoch's widow.* I smiled at the thought. It might be some comfort to her. She could even buy protection for her family with it. I knew where to find her, even if she hid herself away.

All at once the brooch felt light again. I pinned it to the underside of my plaid, where it sat over my heart. Looking one last time around the hut at the dead men and the dying, I saluted them. Now I was ready to go.

The sky was a mucky yellow from cannon smoke. A stink like

rotten eggs filled the air. As I left the hut, I tried hard not to breathe too deeply.

At least the cannon have fallen silent, I thought, though my ears were still ringing from the long bombardment. I looked back at the battlefield, horrified at what I saw there. The redcoats were going across the field, bayoneting any wounded in their path. Some even stopped to strip the bodies of the dead.

Murderers! I cursed them under my breath. "Thieves!"

One of the soldiers looked up and I froze, like a deer under the trees, hoping not to be seen. I knew that if they saw me move, they'd turn their guns on me. Trying to calm my thundering heart, I waited until he turned back to his awful work, then I bent low to escape notice, and ran. South and west, my only hope.

So I fled, running across fields and over paths, jumping ditches and squeezing through thorny hedges that ripped at my arms and legs. I passed dead men, dying men, wounded men, and didn't stop for them. I passed swords that had been thrown away, pistols by the roadside, bonnets and cuarans by the score. But I picked up none of them. I just kept running.

Angus Ban had asked me to stay alive and help rebuild the land. He asked me to choose life. I knew my mission now: to return home, to stand up for my own, to deliver the brooch to the widow Keppoch.

As I went along one stretch of track, I raced past a group of cottages where women and children peered fearfully from small windows.

I didn't stop to warn them. They must have already seen the rout. I wasn't the first Highlander to run this way. *Surely,* I thought as I went by them, *surely the English will spare women and children.*

Then, out of sight of the cottages, I was forced to slow down. My right side felt as if I'd been stabbed. Leaning against a stunted birch, I sucked air into my parched throat. What I would have given for a drink of cold water.

A bugle call and the crack of a pistol behind me brought me bolt upright. I'd no time to stop, to feel pain or weakness. I had to run or I *would* be killed. I willed the pain in my side away, and set off again.

I'd been racing along a broad track since passing the cottages. Though it made running easy, it made me a target as well. Turning onto a dirt track off to the left, I followed it over a small rise.

Ahead of me were a score of Highlanders, shuffling along so worn and ragged, they looked like the straw dummies set out in the field to frighten birds.

One of them—a gaunt, solemn man wearing the bonnet of the Glengarry MacDonalds—looked back and saw me. When he realized I was no redcoat, he limped painfully toward me, then clapped a bloodstained hand on my shoulder.

"Tell me, laddie," he asked quietly, "have ye seen a dark-haired boy a little older than yerself, with a scar on his left cheek? He's my own son, Jamie, and I told him to keep close."

I shook my head, for I hadn't breath to spare for a real answer.

There was a tear in his eye and his hand slid from my shoulder. "I told him to keep close," he repeated, as if the only comfort left him was the echo of his own voice.

"Horses!"

The warning cry made us all jump. The exhausted men mustered the last of their strength and broke into a ragged run.

Only the limping man, Jamie's father, didn't flee but turned slowly to face the approaching riders. There were nearly a dozen of them brandishing sabers and pistols.

"Will ye no come?" I pleaded, tugging at the man's threadbare plaid. "Ye might yet find yer boy."

"Ye go on, laddie," he answered in a hollow voice. "I'll no find him again in this world."

I turned and ran off after the others as the hoofbeats grew closer. Glancing back over my shoulder, I saw Jamie's father raise empty hands in surrender. But the leading rider leaned from the saddle and sliced clean through his throat with one stroke of the saber.

"Halloo!" whooped his companions as they trampled the corpse into the dirt.

I ran down the path with the fleeing Highlanders and we were like sheep before ravenous wolves. Five or six pistol shots rang out and a bullet smacked into the back of the man nearest me, pitching him headlong to the ground.

Then came a swishing sound and something whipped the bonnet from my head. The shock was enough to fling me down. I rolled over and over until I came to rest at the side of the track with my arms over my head. I lay there, unmoving, hoping I would be taken for dead, hoping none of the savage horses would grind me beneath their hooves.

Let me live, I prayed. *I want to live.*

Then the pounding noise of the horses passed by and I jumped up and ran into the tangle of trees by the side of the track.

Just when I thought I'd gotten away, I heard a yell behind me, and looked over my shoulder. One of the riders had broken away from his fellows to chase me. The others laughed and left him to his sport.

"Come here, young rebel!" he shouted as he bore down on me. "Come here you bloody Scot, and take your medicine!"

I was crying now, and the world around me grew wavery. Every minute of life was suddenly precious. I lurched sideways into a hollow and, an instant later, a saber split the empty air where I'd just been. As I dropped into cover, I saw that the whole length of the blade was slick with blood. I waited for a sharp pain, but none came.

Not my blood, then, I thought, then added, *not yet.*

As the horseman passed by, I sucked in air. Cold air into hot lungs. *Dinna let him take ye without a fight.* That sounded like Granda's voice. But he wasn't here. It was just in my head. *Remember, yer a MacDonald.*

I remembered, and swiped the back of my hand across my eyes, clearing them. I saw that I was in a small cavity in the ground, the size and shape of a grave.

"By God and St. Andrew," I whispered, scrambling out of the hollow and racing across the path, slipping into another dip in the ground, this one a maze of undergrowth, enough to hide me. As if by their own will, my fingers found the handle of my dirk and pulled it from my belt.

Meanwhile, the English dragoon had turned his horse around and was spurring it back toward the hole he thought I was hiding in. The horse's hooves thundered along the ground.

"You'll not escape the king's justice, rebel!" the dragoon called.

But now I was on his blind side, waiting . . . waiting . . .

"I'll find you, boy!" he raged. "I'll slice you up like a side of beef!"

The minute he leaned over to scythe at the old hole, his back toward me, I leaped up. Then, with every ounce of strength I had, I rammed my dirk into the horse's neck. The beast reared up with an ear-piercing scream. The trooper was caught completely by surprise. He lost his grip on the reins and was tossed high into the air, then landed on the hard ground with a sickening crack. Maddened by pain, the horse galloped off, the dirk still jammed into its neck.

I stood up and gazed at the fallen dragoon. His sword had gone spinning from his hand to land among a cluster of thorns. I couldn't tell if he were alive or dead, but I'd no desire to get any closer.

"For God and St. Andrew," I whispered again.

Then I ran off and didn't stop until I came to a copse of trees. Squirming down among the roots of a large oak, I wriggled as far as I could into the damp ground, hiding myself in the earth like a badger.

And there I cried.

It was not girlish crying; not soft, wet weeping. It was manful sobs that howled out of me like the skirling of the pipes. A wonder, with all that howling, that the troopers didn't find me. But they were off after bigger game and I was left alone.

By the time I dared to climb out of my hole, the sun had almost vanished behind the western hills and the sky was stained as red as Drummossie Moor. I brushed off the dirt as best I could, made sure no soldiers were nearby, and started my long trek home.

Along the way I came upon bodies aplenty. Most were Highland men, shot down or cut through as they ran. But there were others. Two farm boys—no older than my brother Andrew—lay together in a pool of blood. They'd clearly only gotten in the way of the cavalrymen's merciless pursuit. A hundred yards further along was an old woman who had fallen into the path of their horses.

Strangest of all, I found the stout merchant who'd come from

Inverness to watch the battle. Three deep slashes disfigured his body. He'd hoped to see a fight and had gotten far more than he bargained for. There was no sign of his wife and son, and I prayed they'd been spared. I couldn't wish this slaughter on anyone.

I wandered through the blighted land, feeling as if I were one of the dead myself. And then my head started to ache. With each step the pain grew worse. I felt sick to my stomach and dancing lights flashed before my eyes.

Had I gone through the hell of Culloden without a single fit only to have one here? It seemed so unfair. But I knew I needed to get out of sight before the fit took me completely. Still, it was hard to think with my head buzzing so. Then the buzzing became voices.

"Hoy, who's that there?"

An English voice.

"Catch him, Davy!"

And another.

A trio of redcoats stepped out of the shadow of the trees. Not cavalry but foot soldiers. I saw them as if through a haze. Their boots were spattered with mud, their faces grimed with the smoke of their guns. Even as I swooned, falling to the ground, I could see that their bayonets were sticky with blood.

I thought of getting up again and fighting, but I no longer even had Granda's dirk. And every moment I was sinking further and further toward the dark.

One of the soldiers leaned forward to peer at me through the gathering gloom, his bayonet near my chest.

"Leave him. He's just a boy, not even shaving yet."

"That makes no odds," snarled the first. "He's a rebel."

My arms and legs began to twitch uncontrollably. My jaw

clenched and saliva dribbled down the side of my mouth. I tried to ask for mercy, but could only utter a low, wordless grunt.

"Have we found a mad dog?" asked the first soldier.

"Keep back," his friend warned. "I've seen this sickness before."

"Can't you see a devil's got hold of him?" said the third.

"All the more reason to kill him, then."

"Don't be a fool. Kill this kind of madman, you set the devil loose and he takes the one that killed him."

The soldier standing over me began to shake and the point of the bayonet was wavering, like a blade of grass in the breeze.

"See? See? It's coming over you already."

"Arrrrgh. Only old women believe those stories." The point of the bayonet inched closer to my chest. "But like you say, he's just a boy. We'll let the devil keep him."

They walked away.

Then another figure slipped out of the shadows, one I knew well.

Mairi.

She was all lightness and sparkle. Leaning over me with the faintest of smiles, she brushed my chest exactly at the spot where Keppoch's brooch was concealed.

"Yer carrying a blessing with ye, Duncan," she said. "Take good care of it and I promise I'll guard ye on yer way for as long as ye need me."

The last of the pain and brightness faded and she vanished along with them. I sat up, astonished. Never before had I begun a fit and not fallen away completely into the darkness. Never before had I been awake enough to see and hear all that was happening around me. Never before could I just sit up without help.

I brought the brooch out from under my plaid and stared at it.

The lion's jeweled eyes met mine. Its great mouth was open, as though it wanted to speak.

"What are ye saying to me?" I whispered. But I knew without asking. He was saying that my story wasn't at an end. That I had a duty yet to perform, though I never could have guessed what it would turn out to be.

III. PRINCE IN THE HEATHER

☙ *May–September 1746*

On dark Culloden's field of gore,

Hark! They shout, "Claymore! Claymore!"

They bravely fight, what can they more?

They die for Royal Charlie.

—*Sound the Pibroch,* traditional song

30 ⁊ RETURN TO GLENROY

I walked more miles than I could count, for day after day after day. I didn't dare go along a straightaway. Instead, I went over mountains, through the woods, going south and east toward home.

Every night I lay hidden in a ditch or under a bush, dreading the jab of a bayonet in the dark. Often I heard horses go past, or the march of many feet. I heard English voices shouting out commands and English soldiers cursing. I learned to be as still as a rabbit in its hole or a badger in its sett.

Each day as I walked, I remembered: blood, smoke, and the faces of the dead. At night it was the same. When I slept—when I finally slept—I couldn't escape the dreams. Shattered bone, tattered skin, faces eaten away by musket and cannon shot. The dead and dying visited me and wouldn't let me rest.

Now and again I ran into others who'd fled the battle, all of them weak and pale and hollow-eyed. We didn't speak of that day. What could we say? Besides, whenever we heard the sound of horses, or wagons, or even a deer coming over a hill, we scattered like rabbits.

For food I picked berries and dug up roots, drank from streams and from the wells of villages that had been burned out by the redcoats. Once in a deserted cottage, I discovered some moldy bread and dry cheese in a turned-over cupboard; in another, a full plate of bannocks on the floor under a table. The bannocks were hard as stones. I ate them anyway, after softening them in water.

It was a strange thing to be a fugitive in my own country, hunted by our masters. More than once I thought of surrender. There were redcoats everywhere. Surely a prisoner would be fed, would have a roof over his head. But as quick as I thought that, I dismissed it. I'd already seen Cumberland's justice—men and women and children all slaughtered, their houses burned, their cattle taken. I only hoped that Glenroy might be spared, being so far away and at the end of a small glen. It was a hard place to find.

I lost my way over and over, stumbling through the heather, and clambering over hills, skirting small lochs and wading through cold streams. When I found a river or loch whose course I could follow, I stayed with it until the sun showed me I was headed awry. Then I'd turned south and west again.

But the call of home is strong, and for every wrong turning, I took another the right way until finally I found a path I recognized, up near our shieling.

I bent down and kissed the ground. "For God and St. Andrew," I whispered to the new grass. The rest of the way home I could do with my bonnet pulled down over my eyes.

So I survived to return to Glenroy, and there the worst of my fears came true, for I found nothing.

Nothing.

Our wee cottage—where I'd sat at Granda's knee, listening to his tales; where Ma had stirred the daily porridge pot; where I'd learned my ABCs by writing with a sooty stick on the hearthstone; where Da had taught me songs; where Mairi and Andrew and Sarah and I had slept and eaten and played—the cottage had been destroyed. All that was left was an empty shell of blackened stone. I couldn't go inside, afraid to find my family slaughtered like animals. I put a hand to the wall to steady myself, then turned my back on it and walked toward the byre.

There was little left of it, either, the roof burned off and the door off its hinges. Behind it, the stone dykes that enclosed our garden had been torn down, the acres of crops trampled. I even found our cows, sweet beasts I knew by name—Bessie, Cana, Rona, and Flora Ann—lying along the path between my house and Ewan's.

I started sobbing then. Their throats had been cut, their bodies left to rot. They hadn't even been slaughtered for food. That at least I could have understood. The English soldiers *must* have been hungry. Yet our cows had been butchered simply to destroy our livelihood.

I wandered through the ruin of Glenroy, the smell of burning in my nostrils, a deathly silence filling my ears. There were no people anywhere. Not outside, not inside the cottages, either. I looked.

Where could they be? Had they been taken prisoner? Or had they been marched elsewhere and murdered?

When I finally brought myself back to our broken cottage, I stood for a long moment, still afraid to enter. I who had stood before the guns at Culloden, who had put a knife in a dragoon's horse, who had dodged the English and practically starved on my way home— I was scared stiff.

Finally, I touched the stone where once the door had hinged, drew a deep breath, and went in. My stomach was hollow, there was another hollow in my chest. For a long time I stared down at my feet, afraid of what I would find. I took a deep breath and held it. Then at last I looked up.

No bodies. None.

I let out the breath and a sob at the same time.

I guessed some of the ashes in the broken hearth were the remains of our table and stools. Poking about the sooty debris, I found a little wooden face, charred but still recognizable. I picked it up, then spit on my fingers and scrubbed at the charring. It was all that was left of Sarah's favorite doll, the one Da had carved for her last summer, before the prince came.

Is Sarah still alive? I could hardly bring myself to think it.

"Is Sarah still alive?" There—I said the words aloud, and they echoed in the hollow that had once been my home.

"Is Sarah weeping for her lost doll, or for her lost brother, or Ma or Da or . . ."

I couldn't go on that way or I'd go mad. Instead, I knelt down and put the little carved face back where I had found it. To do anything else felt like disturbing the dead.

It was near dark now, and that seemed right. Right that the whole world should be as black as the remains of my old home. I couldn't stay inside those walls. I walked away with misting eyes until I reached the copse of trees where Ewan and I had played at war.

For a moment I thought I could hear our wooden sticks clacketing together, could hear our arguments and our laughter.

Oh, what I'd give to have those days back again, I thought.

I sank down onto my haunches and rested my head on my folded arms. I began to rock back and forth, humming one of Ma's old lullabies, just as if I were a bairn again. A soft wind accompanied my song.

I'd had enough of being a man.

Suddenly, the undergrowth crackled behind me, and a sense of danger prickled at the nape of my neck.

I reached for my dagger, forgetting that it was long gone.

Grabbing up a fallen birch branch instead—better any weapon than none—I jumped up to face my attacker.

I swung the branch with all my might and it landed with a smack in the flat of Da's upraised palm. We gaped at each other in surprise, and I let my makeshift weapon drop to the ground.

Da's face softened into a loose, lopsided smile, the way it did after his third cup of whiskey. He held out his hands tentatively, as if scared to touch me and find I wasn't real.

"Duncan!" he cried. "Oh, Duncan, I was so afraid ye were dead!" He threw his arms around me, pressing me to his chest. I buried my face in his plaid. Anything, anything to hide my tears.

At last he let go and stepped back to look at me. "Yer thinner than a fishing pole," he said with a weak smile, "and there's enough muck on ye to grow a field of neeps."

I wiped a sleeve across my eyes. "I thought ye'd be angry that I'd run off."

Da ruffled my hair. "I used up all my anger on yer granda for letting ye go."

I looked down at the ground where bluebells were growing all about, and muttered, "It wasna his fault. He couldna stop me."

"Never mind, lad, never mind," he said. "All I feel now is joy that yer safe." He patted my shoulder. "How far have ye been? Where did ye get to?"

"I was at Culloden. On bloody Drummossie Moor."

Da's smile died and his brow grew ridges. "Oh, God, Duncan, after all I told ye, what could have possessed ye to . . ." His voice trailed off and when he spoke again, it was to say softly, "Oh, my poor lad, if only ye'd been spared that horror. Some of the men have managed to make it back with such tales . . ."

"Aye, tales," I repeated in a careful voice. "Maybe one day I'll be able to tell it properly."

He was silent.

I was silent.

We were both remembering battles. Different battles, but somehow the same.

Finally, to stop the pictures in my head, I said, "What's happened here in Glenroy? Was it Cumberland's men?"

"Aye, two days past they came. Lucky those red coats of theirs can be seen miles off by a man on a hilltop. Even so, we'd barely enough time to grab what we could before they came marching up the glen with their guns and their torches. There's been some elsewhere as wasna so lucky. They were caught in their beds, sleeping, and woke to find their houses on fire around them and redcoats at the door to shoot them as they ran out."

"But our folk?"

"All safe. We were lucky, too, for the redcoats came in the daylight. We'd already gotten most of the village cattle to hiding places in the hills. I used the cover of the dark to come down and see what was left."

"It's no much. And our milk cows . . ."

"Aye." He already knew. We passed another silence before he asked, "And Ewan. Is he with ye?"

I swallowed hard.

He looked at me, guessing the worst, but still it had to be said.

"Ewan's dead, Da. Killed at Culloden. A cannonball. I dinna think he suffered, it was so fast." Ewan's death surely deserved better than my poor words, a ballad, maybe, or a lament on the pipes.

"He and his father both killed for the bloody prince," Da said, his voice like bile.

"And all the others. Thousands of them. The best of the Highlands. Was it worth it, Da? Was it worth it?" I remembered Angus Ban saying we'd fight another day, and I wondered if I could lift a sword should that day ever come. My chest heaved with grief and shame, and I began to shake.

Da threw his arms around me once more and didn't let go till he felt me stop shaking. "I'll tell Ewan's ma," he said. "And young Maggie. I'll do it soft."

"Nae, Da, that's my duty." My voice was raw. "They'll want to know how it happened, and there's nobody else can tell them but me. He was by my side. He was . . ."

"As ye think best," said Da. "But I'll come with ye."

"Where are they, Ewan's ma and Maggie?"

"Where we all are—up in the hills. Ye know the place, just past the Great Rock ye can see from the back of the byre. It looks like the end of the world up there. The English never thought to climb so high."

I nodded.

"Let's go now. It will gladden yer mother's heart to see ye well and whole."

"I'll be happy to bring somebody gladness," I said, though I felt neither well nor whole nor glad myself.

We came to the great rock, a crag that stood as high as the Keppoch's rooftop. Da whistled a bit of a pibroch and an answering whistle with the next phrase of the song came from somewhere in the trees.

"We've posted watchers," he said, leading me by the hand. "Though the sassanach are gone on to the next glen, it's better to be careful."

We rounded the rock and there, backed against the tail end of the crag, was a deep hollow. Campfires had been built into the hollow so the light would be hidden by the curve of the hills and smoke wouldn't be seen against the night sky. The smell of cheese being toasted on sticks over the fire made my stomach jump.

"I've no had a real meal since . . ." My voice faded as I tried to remember.

"Dinna mind," said Da. "Ye'll have some tonight." He pointed. "There!"

Before I could make them out, they'd seen me.

Ma called my name and put her hand to her breast, and Andrew and Sarah raced over to me. I picked Sarah up while Andrew clung to my belt.

"Oof!" I said to Sarah. "Ye've gotten heavy."

"And ye've gotten dirty," she answered. "Put me down." Then she and Andrew started kicking each other and Ma pulled them away.

"So ye ran off to battle with yer cousin, did ye?" she said to me, then touched her apron to her eyes.

"Aye, Ma, and I'm sorry if it frightened ye. But I thought it was my duty."

"Och, ye thought it was yer pleasure." She shook her head. "War's sweet to them that never tried it." Then she hugged me so fiercely, I thought my bones would crack, but I didn't tell her to stop.

"Did ye see the prince there?" she said into my ear.

I thought about that, about the glimpse I'd had of him on his prancing pony, before the battle turned into blood and muck and dying men. "Aye, I saw him, but I didna get close."

"And what's become of him now, I wonder?" Ma said.

"Caught, most likely," said Da.

Granda hobbled up, looking far older than when I'd left. He was leaning on a stick now and when he embraced me, he almost over-balanced and fell. But still he wouldn't let Da get the last word. "The bonnie prince caught? With all the Highlands to hide in? Nae, he'll be as free as a bird gliding over the heather."

Da turned on him. "Free to do what? Ye dinna think he can fight another battle, do ye? Ye canna want that! Look at the boy, old man. Look what yer prince has made of him."

"I never said there was to be more war," Granda answered stubbornly. "I just said the prince was free."

"Maybe he's gone back across the water." I hoped that was true, for his sake. And even more, for ours.

We walked over to our fire, which was ringed with stones.

Ma handed me a piece of toasted cheese stuck between two slices of bread.

"Bread! Heaven!" I gobbled it down like it was the tastiest thing I'd ever eaten. At that moment it was.

"We've made an oven out of stones," Ma said. "And bake every day. Though there's scarcely enough for all."

"Never mind," Da told her. "We'll move back down to the village in another few days, after we get the roofs back up on the houses and . . ." It was clearly a conversation they'd had before.

"Where's Ewan's ma?" I asked, after drinking a full pint of water.

"She's sleeping." Ma looked at me closely. "If ye've bad news for her, it can wait till morning."

I knew from her tone that she'd guessed Ewan wouldn't be coming home.

Then Granda insisted I tell what happened at Culloden. He

pulled me toward a stool by our fire. I recognized it as one from our house. So, they hadn't all been burned. "Sit—and let us know where ye stood and what ye saw and . . ."

I was sore tired, and the last thing I wanted to do was talk about that bloody place. "Please, Granda, can it no wait?"

"Nae, lad, ye owe us that. The others all came home with their tales. But I know ye did better than they. Ye had my dirk and the prince knew ye." His eyes seem to glint in the firelight, and Andrew crowded next to him and leaned forward as if into my story.

"I have nae gift for telling," I said.

Seeing Andrew quivering like a dog after a bird, Ma grabbed his arm and led him away. "This is nae tale for bairns," she scolded.

"This is nae tale at all," said Da. "The lad needs his sleep."

But then others of the village came over to hear what I'd been about. Old men and boys my age who hadn't been to the war. And one or two, like the twins and John the Miller, who'd escaped the battlefield before me and found their way home.

So I didn't go to sleep right away, though Da hovered nearby, ready to take me off if I faltered. Instead, I leaned toward the fire, a dram put in my hand, and sipped it while telling them all about the men sleeping in ditches, and the sound of the thundering cannon, about the soldier with the blind eye, and how Angus Ban and Iain and I carried the Keppoch away from the field.

"The Keppoch dead?" Granda whispered. "That grand old man." Though he was much older than the Keppoch had been.

"Godspeed," the men murmured.

"Give the lad some more whiskey," John the Miller said, when I stopped, exhausted, my voice dry.

"He's nae more a lad," Granda said, clearly proud of me. "He's a man now."

But I didn't feel like a man and I drank no more whiskey and I left the telling of Ewan's death for the morning.

Da put his hand on my arm. "Come to bed, son." So I stood.

Granda pointed his stick at me. "What became of my dirk? I see ye dinna have it with ye."

"It's sticking in the neck of an English dragoon's horse."

"For God and St. Andrew," Granda said, and several of the men said it with him.

So I had to tell that story as well, but I told it badly and quickly while I stood. Then Da took me off to bed, a straw pallet by the fire that I shared with Andrew.

Two other things I didn't tell. I never mentioned how the fits that had plagued me for so long had saved my life. And I didn't mention the Keppoch's brooch. There were too many folk gathering around and I didn't know who might be tempted by such a treasure.

31 ❧ BUILDING ANEW

The next day got off to a bitter start. I took my aunt Fiona and cousin Maggie aside, far from the cook fires. We sat on a rock under a stunted larch tree that shaded us slightly from the sun.

I told them how Ewan had died, though I made it prettier than it was, and left out the stolen sword.

"He didna suffer at all," I said. "And he was glad to have won his share of the honor." I tried to put great meaning in the word *honor*, though I felt little.

Aunt Fiona sat stony-eyed and never said a thing, but then she was never one for light talk. Her hair, greyer than I'd remembered, kept falling before her face as if to hide her from what I was saying. Maggie sobbed quietly. When I was done, my aunt stood up and walked off to shed her tears alone in the shade of the pines.

I told Ma how they'd reacted, and Ma said, "I'll comfort Fiona presently. For now we need to leave them to their grief. Now ye go to the fire and get yerself a cup of warm milk to draw away the bitter taste in yer mouth. The cows have just been milked."

"How did ye know about the taste?" I asked.

"It is the taste of someone else's tears," she said. "A mother knows it well."

Just then Da called me over to him, drawing me to the same rock where I'd broken the news to my aunt and cousin. He made me sit down and then sat next to me.

"Last night," he said, his voice near a whisper, "ye didna tell the whole of the tale. Ye never once mentioned having any fits. It's why I so feared for ye, son."

I looked at my hands clenching and unclenching in my lap.

"Well?"

I bit my lip. "I only had one, Da. A small one, and it scarce worth mentioning."

"Only one? In all that horror? Surely yer leaving something out in the telling." His face got a pinched look, like a fox on the trail of a rabbit.

"Why do ye say that?" I tried to keep my voice level, but it rose and broke on the last word.

"All the while ye were telling yer tale, yer hand kept reaching for yer plaid, for a spot over yer heart."

I gulped and my traitor hand went back to the same spot. "A bit of trouble digesting the cheese," I said. "After so many days of starving."

"Nay, lad, yer doing it again." He reached over and touched my hand.

I knew I had to tell him. And I *wanted* to tell him, too. "I've been meaning to say something to ye, for I've a duty yet to do. I just didna know how to say it."

"Just speak, son. I'll no say anything but keep yer confidence."

Nodding, I reached under the plaid and unpinned the brooch, holding it before me in the flat of my hand. Though the day had gone grey, the sun hiding behind a dark cloud, the gold casing shone.

"I think I've seen its like before," said Da.

"It was the Keppoch's, given to him by Prince Charlie."

"Ye didna steal it, Duncan?"

I shook my head, and quickly told him how I'd come by the treasure.

He reached out one finger to stroke the brooch. "It must be worth a prince's ransom."

"I've thought of that," I admitted, "and of what we could buy with it."

Da nodded slowly, imagining out loud the possibilities just as I had, and rejecting them one by one. He finished, saying, "We could take money for it, but there would be no honor in that. We must keep it safe for now. With the redcoats combing the hills, we dinna want it falling into King George's hands."

I was so relieved, I told him the rest. "I need to give it to the Keppoch's widow."

"Aye. That's the right choice," Da agreed. "But ye canna go till the hills are free of the soldiers."

We sat for a moment, considering. Near us on a branch of a pine tree, a hoodie crow cried out to its friends, a sharp, loud warning.

"There's a hiding place among the rocks above Glenroy," said Da. "I used to keep things in it when I was yer age, though nothing so precious as this."

"Is it safe?" I asked.

"I would have thought Glenroy safe once," Da said. "But there's nowhere totally safe these days."

I nodded. "But safer than the village or under my plaid. We'll hide it there. I trust ye, Da." Then I sighed. "Ye do believe I'm doing right by bringing it back to the widow Keppoch?"

"Well, the thing is yers now, son," he replied. "Ye must do with it as yer conscience dictates."

So we hid the brooch in the rocks, telling the others we were going down to salvage what more we could from the cottage. We wrapped it in a piece of cloth torn from the bottom of my sark, then placed it carefully in a small cavity that we blocked with a loose stone. No one could have told there was anything there at all.

Then we went on down to Glenroy, slowly and carefully, being sure that there were no soldiers about.

I picked up the little doll's head from the ruined hearth to give to Sarah, and we found more neeps in the field. Dad cut up our poor cows, what little meat was left on them that hadn't been got at by scavengers—crows, buzzards, foxes, and the like. What was not too rotten. And we found a cart to haul it away. It was a hard return.

The Duke of Cumberland's burning and slaughter went on for many days. We heard about it from stragglers who managed to find us up in the hills. They told us of bodies stripped and violated, babies dashed against the rocks, and women hanged for nothing more than milking cows. The stories frightened us all.

"Is there to be no end to it?" Ma asked, her hands over Sarah's ears.

We sat around our fire, with Aunt Fiona and Maggie now part of our family, for we didn't dare let them be alone. Aunt Fiona stopped eating unless fed. She'd stopped sleeping unless led to her bed by Maggie. And though she didn't weep, she looked as if she wanted to. The only one she seemed to take to was Andrew, who sat with her and let her stroke his hair. And when she called him Ewan by mistake, he never corrected her. That made Maggie weep even more.

Strangely enough, though, it was the stories of the English depravities that brought Aunt Fiona back to the living again. Each new story seemed to make her stronger. So we took turns telling them, though Granda's were the best.

Then one night Aunt Fiona took off and we never found her, though we searched for days. We could only guess where she'd wandered to.

"Gone to kill some redcoats," Maggie said, almost relieved.

"She'd never do that," Ma countered. "More than likely she's found some quiet spot and there to grieve till she dies of it."

Over the next few weeks the raids eased off, as if even the English soldiers tired of their sport.

Gradually we all returned to Glenroy, or what remained of the village.

"Angus Ban told me to rebuild, Da," I said to him. "I want to help."

"Yer a man now, son," he told me, running his fingers through thinning hair. "Of course ye should help, whether Angus Ban willed it or no."

"Me, too," said Andrew.

I patted his head, then turned to Da. "He can run errands and fetch tools and . . ."

Da smiled. "Of course he can. With ye away, he did all of that and more."

So, at our father's side, we fetched fresh stones to remake the broken walls. We gathered together the cattle that had been scattered in the flight from Glenroy. Doors were rehung on the byres and roofs rethatched. We worked side by side with our neighbors, they on our house, we on theirs. If any good came out of what had happened, it was that the MacDonalds of Glenroy banded together as one big family—not in order to make war, but to secure our village once more.

We even fixed Ewan's cottage for Maggie, hoping Aunt Fiona would return one day to live in it.

We heard more tales of horror, of course—of hangings and captured rebels being transported overseas to the colonies. Of great houses sacked and lairds beheaded and whole villages of people put to the sword. Of clan leaders making peace with the old king.

But at last Cumberland went home to London. One tinker, who stayed the night, said Cumberland had received his father's thanks for the bloody work he'd done.

"Work!" Granda was furious. "What we are doing here in the village is work."

But I understood what the tinker meant. The soldiers at Culloden had gone about their slaughter as if it had been no more than honest labor, and we Highlanders no more than cattle.

Granda nursed his anger with cups of whiskey and when he'd had enough, he went outside into the charging rain. Standing unsteadily by our door, right fist in the air, he raged against the lairds, crying, "Making peace with King George is like lambs thanking the butcher."

I went out to lead him back inside. "Granda, let it go. The lairds are making peace so their people can return to their farms and their lives."

But Granda would have none of my soft talk. He shook off my hand. "I thought better of ye, Duncan. We Keppoch MacDonalds didna make peace and we are here safe at home." And then he

added, "Look at our new Keppoch, a fine lad. A braw lad."
Meaning that Angus Ban—like a few of the other chiefs—remained
a fugitive in the hills, living like a bandit, dodging the redcoat pa-
trols that hounded his tracks.

But I guess Granda wanted it both ways, and didn't see any con-
tradiction in what he said.

Word came by another tinker later in the spring that the
Highlanders were to be forbidden to bear arms by King George's
law.

"And what are we to do without our muskets and swords?"
raved Granda, who had neither anyway.

"On pain of death," Ma warned him. "That's what the tinker
said."

Granda laughed angrily. "Och, woman, the only pain now is
life, no death." But when the redcoats came through, he said nothing as the swords and dirks were collected, for at least they hadn't
burned us out again.

Da never entered into any of these arguments with Granda but
sat by the hearth, arms crossed over his chest, staring at the fire.
More and more often, though, I sat with him and let Granda rage
alone. After all, there was no changing him. I understood that now.

Ma had once said, "War's sweet to them that never tried it."
Well, we'd all three tried it, and come to different conclusions. Da
was right, though, there was no sense in arguing over it. We all had
nightmares of what we'd seen.

But the day came that Da agreed with Granda. A law was passed
against the wearing of the tartan and the kilt. A runner sent by
Clanranald came through the glen to tell us.

"A fine or even jail if you dinna comply," he said, after drinking some whiskey and eating a joint of lamb. Ma was furious to have fed him so well for such dire news.

"Are we to be naked then?" Da complained. "For I swear I'll never put on those bloody trousers. They pinch in all the wrong places."

"And take forever unloosing," I pointed out, "when yer bowels want to empty."

Ma clouted me hard on the back of the head for saying that, especially at the table, but Da laughed.

"Duncan's right, ye know. And if they force us to wear trousers, I'll go about in my sark alone."

Andrew and Sarah crowed with delight, Sarah shouting, "Da's got nae kiltie, Da's got nae kiltie."

"Alisdair, ye'll do nae such thing," Ma said, hands on hips.

"Dinna fash yerself, woman," Da told her, "the sark covers my privates, so why should ye worry?"

But of course he put on the trousers. As did Granda. As did I. However much they chafed, we wore them. As we wore this hard peace. And after a bit we got used to them. After a bit we got used to everything. But we bore each new humiliation like a dull knife in the heart.

32 ❧ THE BROOCH

Summer came, heedless of our humiliations and sorrows. The hills pulsed with life. New crops grew steadily in the fields. Glenroy was abustle as if it had never been burned. I worked with Da side by side and hardly ever thought about the war and its aftermath, or the promise I'd made to bring the Keppoch's widow his brooch. Truth was that the family and the village were more important to me than honor, than promises, than war.

I dreamt less and less about Culloden. Life went on, tied to the seasons. Summer was soft, the sun was warm, and only enough rain fell to make the harvest hopeful, and not turn its feet to rot. What I had once despised, I now prized.

We had lost our milk cows, but Maggie gave us two of theirs—Molly and Moog. "Till Ma comes home," she said. Then she smiled shyly at me. "Or I get married."

I blushed.

Weeks at a time I spent alone in the shielings, tending the cows, milking, churning the butter. I found I had fewer nightmares there. The quiet was healing. The only sounds were Molly and Moog lowing and birdsong in the bright, pearly mornings: curlews singing their names, a single cuckoo loud and echoing, and a flock of peewits who called over and over to their mates.

In all that time I had but one fit, and that up alone at the shieling, looking out over the Gloaming Pool. It wasn't a long blackout, not like some, and I came through without a single scrape.

Everyone in Glenroy was working so hard, it should have been possible to forget the ills done to us. But like a wound not yet scabbed over, we kept rubbing ourselves raw with stories. I heard them each time I came down from the shieling, carrying my butter and cheese.

I heard about Bonnie Prince Charlie fleeing to the western isles, going off to Skye, and to Lewis. The man who'd told Da the news—when he was off to a market at the foot of the glen—said that the prince had been hoping to find a ship bound for France.

"France!" I said. "I hope he made it." Then I gave a short laugh that had little mirth in it. "I hope France is far away." As I spoke, I was staring at Ewan's cottage.

But Da said the bonnie prince hadn't actually gone at all. As we walked into the cottage for dinner, he added, "The English navy's kept him penned in. And kept out any French ships."

Our cottage was once again cozy, and the stones made it cool, even in the summer heat.

"So where is he?" I asked, sitting and reaching for a bannock. Ma slapped my hand. Grace hadn't been said yet. I smiled at her. "It canna be so easy to keep a prince hidden."

Granda was all smiles and put a finger to his lips. "He's here."

"The prince is here?" Andrew asked.

"In our cottage?" asked Sarah.

I laughed. "Well, no *here*!" I pointed to the floor.

"We could invite him . . ." Sarah said wistfully. "*Ye* could invite him, Duncan. Yer the one who's spoken to him."

"Ye wouldn't want him here, Sarah," I said, "Where princes go, trouble follows."

"To think I'd live to hear a MacDonald say such a thing," Granda muttered.

Still, Sarah's comment made us all laugh. And from that evening on, whenever someone in the family mentioned the latest story about the prince, one or another of us would cry out, "We could invite him . . ." and all fall about laughing again. Even Sarah.

The rumors about the prince continued well into August. He was here, he was there, he was behind every gorse bush in the Highlands and dancing nightly at every ball.

Ma said once, "Next he'll be a bogie to frighten the children."

I didn't tell her that sometimes, in my dreams, he was just that.

Andrew began spending more time up in the shieling with me. He was so eager to be thought a man—though ten is hardly that— he stuck to the chores and soon became better at making cheese and churning butter than I had ever been. So, I turned my thoughts once again to the brooch, thinking that if Andrew could handle my chores, I had time to deliver the treasure to the Keppoch's widow.

I left Andrew watching the cows by himself and took the latest butter and cheese down the hillside to Glenroy. There I found Da hoeing between the neeps.

"That's a goodly crop," I said, admiring the dark earth as well.

"If the rains keep coming and the craws stay away," he said. As he spoke, there came a chorus of rooks and crows from the nearby trees.

I saw he'd put up another bird-scare. "Andrew's doing well enough."

He nodded and kept on at his work lifting the weeds away with his wooden spade.

"I'm away then."

"To Keppoch House?" He knew.

"Aye."

He never stopped working, but said, "I'd been wondering when ye'd go. There are still soldiers about."

"I'm wearing the bloody trousers, Da. They'll never know me for a rebel."

He wiped the sweat from his brow with the back of his hand. "Keppoch House might not be standing."

I nodded slowly. The thought had occurred to me. "I know where to find the widow if she's no there."

He straightened up and looked at me closely. "And where would that be?"

For a minute I thought to keep it hidden from him, but I needed his help finding the place. "At Loch Trieg. In a cave."

"Loch Trieg." He mused a moment, then looked up at the threatening sky. "Good fishing there. But it's a full day's walk from the Keppoch's house, due east and then south. Dinna go into the mountains, mind."

"Thanks, Da."

"There's high cliffs and plenty of caves. It willna be easy to find the right one." His mouth was suddenly drawn down.

"I'm sure she'll be at the house."

"Aye, there's been no word of trouble there." He forced a smile. "Mind ye be quick about it. A day or two down and another two back. No more. Yer mother will worry otherwise. Besides, there's the harvest to bring in. Andrew's not up to that alone." He looked away, at the field, at the sky, at the road. Anywhere but at me. I understood. He was afraid to let me go again.

"I'll be back soon."

"I'd go with ye, son, but . . ." He stared pointedly at the field of neeps and then beyond, the fields of barley already starting to tuft. They'd been replanted after the soldiers had done their worst. But whether they'd be ready before the heavy rains came, no one knew. "Best say something to yer mother."

"She willna mind. I'll be quick," I assured him.

"Be *careful* above all else," said Da. "There are still redcoats out hunting for Prince Charlie."

"He'll be safe," I told Da, "as long as he's among Highland folk."

He took me by the shoulder. "Dinna be too sure of that. There's a reward of thirty thousand pounds offered for his capture." His brow made furrows as deep as the ones he was hoeing. "*Thirty thousand!* That's a temptation for any man."

"Any man that disna value his honor more," I said.

I went up over the hillside just as the clouds were swept away. There'd be no rain today. I checked behind me that no one was watching. Then I went over to the jumble of rocks and lifted away the stone that disguised the safe. Underneath in the hollow, the brooch lay wrapped in its strip of cloth. I took it out and replaced the stone before unwrapping the brooch. It gleamed in the sunlight and the lion looked at me, defiant as ever with its blazing red eyes.

"We have a journey to make, a promise to keep," I muttered.

"Ho, there, Duncan!"

I spun around, sticking my arm behind my back to keep the treasure out of sight.

"Granda, what are ye doing here?"

"I'd as well ask ye the same," Granda said, hobbling up the other side of the hill.

"I came to look for one of the cows that strayed," I said. "Moog is a roamer." My fingers tightened around the brooch.

Granda made a great show of peering in every direction. "I dinna see any cows. Of course my old eyes are poorly. Maybe it was a lion ye came for."

I was so startled, I nearly lost my footing on the rocks.

"It's easy to fall when ye've got yer arm twisted back like that." Granda chortled.

"I'm just scratching," I said lamely.

"So it's no the Keppoch's brooch yer hiding behind yer back." He held out a hand.

I brought the brooch out and let it lie in the flat of my palm, but I didn't give it to him. "How did ye know about it?"

"Och, I could see ye were brewing something up with yer da all those weeks back."

"But this is a *secret* hiding place." I sounded like Sarah, my voice close to a whine.

Granda laughed. "That's what yer da thought when he was a wee lad, but I knew about it even then. I used to take a peek and see what he'd hidden there. It usually wasna much—a button, a bit of yarn—but he was only young then." He paused. "Shortly after ye and yer da went down to Glenroy that time, I had a wee peek. I've been checking the treasure safe every week, whenever ye come down from the shieling."

He came closer and lowered his face to the brooch until his nose was almost touching it. "Yer da's found better things to hide these days. I suppose the Keppoch gave it to ye at Culloden."

"In a way." I shrugged.

"And now yer to take it where it belongs. Ye know where that is, do ye no?" He looked up into my face, his eyes piercing. "To the prince himself."

"Nay, Granda, I'll be giving it to the widow Keppoch. By rights she should decide what's to be done with it."

Granda nodded. "That sounds fair-minded to me. But ye better hurry. Ye'll want her to have it while the prince is still about. She can get it to him if he needs it."

"Ye mean before he's caught?"

"Dinna be daft! I mean before he *escapes.* Every jewel will help buy him a ship's passage to France." Granda was trembling with his plan. "Ye'll be a hero, lad. A hero!" He was on fire now, I could hear it in his voice. "The English may take our land, our swords, and our plaids, but they willna have our prince. Not if we can help him." He reached over and closed my hand around the brooch. "So take that brooch to the Keppoch's good lady and she will get it to Charlie's people, who will see him safe out of the German lairdie's hands."

I wrapped up the brooch and stuffed it under my shirt.

"And before ye leave," said Granda, "speak to yer da about it. I dinna want to take the blame of yer going this time."

"I already have."

He looked surprised, then pleased. He gave me a swift hug. "For God and St. Andrew," he whispered in my ear.

Ma sent me on the way with a bag of oats, a skin of water, some cheese, a loaf of bread, and Da's hunting knife.

"Be quick," she said before hugging me.

"As quick as I can," I said, and kissed her on both cheeks. "Maybe even quicker."

The journey to Keppoch House took a full two days. The air was full of the sharp smell of wild onion, and the roadside ablaze with purple foxglove. I could see a maze of hoofprints where a herd of deer had crossed the path and a scattering of pointed, black rabbit droppings. The acrid, sour odor of fox lay over all.

As I walked along, the sound of the River Roy rumbling over its old course kept me company. Above me a circling eagle gave its hearty cry. The days were beginning to draw in now, and the nights were coming earlier, which meant I had less time to walk, so I didn't stop to eat what Ma had packed for me. Instead I ate as I went. I'd promised to be quick on this journey and meant to keep that promise.

Oddly, I felt lighter of spirit as I got closer to the Keppoch's house. I hadn't realized it, but the brooch had been a burden. Once I'd delivered it to the widow, I knew I could go back home feeling free, my war truly over.

• • •

Coming over the hill to the Keppoch's house, I smelled the burned air even before I saw the destruction.

Oh, God—no! I thought, then said it aloud. I began to run, praying as I went, "Let them be alive. Let them be alive."

By the time I got to the site, dark was coming on fast, but it was all too clear what had happened. "The bastards!" I shouted, not caring that any soldiers could hear me and know me for a rebel. "The bloody bastards!"

Ahead of me, the shattered ruins were no more than blackened brick. Even the garden walls had been dragged down and scattered, the gardens themselves razed to the ground. Where we had camped nine months earlier, singing the old tunes in an orchard filled with apples and pears, there was now only a desert, the trees chopped down near their roots. Cumberland's men had done their work here as thoroughly as they had in Glenroy.

Och, the poor widow, I thought. *Poor Angus Ban.* For they'd more to lose than we villagers. I wondered why no effort had been made to repair the damage. Perhaps, I thought, the English had killed all of the Keppoch's men. Or perhaps rebuilding anything so large was more work than the widow's people had the heart for.

I searched through the ruins carefully before the light faded entirely, but found no bones. That was a small comfort.

But what if . . . I thought, *what if they've all been captured? Wouldn't we have heard of it?* One part of me said yes. The other no, for we hadn't been told about the burning of Keppoch House, either. Still, by the smell of it, the thing had been done recently. So perhaps the news was yet to reach Glenroy.

I stopped and looked up at the darkening sky. A single star glittered there.

Perhaps they've gotten clean away. Perhaps they reached a place of safety. And that meant the cave at Loch Trieg. Another day's walk, east and then south, Da had said.

I thought about leaving at once, but feared making my way in the dark in an unfamiliar place. A fox yipped somewhere beyond the trees and was answered by another.

Better to look for shelter and leave at first light.

I finally found an old sheep pen that nobody had thought worth demolishing. As I lay down under a sky now brilliant with stars, I remembered how beautiful the Keppoch's house had looked. How stately, like the palace of a faerie king. It had served the best of Highland hospitality to us. Now the Keppoch was dead, and his house razed.

I fell asleep and the Keppoch, Prince Charlie, and the butcher Cumberland were all dancing together in my dreams.

I left before daylight, the sky a dark, moody grey slowly leaching into blue. Keeping the mountains on my right, I walked east, crossing a dozen or more streams, until I reached the tip of Loch Trieg in the afternoon.

From what I could see, it was a small, narrow loch shaped like a tree limb. The sun was still high in the sky, spreading a golden sheen over the surface of the peaty water. Small black-headed ducks swam in and out of the reed beds lining the shore.

Loch Trieg seemed like Eden until I came around a bend in the shoreline and saw a trio of fishermen's huts burned to the ground. If any of the Loch Trieg fisherfolk were still alive, they'd not found the courage to return.

Rugged hillsides rose up like fists on every side of the loch, out of a thick blanket of heather that was just beginning to turn purple.

I looked at the slopes, recalling a story Granda once told me about the Loch Trieg caves. Giants or trolls, I suppose, like most of his tales. "The caves run so deep," he'd said, "that after ye've followed them for an hour, ye can hear the fish wriggling in the water over yer head." I remembered how that image had made me giggle.

But I was not giggling now. I wanted to find the cave, hand over the brooch, and go home.

Still, it might take me days trying to search those cliffs. Days to worry my mother. Days that might draw Da out to find me. I didn't even know on which side of the loch the widow's cave lay. Shading my eyes against the sun, I stared in turn at the eastern and western hills, concentrating with all my might. Finally, I could just about distinguish dark places on the eastern slope that *could* be caves and started toward them.

Now that I was so close, the walk around to the eastern slopes seemed to take forever. A slight wind had picked up, ruffling the loch. Overhead gulls wheeled and screamed, then dove down into the dark water.

I left the loch behind and walked quickly to the base of the eastern hills through the tough, springy heather. Everything seemed deserted and still. Even the wind had stopped, and for once the gulls were quiet. Was that a good sign or not?

I wondered briefly if I should call out, rather than take my time searching. But if the widow Keppoch's people were deep inside a cave—deep enough for fish to wriggle overhead—would they hear me? Besides, yelling would certainly alert any English soldiers in the area. I couldn't take the chance. It might cost me a day or more searching both sides, but it was the only way I could be certain not to give the widow's hiding place away.

Ma will have to wait, I told myself.

Suddenly, I worried what would happen if I were caught, and this far from my own home.

Then I laughed. I wasn't wearing a bonnet with a MacDonald crest, and the trousers made of darkened wool wouldn't give away my clan. Without realizing it, the English had given me a disguise.

"I'm a fisherlad whose hut was burned down, so I'm searching for birds' eggs," I practiced. "Gulls' eggs, sir, and terns' eggs." I doubted the English would know any better. *Gulls' eggs and terns' eggs.* I chuckled.

In places the heather at the base of the cliffs was up to my knees, and it was hard going. The undergrowth clutched at my legs and for the first time, I blessed the trousers I was wearing. If I'd a sword, I might have hacked a path for myself. But, of course, we weren't allowed to carry swords anymore. And any hacked path would show the English where to follow. Besides, as a fisherlad, what would I be doing with a sword anyway?

Gulls' eggs and terns' eggs.

From somewhere close by, I suddenly heard a whistling, like the cry of a curlew. I glanced around but saw no sign of any bird. Then another curlew piped up from the opposite direction. I couldn't catch as much as a glimpse of it, either.

I cursed the hard ground, the high heather, my fear of the English, and then too late I heard something wriggling along the ground directly behind me. Before I could turn, I was seized from behind by a pair of burly arms, and the point of a dirk was pressed to my throat.

To come all this way to die. My heart jumped in my chest and I tried to think what to do. "Gulls' eggs and terns' eggs . . . " I tried to say.

Just then a second figure rose out of the heather ten yards in front of me, as if he'd sprouted from the earth. He was wearing a kilt and plaid, though they were both darkened with mud and dye. He held a broadsword in his hand. His face was pocked and homely and I knew him at once.

"Angus Ban," I croaked.

"Leave off, Iain," Angus Ban called to the man who'd captured me. "Can ye no see this is a friend?"

"I can only see the back of his head," Iain replied gruffly. "And it's a noisy head at that. Gulls eggs' and terns' eggs, what's that supposed to mean?"

"Well, it's the back of a *friendly* head," said Angus Ban.

Iain let go, turned me around roughly. "Aye, I ken him now. It's the lad from Culloden who helped carry the Keppoch." He slipped the dirk back into his belt.

"Duncan of Glenroy," I said, not sure if Angus Ban would remember my name. Then I added quickly, almost babbling, "And I was going to tell any English soldiers that I was looking for gulls' eggs and terns' eggs up in these cliffs."

Angus Ban gave a short, sharp laugh that he turned quickly into a cough.

"There's no such nests here," Iain said.

"Aye, but would the sassanach know that?" Angus Ban said. "The boy's got a good head on his shoulders."

"Then why say it to us?"

"Ye came up too fast for me to make a proper greeting," I told him.

"Too fast?" Iain spit to one side. "Ye were spotted two miles off."

"Ye wouldna have got this far if ye hadna appeared so harmless," said Angus Ban, sheathing his sword and striding toward me. As he did so, the wind started up again, shaking the heather.

"Harmless?" For some reason I was almost insulted, though harmless was exactly how I'd been trying to look.

"Aye, harmless, a boy just larking about, wearing a silly pair of trousers. We thought we'd sneak up and take a closer look, all the same."

"I'm glad ye used yer eyes before yer dirks," I said, rubbing the spot where Iain had set his blade against my throat.

"I'm glad to see ye safe, laddie," said Angus Ban. "But ye've picked the wrong place for an afternoon stroll."

Hardly a stroll, I thought, thinking about the hard climb up to the cliff base through the rough heather. "I've come to find the widow Keppoch. First I went to Keppoch House, but it was burnt to the ground, and then I remembered ye telling Iain that yer family should hide out here at Loch Trieg."

Angus Ban leaned toward me, one hand resting on the basket hilt of his sword. "Ye've good ears, lad, and an inconvenient memory. What business have ye with my stepmother?"

I decided that I could surely trust the Keppoch's own son. Besides, I had no other choice. "I've this to give her," I said, reaching inside my sark.

Iain started suspiciously and pulled out his dirk again. I stood stock-still, fearful of triggering another attack.

"Be easy, Iain," said Angus Ban, gesturing him to put his weapon away.

"There's many as think they'd be doing King George a service if they shot ye dead," Iain growled.

"Tush! He's nae room for a pistol in that sark," said Angus Ban. "Come on, lad, let's see what ye've got."

Keeping a wary eye on Iain, I slowly drew out the little bundle and unwrapped it gently, as if it might break.

Angus Ban's eyes grew wide at the sight of the lion brooch. Reaching out a hand to touch the treasure, he stopped short of taking it from me. A groove formed between his eyes and he got very quiet.

"Ye stole that," Iain accused.

"It fell to the floor in the hut, under the table we laid the Keppoch on. I picked it up," I answered sharply, furious that my honor should be questioned.

Angus Ban smiled ruefully. "I must have overlooked that in my hurry to get clear of the battlefield." He made a strange sound through his nose, like a horse or ox. "I hardly deserve to see it again for my carelessness."

Iain started to speak and Angus Ban raised a hand to silence him, saying, "Did ye no think to sell it and keep the money for yerself, Duncan of Glenroy?"

"I didna," I declared hotly. Then added with more honesty, "Well, no for long."

"No, of course ye didna," said Angus Ban. "Ye already proved the quality of yer honor at Culloden."

"We'd best get out of sight," Iain advised grimly. "The redcoats will be long out of their soft beds and on patrol." He wet his forefinger and held it up to the wind. "And they'll hear us halfway down the lochside, the way this wind is blowing."

"Ye nag like a wifey," complained Angus Ban, though his face was now wreathed with smiles. "But we'll humor ye just the same. Come on, Duncan of Glenroy, I'll take ye to a place where Scotsmen are still free."

34 ✤ THE CAVE

ngus Ban led the way up the rocky hillside, while Iain stuck close to my back, probably making sure I didn't run off with the Keppoch's treasure. The sun was once again gone behind a cloud and there was little to keep the wind off us. I was sweating from the climb and the chill air swept across my back. It was not a good combination.

Suddenly, before I was ready for it, we came to a break in the heather where several caves pocked the crags. We headed for the largest of these, the entrance about as high and as wide as a rowing boat stood on its end.

"I'll wait here and keep watch," said Iain, crouching down among the heather. He disappeared so thoroughly, I was astonished. No wonder the redcoats hadn't found the Keppoch's family.

I followed Angus Ban into the cave. At the point where the sunlight failed to penetrate, oil lamps had been lit and placed inside carved alcoves in the rock.

We walked quite a ways in through a narrow tunnel, first straight ahead, then on a downward slope. All the while I was thinking about Granda's fish swimming over our heads. The walls—which were about an arm's length from me on either side—looked slick and wet, but that could have been a trick of the lights. Still, there was a cold, damp feel to the tunnel and I wondered how a lady like the widow Keppoch could stay in such a place.

Suddenly, the tunnel opened out into a large chamber where tapestries had been fixed to some of the walls. Rugs had been laid on the stone floor, and chairs and cushions placed around. The chamber almost looked like the parlor of a great house, or so I imagined. Certainly, the tapestries and rugs made the room a warmer place than the cold, dank tunnel. *So,* I thought, *here is where she must stay.*

In the center of the room was a large table, upon which stood baskets filled with cheeses, berries, and bread. A glass pitcher filled with a golden-colored liquid nestled beside the baskets. And next to that was a large glass bowl with a bit of some rosy water in the bottom. I had never seen such beautiful things.

Nearby, a smaller table was piled with children's toys.

A pretty woman carrying a wee baby came into the room. She wore a simple gown decorated with ribbons of bright tartan, and her long brown hair was tied behind in a bow.

"Angus, yer back early," she said, her voice echoing lightly off the cave walls.

Angus Ban bowed to her respectfully, and I suddenly recognized her as the young woman who'd been so huge with child at the Keppoch's house. Four youngsters came after her, one bouncing a ball and another carrying a hoop. The smallest child broke away from them and went over to sit at the toy table and draw on a slate. Behind the widow trotted a maid, who sat down at a spinning wheel and began winding yarn. They were soon joined by a pair of servants and an armed guard, his arms crossed over his chest.

It was all so homey, yet so far beyond anything I had ever known—and in a cave as well—I found I couldn't speak.

Angus Ban signaled me forward. "Stepmother, may I introduce young Duncan MacDonald of Glenroy. He was the lad I've spoken of, the one who helped us carry Father in from the field."

I bowed silently to the lady, thinking that she was awfully young to have been the Keppoch's wife. "Lady Keppoch . . . " I began.

"It's the Widow MacDonald," she said, sitting down and bouncing the baby on her knee. "Our Angus is the Keppoch now."

Not knowing what else to say, I pointed to the child in her lap. "Is this yer baby?"

She stroked the child's feathery, golden hair. "My bonnie Charlotte," she said, "the daughter the Keppoch never saw. She's been a comfort for me since the loss of my Alexander."

Alexander, I supposed, was the Keppoch's born name, though I'd never heard it used before. The widow's sweetness, though, unloosed my tongue. "He . . . he was a noble man," I said. It hardly sounded enough. "A fine, strong leader and . . . "

"And did ye truly help carry him to his final rest?" she asked.

I nodded, afraid to say anything more since I didn't know how much Angus Ban had told her of the Keppoch's death.

"Well, what a way to welcome such a brave gentleman to our home. Have we none of the hot punch left?" She turned to the serving maid who was unsnarling some of the yarn.

"What's left is barely warm now, ma'am," the maid replied.

"Make nae matter of that. I'm sure this young man is too well-mannered to pass comment on it. And the warmth will do him good. Fetch him a cup."

The maid disappeared into a shadowy corner and came back with a silver cup, which she dipped into the glass bowl, then brought to me.

I had never drunk from anything so fine, and handled it gingerly, as if my touch might tarnish the metal. The punch tasted like fruit—apples and pears—with more than a hint of brandy. The fire it stirred in my breast gave me the courage to address the lady.

"This is the bonniest cave I've ever been in," I told her. "My father's house isna half so grand."

"We were warned the redcoats meant to burn us out, and so took what we could before they came," she said. "They might make fugitives of us, Duncan of Glenroy, but they'll no turn us into animals."

I thought her the most splendid woman I'd ever met.

"I've told ye these furnishings would sit better at Inch House," said Angus Ban, pointing to the table and chairs. "Everything's ready there for ye to move in." He turned to me. "Young Duncan here would tell ye so himself."

"I . . . I . . . " I could tell her nothing.

"And leave ye to live in bare lodgings, Angus?" she joked. "Without my civilizing influence, ye and yer friends would be little better than foxes hiding in the hillside."

"Och, but ye shouldna be living as less than a lady. Father would hate this." He gestured to the one wall without a tapestry on it. The bare stone looked grim and damp.

"There will be nae rest for us at Inch House or any place else as long as the prince is still loose in the hills," she answered him, her cheeks flushing as she spoke. "The English would be at the door of Inch House every hour of the day, searching, questioning, looking for any excuse to haul us off as traitors to King George. As if we know where the bonnie prince stays."

"Then he's no in France yet?" Granda and Da and every visiting tinker had told us so. But to hear it from Angus Ban's lips made it real.

"Nay, no in France yet," Angus Ban said. "He's still leading them a merry dance all around the islands and up and down the glens." He grinned. "They dinna need us to tell them that."

His two younger brothers had left off playing with the hoop and ball, edging closer to the conversation. The older of them piped up, "The prince dressed himself as a lassie."

"Aye, called himself Betty Burke," put in the other.

I turned to Angus Ban. "Why did he do that?"

Angus Ban laughed. "Let the lads tell you about it. It's their favorite tale."

The lads were quick to comply. "Our kinswoman Flora MacDonald was with him," said the first.

His brother added, "He escaped from the English wearing a disguise. They rowed off to the island of Skye, in skirts and all."

Both lads danced about their mother, swinging their arms like ladies swishing their skirts.

"Off with ye, lads, and back to yer games," the widow told them. "We're talking serious business here."

"Is it true?" I asked her as the lads scampered away.

"True enough," she said, holding out her hand for the silver cup, which I gave to her.

"Young Duncan's brought a gift for ye," said Angus Ban. "A very special gift."

The widow gave me a curious stare. "A gift? He's a very noble young knight indeed." She handed the cup and baby to her maid.

"I hope it brings more joy to ye than sorrow, ma'am."

"Well said," Angus Ban put in.

I brought out the brooch and handed it to her, peeling away the wrappings as I did so. A tear bloomed in her eye and she took the brooch in cupped hands, as if it were a fragile bird's egg.

"I remember how proud Alexander was when he came home with this pinned to his plaid. 'A gift from Prince Charlie himself,' he said, 'brought all the way from France.' See, it has a lock of the prince's own hair." She touched a finger below her eyes and flicked away the tear.

"I was so set on saving his weapons," said Angus Ban, "I never minded his treasure."

Lady Keppoch pressed the brooch to her breast, then set it on her lap. "I'm no a warrior to wear so fine a crest as this."

"Yer as brave as any warrior I know," said Angus Ban.

I wished I'd been quick enough to say such a thing.

For a moment we were all quiet, thinking about the brooch and—I expect—about the Keppoch as well.

A shadow passed across the chamber entrance and Iain entered. "There's a visitor to see ye," he said, ushering another man in behind him. "He says his business is urgent."

The newcomer was a broad-shouldered Highlander with a grim face, curling black beard, and sharp grey eyes. He, too, was still wearing a kilt, but like Angus Ban and Iain, his was dyed brown.

"McNab!" Angus Ban exclaimed when the man stepped into the light. Then quickly he explained to the widow, "It's McNab of Innisewan." He turned back to the man. "McNab, ye rogue, what's flushed ye out of yer bothy?"

"Nothing less than the safety of the prince!" McNab replied.

Clutching the brooch, the widow stood up. "Ye have news?"

McNab nodded. "I have news, ma'am. He's been hiding out east of here, near Ben Alder, under the protection of Cluny McPherson. But now a French ship has finally beaten the English blockade, so he's off to the coast to board it."

"And then to France?" the widow asked.

"God willing." McNab's face was dour. "Where the redcoats dinna dare go."

"At last!" she cried.

Angus Ban clapped his hands together, a sound which echoed around us. "But that's good, man, that's good."

"Nay." McNab's dour face got grimmer. "For the redcoats have got wind of it and they're closing fast. The prince needs men around him, brave men, loyal men, to protect him."

"Men who know their way through the heather?" Angus Ban asked.

"Aye."

"Men who know this countryside will be more valuable to him than swords," said Lady Keppoch. "Ye'll go to him, Angus?"

"As fast and straight as the crow flies," Angus Ban answered.

"And what about ye, Duncan MacDonald of Glenroy?" She turned to me. "How well do ye know this country?"

"As well as I know the fingers of my own hand," I told her, which was a terrible exaggeration. Mostly I knew my own glen.

"Ye'll go, too, then. And take this with ye." She wrapped the brooch up in its cloth and handed it back to me.

I would have done anything for her. Even go to the prince, once more into the teeth of danger.

Angus Ban put out a hand to stop her. "It's yer brooch by right," he protested, "and ye may have need of such treasures yet."

"Our prince has greater need than any of us," she replied. "Let him take it as a charm, if he will. Or sell it for food. Or use it as a bribe. It will prove its worth yet." She pressed the brooch into my palm. "Will ye take it to him, young Duncan, and my prayers with it?"

"Aye, ma'am, I'll go," I said. "And carry yer treasure as ye wish."

"Then we'll both go to join Prince Charlie's last army," said Angus Ban, offering me his hand. We shook firmly and then he turned to give orders to his men about keeping watch here while he was gone.

I stuffed the brooch back into my shirt, remembering what Mairi's ghost had said: *It's a blessing ye carry with ye, Duncan.*

I hoped for all our sakes it was.

35 THE BOTHY

The three of us traveled east, then north into the hills and forests, letting McNab lead the way. He knew the swiftest route to the prince's hideout, knew where the streams could be most easily crossed and where narrow gaps gave passage between the frowning crags. We ducked under curving bushes and low-hanging trees on paths that ran like tunnels through the foliage. The tracks would have been impossible for the redcoats to spot, but the local clansmen knew such hidden paths well, using them for passing messages among themselves as well as smuggling weapons and money for the prince's cause.

I kept up. I had to—or else I would have become totally lost. And no one would have had the time to seek me out.

We spent the rest of that day traveling, and, after a half-night's rest, were off again and never on any recognizable road. I should have been exhausted, but our spirits were so high, it was hard to feel tired. I said so to Angus Ban in a low whisper.

He whispered back, "Harder, I think, to walk along a broad road all day, especially with redcoats to either side." He was silent for a moment, then added, "It was by using tracks like these that the prince evaded Cumberland's searchers, all the way from Moidart on the western coast to Badenoch on the far side of Loch Ness." His hand described a large arc.

"And now back again," McNab added quietly.

I sighed. "That's a long way."

Iain whispered, "Long and hard and dangerous."

"But he never went alone," McNab said. "We wouldna let him."

As the second day started to darken toward dusk, we crossed yet another small stream. Wading through it, I began to think about the prince. What courage it must have taken, going from Culloden to the coast and back twice more, with the redcoats fast behind him. And the anger I had held since that awful battle began to turn to admiration again. Yes, I still wanted him gone to France, but for his own sake now, as well as ours.

"He's been rumored dead more than once," said Angus Ban, when we reached the other side of the stream. "But a rumor's nae fact." He laughed, which lent his homely face a kind of beauty.

"And nobody's betrayed him." I had to marvel at that. "Not for all the gold offered by King George."

Iain's face turned hard. He spat. "That for German Georgie!"

"What do ye know of the gold?" Angus Ban asked me.

"Thirty thousand pounds, it's said. I can hardly imagine such a sum."

He clapped me on the back. "It would make ye the equal to any laird."

I gave him a startled look. "But a laird is born to his title."

Shaking his head, Angus Ban retorted, "There speaks a true retainer. Laddie, lairds can be broken and built up again. A man with money can make his way anywhere in the world. That's what makes this so miraculous—that nae Highlander has given even a hint of the prince's whereabouts. Nae money, nae torture, nae exile has made the Scots talk."

"Hush," McNab said. "No more speaking here, either. We're coming to a tricky part now. Even trickier in this fading light."

We dropped to our bellies and began crawling through the heather. It wasn't easy, for the stuff was dense and tangled.

I kept wanting to sneeze and had to hold my nose for fear of giving us away. And all the while, my heart was beating as loudly as it had at Culloden. I thought about Ma and Da waiting at home, thinking I'd be back this evening, or the next. I thought about the bonnie prince somewhere ahead of us, waiting to be guided to the coast.

Is he worth it?

He better be!

McNab raised his hand and we paused, side by side, to stare through the gathering dusk at a rough-built, square bothy lying on a low rise some twenty yards ahead of us. Sheltered among the holly trees and high rocks, its stones caked with moss, the bothy was smaller than my cottage. From a hole in its turf roof a faint streamer of smoke trickled out, disappearing when it reached the tops of the rocks. There was no light at the window, no sound from inside, no guards at the door. Except for the chimney smoke, the place seemed utterly deserted.

"There it is," said McNab, starting to rise.

Angus Ban took McNab by the shoulder and pushed him back down, till we were hidden in the bracken. Slipping out his pistol and cocking it gently to make as little sound as possible, he whispered, "Are ye sure, McNab? It could be a trap. The place is too quiet by half, and who's the daftie who set that fire?"

"I'm as sure as ye are of yer own name," McNab whispered back. "John McPherson himself told me to come here. The prince is waiting for us."

Angus Ban rubbed his chin thoughtfully. "Duncan, lad, go up and take a wee peek in the window."

"Me?" My voice choked the word.

"Yer harmless looking," said Iain. "Tell them 'gulls' eggs and terns' eggs' if they ask."

Angus Ban stifled a laugh.

"Suppose whoever's up there doesn't think me that harmless, say?"

"Then run like the devil and we'll give ye cover," said McNab, grinning.

"Or see ye avenged," Angus Ban added mischievously. He waved the pistol by way of reassurance, but it gave me little comfort.

I stood and started toward the bothy, keeping low and fixing my eyes on the door. It seemed a long way down and too open by far. I didn't betray those behind me by so much as a glance back. A hoodie crow flew off to my left, which made me flinch, but otherwise I kept on until I was close enough to be spotted by anyone inside.

Realizing then that I was coming upon them like a bandit or an enemy, I straightened up and held my arms out from my sides to show that my hands were empty and I had no weapons concealed about me. *Except Da's knife,* I thought, which was stuck in my hose and hidden under the awful trousers. *Well, at least they're good for something.*

I stood stock-still, awaiting some reaction from inside the little shelter. My heartbeats measured out the time as I waited for the crack of a pistol. I took one step more toward the bothy, then another, until I was no more than an arm's length from the door.

Surely, the prince has long since moved on, I thought. *Or, more likely, McNab has been misled.*

I took another step closer.

But what of the chimney smoke? my more cautious nature warned.

The last remnants of an old fire, I told myself. *See how thin it is.*

I turned toward a low window and at that moment the door was flung open. Out jumped a red-bearded figure in Highland garb. He wore a dirty sark with a plaid wrapped round it, a black kilt, and worn boots held together with string. A plain blue bonnet sat on his head, like a bird perched on a tree limb. On his belt hung a sword in its sheath and a pistol was stuck down in the belt. Thin and young as Angus Ban, his eyes burned as if he were possessed.

I stared for a second, then stumbled backward, tripping over a mossy rock. "Yer . . . Yer Highness," I stuttered in Gaelic as I fell.

The prince let out a rich laugh as two men with muskets emerged from the holly bushes at the rear of the bothy and two others came out the door.

"I told you not to worry. Here's your redcoat scout, gentlemen," the prince told them in his halting English. "It turns out he's a fine Highland lad."

Brushing off my clothes, I got slowly to my feet and then looked down to hide my embarrassment. Prince Charlie didn't seem at all like the grand figure I'd seen at Glenfinnan and Culloden. Still, he was a prince. I stood and touched my forehead. "Yer Highness," I said again, this time in English.

A tall, handsome man with sharp cheekbones and gentle eyes limped to the prince's side. I recognized him at once. It was Lochiel, who'd stood between the prince and me that night at Glenfinnan.

"There's nae shame in being cautious, Yer Highness," he said.

The guards suddenly raised their muskets and squinted down the barrels. They'd spotted Angus Ban and McNab climbing toward us.

"Easy, lads," said Lochiel in Gaelic, placing a finger on one of the guns and pushing it down. "Even in this light I recognize the old Keppoch's son."

Angus Ban hailed Lochiel, then he and Iain and McNab fell on one knee before the prince.

"Up, my friends, rise up," the prince told them. "If there are spies hiding on the hilltops, you'll be telling them exactly who it is stands before you."

I took a deep breath. At least I hadn't been the one to make that mistake.

We were ushered into the bothy, where, by listening to the conversation and asking a few whispered questions of Angus Ban, I soon learned who the prince's other companions were.

The stocky man who stayed close to Lochiel was his brother, Archie. A doctor, his services had been sorely needed when Lochiel had been carried off the field of Culloden, shot through both ankles.

Then there was Cluny McPherson, hawk-nosed and fierce, of whom I'd already heard tell. Also his brother Donald, Aeneas MacDonald of Lochgarry, and Allan Cameron, a young officer of Lochiel's clan.

There was scarcely room for us all in the bothy. It was lucky, I thought, that Cluny's four retainers were outside on guard duty, or we'd hardly be able to breathe.

At one end of the room a brace of pheasant had been spitted over the fire, the reason for the smoke. The smell was so delicious, my belly began to growl.

When he saw me eyeing the birds hungrily, Cluny told me proudly, "Prince Charles snared them himself." He sounded as if he were bragging about his son rather than his prince.

"I've always been a keen huntsman," said Prince Charlie, "but never before have I had to hunt to keep from starving."

"Starving?" Lochiel said. "Why, just three days ago, my lord, I served ye a feast in another hut. Ye said, as I recall, 'Now I live like a prince.' "

Prince Charlie smiled. "A feast, yes—with mutton and an anker of whiskey, butter and cheese. Such cheese. And ham. And minced collops, too."

There was a wave of good-natured laughter at this description, and a jar of whiskey was passed round the company. I couldn't tell if there had really been such a feast or not.

"Take a care, lads," Lochgarry added, "and dinna drink yerselves silly. The prince is a fine tippler. Why, as he tells it, he drank cold brandy out of seashells at Corradale and sent the others to bed, standing alone at the end of the night."

Everyone but me laughed again, the prince heartiest of all. It seemed an odd thing to do, laughing about being drunk, when all about us lay danger. I suppose after all these months, the prince and his friends had become used to this outlaw life, but I doubted I ever could.

Angus Ban must have understood my concern, for he clapped me on the shoulder. "Have ye never heard it said, lad, 'Laugh at leisure, ye may weep at night'?"

Indeed I had. "My ma says it often, sir. Usually when there's plenty to weep about."

They laughed even harder.

The pheasants were cut into small portions and given us to eat by hand, along with some stale bread and a few crumbs of cheese. The prince ate a whole piece of white breast meat, sitting on one of the two stools in the bothy. Lochiel sat on the other. Everyone else stood around, sharing the rest of the pheasant. Even Cluny's retainers had a bite. It was the best meat I'd ever had, even if it was only a couple of bites.

Once the meager meal was over, and everyone had wiped their hands on their plaids or breeches, Angus Ban gave me a nudge. "Give the prince what ye have, lad, and tell him yer name."

The prince looked up at me. "Have? Have?" He shook his head. "Do I understand this *have*?" But he said it smiling.

Cautiously I approached him. My heart was hammering as hard as it ever had in battle. I held out the brooch.

"What is this? I recognize this." The prince turned to Lochiel. "Do I recognize this?"

Lochiel leaned forward to see what was in my hand.

"I am Duncan MacDonald of Glenroy, my lord. This comes from the Keppoch MacDonald. He died for ye, sire." I glanced quickly back at Angus Ban, who nodded for me to continue. "His widow says that . . . " I hesitated, trying to remember exactly what she'd said, though I remembered her face clearly. "That ye'd have greater need than any of us for it." I took a deep breath and the rest came out all in a rush. "And she said that ye could use it as a charm or sell it for food or use it as a bribe, and her prayers go with it."

The prince took the brooch in his hand and admired how it shone in the glow of the hearth fire. "This lion, he reminds me of the old Keppoch himself," he mused. "Steady-eyed and brave." He suddenly seemed of two minds whether to accept the thing. "This was a gift," he said, "and surely must pass to the widow, or to you, Angus, the son."

I wondered what Angus Ban would say. For how does one say no to a prince?

Angus Ban waved the brooch away. "I knew my father's mind, my prince, and if he were here among us now, he would press the brooch upon ye with all the strength he had. There may be one last favor needed to get Yer Highness to safety, a favor that canna be bought by loyalty but gold would make the difference."

"It's true, true," the prince answered solemnly, "that on a few occasions, when I was out of money, there were those unwilling to shelter me." He smiled wryly. "Though how can I blame such poor souls? They feared the fire and the lash."

For a minute I was furious. "Some refused their prince shelter?" I said. "What of Highland hospitality? What of honor?" And then, remembering how only that morning I was hoping the prince would soon be gone, and no longer endangering Scottish lives, I felt deeply ashamed. I was lucky the fire was already too low for anyone to see my cheeks burn with the memory.

"Well said, lad," Lochiel interrupted, "but remember there's nae Highlander who's spoken a word to put the redcoats on the prince's trail, neither for fear nor greed."

The prince turned the brooch over in his fingers. "It is true there's a march of hazards ahead," he said, "and a bauble like this might serve me well." He looked directly at me. "I'll keep it for now, and I'll remember your honesty, young Highlander. Duncan, you say?"

At the mention of the march, the men all suddenly turned to business and I was no longer in the prince's eye. We made a circle around the prince and Lochiel, shoving the table to one side. The doctor poked up the fire with a stick and it flared to life again.

"What's the route?" asked Angus Ban.

"North and west," replied Lochiel, "to my house at Achnacarry. Or what's left of it since Cumberland's men passed that way recently. Only we must go over the hills and not along the main roads."

"Of course," Angus Ban agreed. "If your poor legs can manage."

Lochiel gave him a dark look. "They'll manage."

"Then we should go soon," said Cluny, making a fist of his right hand, "and use the cover of night. Sleep will be a luxury. No telling how long the ship can wait for us. Days perhaps. A week may be too long."

"How will we find our way at night?" I asked. I said *we*, though I didn't really expect to be taken along.

"That's why we need men who know the country well," said Cluny. "McNab for here, and ye others as we go further west. Even ye, laddie. A body on his own land is the real jewel in the prince's hand. Not that bauble, for all it's a pretty thing and well meant."

I knew he was right, but still it rankled. For the widow's sake, if not my own.

"Ye could stick a bag over McNab's head and with his bare feet he could feel his way from here to Loch Trieg," Angus Ban joked.

"Further," said McNab in his growl of a voice.

It was just the right thing to say, for we all laughed heartily and any lingering tension about the coming trek west was immediately set aside. And I knew that I would go with them whatever the consequences.

36 ❧ JOURNEY BY MOONLIGHT

In fact we waited till after midnight before leaving the bothy. McNab had us take the time to bury the bones of the pheasants and scatter the ashes of the fire. We overturned the stools and set the table against the hearth. The place looked as if no one had been there for ages.

"I dinna expect the Butcher to find his way here," McNab said, "but one canna be too careful."

We left single file, with McNab, Cluny, and the prince at the fore, and Lochiel and his brother at the rear.

It was hard going for five hours, with black tree branches slapping us in the faces, and us startling at every sound. We got as far as another, even smaller, bothy, where we spent the bright hours of the day sleeping curled up on the floor. The little building echoed with snores.

I was soon ready to believe that Angus Ban had spoken in truth, not in jest, when he said McNab could lead us with a bag over his head. Even through the thickest of red pine woodlands, or over small heather-spattered mountains, or down the narrow glens where water gushed over rocks into tumbling cataracts, he led us as surely as if the sun were shining. I wondered if I would be so certain of the way when we reached Glen Roy and it was my turn to lead. Of course, I knew the shieling meadow well, and the paths up and down into the village. And I knew how to go around the Gloaming Pool. Well around, for Mairi's spirit still haunted that place. But as for the rest . . . well, I would worry about that later. For now I had trouble enough keeping my head down and watching where my feet were planted.

The only delays we had were when we rested from time to time to allow Lochiel to catch up. Leaning on his brother's shoulder, he made a manly effort for one who'd been so badly crippled, and I never heard him complain. In fact, Lochiel was always the first to insist we carry on, even though the prince urged him to spare himself.

"Ye'll need me to get across to Achnacarry," was all Lochiel answered.

Several times the prince tried to move on before the men thought it safe, and he was cautioned by them all.

"We canna be sure where Cumberland's men will be," Angus Ban explained.

"Or the Butcher himself," Lochiel added.

Each time the prince heard them out, then turned and smiled at me, shrugging. "Young Highlander," he said, as if he'd forgotten my name, "I have been through this before. These men are not so much my subjects but my councilors. I must be ruled by them."

One time, overhearing him, Angus Ban told me, "The prince is rightfully fearful that an English patrol might find the ship before we get there. So we must hurry. But not"—and he turned to the prince—"without caution, sir."

Prince Charlie put up his hands and smiled. "Am I not the most cautious of men, young MacDonald?" he said to me.

"But this may be your last, best chance, sir," I said, thinking about the French ship.

"This may be *Scotland's* last, best chance," Prince Charlie said.

• • •

By morning we had reached the Forest of Moy, a tangle of pine and larch, beech and birch. We used the shelter of the trees to continue our journey. But at noon we finally stopped for a brief but welcome rest. I was so tired that every now and then I simply nodded off, still walking.

Angus Ban caught my arm. "Soon, lad," he told me, "soon. We're very near Glen Roy. Ye'll be needed then. I know the lower part, but it's up in the high trails we'll want yer help. And when ye've got us to the other side, we'll send ye home again."

At our resting place that time, Lochiel was persuaded to sit a bit, his brother beside him. But Cluny paced the while as if he feared once down, he'd never rise up again. Only Iain refused to stop, going on ahead to scout.

As soon as Iain returned with the news that all was clear, and not a redcoat in sight, Angus Ban had us up and on the move again. Archie helped Lochiel to stand, neither of them betraying any pain on their faces.

Surprisingly, the prince was the most energetic of us all, always ready for the march to continue, always ready with a smile. I watched him often, as he spoke to one man after another. It made me like him, how he disguised his own weariness for the sake of us all. Surely there must have been times, during his months escaping the English across the Highlands, when he felt as miserable and alone as I had making my way back from Culloden.

It is his concern for those about him, I suddenly realized, *that makes him a great prince.* And then I had a further thought: *He will make a great king.*

Thinking that made me smile ruefully to myself. He would make *no* king at all if we didn't get him to his ship in time.

• • •

By that evening, with a clear sky and an almost full moon beaming down on us, we'd passed by broken walls of crag and cliff. We'd crossed sodden meadows, fed by water tumbling in white tracks down the mountainsides.

Finally we arrived at the eastern foothills of Glen Roy. I'd never come upon it this way before.

"What is that?" asked the prince of Angus Ban, pointing to a place where something had cut under a tussocky plateau.

"We call those the Glen Roy beaches," Angus Ban said.

The prince laughed. "Beaches? And no ocean for many miles."

"They say that there was once a lake here, and when it dried up, it left parallel beaches behind."

I'd never heard of any such thing before, and wondered that the world—even my familiar part of it—should be so wide. Then I thought how the familiar hillsides looked almost sinister in the growing dark.

We were all exhausted, though none showed it as much as Lochiel, who was pale and drawn, the bones of his skull clearly outlined on his handsome face.

Angus Ban called a halt. "We'll stay here and set out again before dawn." He glanced at the prince, who nodded his agreement. "Since we'll be high enough in the glen to escape the attention of the redcoats, we should be able to make good time. With luck, we'll reach Loch Lochy by nightfall. There should be several small rowing boats on the loch, and once across, we are but short miles to Lochiel's home."

Crossing all of the glen is easy enough to do on the broad road by the Keppoch's house. But it would be hard going, being that quick while scrambling over the hills. Angus Ban was making a plan by what he knew. But if the lower glen was his country, the high glen was mine. Even by daylight the way might be hazardous. And once we left the part of the high glen that I knew, I'd be guessing which way was easiest, fastest, best. I wondered if I should say anything to them about my fears.

"Another day only," the prince said, smiling. "That is good, dear Angus."

"Another day only to Lochiel's," McNab reminded him. "Then three more days till the coast."

"Have we time? Have we time?" the prince asked.

"We have time, sir," Angus Ban said.

After that promise, I didn't dare say anything. I bit my lower lip and thought: *If I set my back to the east and head due west, I can manage.*

The prince started to climb toward higher ground. "Can we see the loch from up there?" he asked.

Angus Ban quickly blocked his way. "The moon's nearly full, my prince," he said, "and as of last week, Lord Loudon's camp of redcoats wasna far distant. Ye could be too easily spotted up there."

The prince looked disappointed and reluctantly turned back. Catching my eye, he shrugged, smiled, and whispered, "My council again."

This time I smiled back. Who could resist him? I wondered if princes were born to that charm, or had to learn it. Then I remembered that Butcher Cumberland was King George's youngest son, which meant he was a prince, too. *No charm there,* I told myself with a shiver.

Before we wrapped ourselves in our plaids and curled up for the night, Prince Charlie unaccountably came over and sat by me. He took off his bonnet and his wig and gave his scalp a vigorous rub.

"I swear, lad, there's more lice and midges than grains of sand in this country."

"Ye'll be glad to be gone then," I said.

"Glad? No," he answered, replacing his wig. "This is my father's kingdom. And mine. When I was your age, I learned about Scotland and England from the finest tutors. I knew always that one day I would have to come here to win back the stolen throne." He gave me another smile, this one less charming and more full of regret. "To come here was not so hard. But to win the throne back—ah, that has not been easy." He got a faraway look in his eyes. "I expected to rule this land someday, not to love it. But love it I do."

"I love it, too, sir."

He leaned toward me. "Then we have much in common, young MacDonald."

Suddenly, I realized he was right, though perhaps not in the way he thought. We were both lads who had gone to fight in our father's places, and found the battle wasn't quite what we'd reckoned on.

"Are ye so sure of yer kingdom now, sir?" I asked.

The prince glanced around at the rugged men in their muddied clothes who were settling down under the towering pines. Then, he watched a moment as a flock of peewits flew over. "Perhaps . . . perhaps there's not much of a court here, but there's never been braver subjects."

"My da once said that courage begets courage," I told him. "He said that nae man ever raced to follow a coward. And think how many brave men have followed ye across the country and into that far place where none return."

Prince Charlie smiled at the compliment. "Stout lad," he said. "You do not falter, even when grown men do."

"Oh, I've stumbled, Yer Highness. And I've made a harder jour-

ney than this," I said. "Much harder." I said no more than that. It
would have been unthinkable to remind him of Culloden now,
adding past horror to the hard present.

Perhaps he was thinking of it anyway, for suddenly he gazed up
at the moon and said, "I'll pray God keeps us safe this night. Just the
one more night till we cross the lake. You can be free of this particular danger then, boy."

I must have looked startled. *"Me?"*

"Ah, yes—I know you leave us once we are at the loch. And I am
glad for it, for you have much life ahead of you yet." He smiled,
just a young man now, thinking of his friend's safety before his own.

"Just the one more night," I repeated. Then I smiled back.
"That reminds me . . . " I hesitated.

"Reminds you of what?"

I took a deep breath. "Of one of my granda's stories."

"A storyteller, eh?" said the prince. "All the stories I know come
from books."

"Not the ones my granda tells. They're passed from lip to ear
and from heart to heart, with nae paper in between."

The prince chuckled good-naturedly. "And which heart-to-
heart tale are you reminded of this last night?"

"The tale of Sandy MacDonald," I said quickly. "He was a fish-
erman of the western isles. His wife Kate was the most beautiful
girl in all Scotland." I paused.

"Tell it to me, my brave Highlander." It was a royal command.

Of course I had to continue. "One day," I said, "when Sandy was
out in his boat, he overheard a pair of sea imps plotting to steal his
wife away that very night. They planned to leave a wooden image in
her place." I stopped to glance at the prince, afraid he might find the
tale foolish to his sophisticated ears, or my telling weak.

He had pulled up his legs and was resting his chin on his knees. His eyes were fixed intently upon me and he looked for all the world like Andrew or Sarah sitting at Granda's feet as he told his tales. Seeing this, I carried on with more confidence.

"Well, Sandy rowed right back to shore and raced home," I said. "He barred the door, and shuttered the windows. He wouldna let his Kate go outside. That night the imps sneaked up to the door and in wheedling tones told Kate her husband was hurt and had need of her. Yet there he was beside her and she didna move. So they told her one of her friends was ill, and next that the byre—the barn—was on fire, and all manner of other lies meant to draw her out. But she didna go, for Sandy held her fast."

The prince nodded, as if bidding me to go on. So I did.

"All that night—just that *one night*—he wouldna let her open the door. When the dawn came up, the voices stopped. Then he and his wife went outside together and there, in a corner of the yard, they came upon the stump of an old ship's mast carved with such skill, it was the very likeness of Kate MacDonald."

"I'm glad a happy ending came," said the prince. "Sandy MacDonald deserved to keep his wife."

"Aye, he did."

I didn't need to add that the prince's friends—just like Sandy MacDonald in the story—had done all they could to keep him safe, sometimes in spite of himself. If he guessed it was what I meant, he didn't say. But that wasn't the only reason I'd thought of that particular tale. I'd been wondering which prince we would be left with at the end of our story. Would it be this caring young man, or the charming hero from across the sea?

Which one, I puzzled, *is the true prince and which only a wooden copy? And would any of us know the difference?*

The prince got up and nodded to me. "One day," he said, "I hope to see you a captain in my army."

"A captain," I mused aloud, and he seemed satisfied with that.

Then he walked over to Lochiel and Archie, finding a spot by them where the stones were not too hard.

A captain, I thought, as I lay down and folded myself up in my plaid and slept. I dreamed I was wearing a bright blue uniform decorated with gold piping. I wore a wig like a gentleman, and a three-cornered hat with a white cockade pinned on. My sword was a gentleman's sword, with a basket hilt and watering down the blade. I had a *sken dhu* in my stocking, not a poor man's dirk, and it, too, was made of the finest steel. A musket poked its handle from my belt.

I woke suddenly and found myself staring up at a sky full of stars, thinking: *It's fine to be a captain in the army, as long as there's no war.*

37 ❧ GLENROY

Angus and McNab had us up before dawn. "Up, lads, up," they said. "Before the red-coats wake."

A mouthful of oatmeal stirred in a cup of cold water was all the breakfast we had time for before we were clambering once again over heather-clad hills. This was to be the last leg of our journey; the weight of it—and the hope—kept us all from speaking.

When we came over the top of one hill, we could see the River Roy below us. The crimson glow of daybreak shimmering on the running water had turned it bloodred, like a river in one of the old ballads.

I hoped it wasn't an omen, and shivered at the thought.

Once we'd reached the riverbank, Angus Ban paused, looking about carefully. "We canna stay out here in the open." He turned to me. "This is yer country, lad. Show us the way."

It was true. I was home.

"This way," I told them, pointing. "There's the best place to cross. Over the rocks, beneath that outcropping."

I took them to a spot a quarter mile upriver, where a natural fortress of stone guarded the ford. A series of flat rocks made a path across the river and a man could follow them step by step to the other side without so much as wetting his feet. Even for the limping Lochiel the going would prove easy. It fact it was an easier passage than many we'd had up till that time.

"I dinna like it," Iain said. "We're too exposed to any soldier on the hills. Let me go first to draw any fire."

"Do it," Angus Ban said.

So Iain went across, but though we watched the hills carefully, there was no movement, no flashes of light. Still, we each looked around before making the crossing and I went last. As soon as we reached the far bank, Angus Ban hurried us on brusquely.

"Have a care, Keppoch!" the prince chided him. "The gentle Lochiel still bears the wounds taken in our cause. The poor man can go no faster."

I saw Angus Ban bite back an impolite reply. "Yer pardon," he said. "I was only thinking of Yer Highness' safety." He pointed to the surrounding hills. "There may be eyes everywhere. We do not have time to tarry now. It is more open here, more dangerous."

It was a reverse of their argument a day before, with the prince cautioning us to slow down, and Angus Ban pushing us forward with haste. They were both right, of course. We had little time to spare. But we needed Lochiel well enough to travel. And there just might be English soldiers hidden among the crags or tucked down in the bracken and heather. They'd been there only days before, burning Keppoch House.

I glanced around at the familiar hillsides, my eyes alert to any movement, but I saw no sign of redcoats anywhere. "Sir, it seems safe to me."

The prince waved his hand at the glen. "See, dear Keppoch— Lord Loudon's men are still abed. We have plenty of time."

"Haste is still the wisest course," said Angus Ban, drumming his fingers on the butt of his pistol. "They'll awake before long, and there is nae telling where they have set their cordons."

"And we still have a long ways to go before—" I began.

Just then something exploded from the undergrowth. Startled, we all scattered for the trees before we realized it was only a dusky-coated deer, its hooves drumming on the ground. After it came a second, smaller deer.

My heart was nearly bursting my chest.

The prince was first out from behind his tree, chuckling to himself. "I take your meaning, Angus. No need for such a demonstration."

We all laughed, but quietly.

"This way," I said, once my heart stopped hammering. I pointed up the hill where a narrow path led through some trees.

"Good start," Angus Ban said. "The path, not the deer."

We climbed up the far slope, winding past the rock fortress, clearly going too slowly for Angus Ban's liking. I could read his face now, and his lips had thinned down, a sure sign he was upset. But Prince Charlie was strolling up the trail casually, chatting with Lochiel and Archie, admiring the scenic glen. He had such a confident air, as if he were already safe on the deck of a French ship. Angus Ban, who was next to Cluny and me, shook his head and made a *tch* sound with his tongue. Then he went back to chivy them along.

I had moved closer to Cluny's side at the head of our little company, and we'd just left the shelter of trees under the grey sky and come upon an open heather- and rock-strewn hilltop. He drew a sharp intake of breath.

"Damn!" he swore, and whipped out his pistol, cocking it in the same movement. Then he turned around and shouted to the prince and Angus Ban and Lochiel and the others, "Fly! Fly! We are discovered!"

I turned to my left and saw what had alarmed him. On a hill down below us, to the west of where we stood, a party of redcoats was just topping the summit. Their scarlet uniforms made them easy to spot. Their captain had seen us as well, though in our dark plaids we would have been less easy to find. He was crying "Halloo!" to bestir the rest of his men, who must have still been out of sight over the brow of the hill.

The prince stumbled, then paused to straighten his wig and bonnet. The rest of our party surrounded him, to shield him from the sassanachs' view. If they only thought they had rebels to chase, they might just come after us in a haphazard manner. But if they knew it was the prince, they'd race over the hills and never stop.

I had to think fast. If we went back into the sheltering trees, we could only go down and perhaps meet the soldiers coming up. Yet to make our way over the slope of the open hill, skirting heather and rocky scree, gave us no cover. But over the next hill stood our shieling. And from there, I could lead us all to safety. I was sure of it.

"Follow me," I cried, and began a scramble up the hill, staying as low as possible. They followed right behind me.

Now on the brow of the distant hill, the redcoats set their muskets to their shoulders and fired raggedly, without time for a straight and ordered battle line. At this distance, they had little chance of hitting us, but the noise of their guns would surely summon any other soldiers in the area.

"Hurry!" Angus Ban cried, though none of us needed urging.

One of the McPherson men stopped to turn and shoot back. Cluny slapped him about the head and pushed him on. "Yer wasting good powder!" he growled.

"We have to get over the brow of this hill!" I cried, and Angus Ban nodded, herding us on with a frantic wave of his pistol.

We passed swiftly over the crest so our pursuers couldn't get a clear shot at us, then we huddled all together for a quick plan.

"Which way now?" McNab was panting heavily. The question was for me.

Before I could catch my breath and answer, another shot rang out.

I searched behind to see how the redcoats had managed to close so quickly, but it was Archie who saw where the shot had come from.

"There! There!" he cried, pointing.

A second squad of sassanachs was making its way along the hilltops from the other direction, from the north. The soldiers outnumbered us by a dozen or so.

"We've fallen into a trap!" Lochiel exclaimed.

The prince drew his sword and pistol and shook them resolutely. "I'll fight on till they kill me," he declared. "I'll not let them take me prisoner."

I pulled out my dirk. "Nor I," I said, the captain by his king.

I was sweating now and wiped my forehead with the back of my hand. We had soldiers on either side of us.

Angus Ban faced the prince squarely, determination writ large on his homely face. "It's best no to die at all when there's nae call for it," he said. Turning to Cluny, he added, "Ye and yer boys hold off the ones on our tail. The rest of us will mix shots with the others, then lead them off."

"Aye, we'll give them a fight," Cluny agreed.

Angus Ban turned back to me and said sharply, "Duncan, ye know *these* hills better than any of us. While we keep the redcoats off yer backs, ye must lead the prince to safety."

To safety? When there was none?

"Will ye try, lad?" Angus Ban said.

"I'll try."

Placing a hand on my shoulder, Angus Ban's tone softened. "Duncan, keep him safe. All Scotland is depending on ye."

I nodded, but my heart was suddenly racing.

"It is not in me to leave the rest of you fighting in my stead," said the prince.

"If anything happens to ye, then we're fighting for naught," said Angus Ban. "We'll hold them off as long as we can, then we'll make a run for it. We can outrun these sassanachs easily." It was a boast, of course, but true.

Lochiel added, "The English can march and turn, but there's nothing for speed like a Highlander on his own hills, sir." Then he smiled, and all the weariness on his handsome face disappeared. "Ye know the cove on Loch Lochy?"

"I know it," said Prince Charlie. "I'll look to see you there."

"Tomorrow eve at the latest," Lochiel said.

"It is done," the prince said. He offered his hand first to Lochiel, then Angus Ban, and they shook like parting friends. *Just in case,* I thought, *he might be saying a last farewell.*

"Come on, sir," I said, tugging at his sleeve.

This time he was the one to wipe the mist from his face.

Cluny and his men took up positions among the boulders on the slope behind us, aiming down the length of their muskets. A shot rang out and then a second, but we were doing the firing, not the English. A small breeze brought me the acrid smell of gunpowder and I was suddenly, horribly reminded of Culloden.

I said a small prayer under my breath.

Angus Ban grinned. "That old poacher will show them a thing or two." He nodded at me. "We're off, lad. Now the prince is yers." Without more ado, he and the others turned and went back over the hill to face the troops who were closing from the north.

"Come, sir," I said to the prince. "Follow me." Then, crouching low so we were masked by the heather, we left our companions to fight. "Dinna worry, sir," I said over my shoulder. "These are the very hills where my father's cattle graze. I know every track and trail."

We crawled further through the heather, the little purple flowers grazing against our shoulders. "With luck," I called back to him, "the redcoats will be too busy dodging bullets to see us separating from the rest."

"With luck," he repeated.

"Here's a track I know well, sir, along this waterfall course. The small trees will hide us till we get over the next hill."

We rested for a moment under the trees. Behind us we could hear shots being exchanged.

I spoke more boldly than I felt. It was true, I knew these hills. But I also knew they wouldn't hide us for very long. They were too open. We needed the cover of real trees. "Hurry, sir."

We continued up the waterfall, our feet splashing through the pools, but the trees got even sparser as we neared the top. Their straggly branches seemed to be pointing at us like traitorous fingers.

"Only a little further, sir," I called, encouraging us both, but we would soon be out in the open again. "Then a quick run over the hilltop and into my family's shieling."

"Shieling?"

"The summer meadow where we bring our cows, sir."

"You *do* know this country," he said.

We ran with our heads down as if a demon horde were behind us. As we ran, I could still hear the crack of firearms echoing over the hillsides, and I glanced back to see if there was any sign of our companions. But there was no movement at all, except for some buzzards flying lazily overhead.

Then we crested the hill and made it down the other side. Standing under a stunted pine, we tried to catch our breaths.

"See, Yer Majesty," I said, when I could speak again, "now we have the whole hill between us and the others."

"God keep our friends safe," said the prince, making the sign of the cross over his breast.

I repeated his prayer to myself, thinking at the same time of all those who hadn't been kept safe: Ewan and his da; the Keppoch; Sandy, the man with the white eye; all the Highlanders facedown in the mud of Drummossie Moor; and those burned up in the hut where the Keppoch lay. I tried not to think of them because thinking made me angry at the prince. Now I liked him and now I needed to keep him safe. But that didn't stop me from keeping a running tally of the dead as we walked along the shieling.

"Where do we go now?" he asked.

"Down this path"—I pointed—"lies our village. But before we get there, there's a cutoff that goes west."

"And west," he mused, "is Loch Lochy."

I thought about Loch Lochy and how I'd leave the prince there and return home. *Home,* I thought, suddenly wondering if Ma and Da were worried about me. If they'd given up on me. If they'd gone looking for me. And because I let my thoughts go wandering off, I nearly got us killed.

As we rounded a bend where my cows had often strayed, well past the Gloaming Pool, we found ourselves suddenly confronted by three burly redcoats. They appeared without warning on the path below us, about a hundred feet away.

Immediately, the tallest soldier spotted the prince's sword and pistol and cried out, "What! Hoi! Rebels!"

The nearest of them had a pair of rabbits slung over his shoulder and I guessed they had risen early to go foraging for game. At the sight of us, the near one shrugged off the rabbits and raised his musket, pulling back the hammer as he did so.

I lunged at the prince and gave him a shove as the gun cracked the air. The bullet tore through my left sleeve and cut across my arm like a hot blade.

For an instant, I reeled back with the shock of it. I wanted to shout to the prince to run, but my teeth had clenched with the pain and I couldn't seem to unlock them. As I swayed, a firm hand grabbed my arm and hauled me back up the slope.

"Come, young MacDonald," the prince urged, "you're not done with me yet." The courage in his voice lent me fresh strength and I hurried with him.

"One side there, Hawks!" barked another of the soldiers. "Let me get a clear shot!"

A second musket boomed out, but in his haste the man had aimed wide.

"Come, sir," I called to the prince, taking over the lead. We clawed up the heathery slope. Scraping through the brambles, I cut my palms on jagged pieces of flint, but it hardly mattered. I could barely remember the pain from that shot along my arm. I had no time for it. *We* had no time for it.

A third musket fired and I heard the smack of a bullet on a nearby rock.

"Which way, lad? Which way?" the prince demanded urgently as we scrambled over the crest of the hill.

"Just follow me." I could only think of one route of escape, the last place in the world I wanted to go.

Not taking time to reload, the redcoats had shouldered their guns and were now climbing up after us. They couldn't be more than a couple of hundred feet behind us.

"Over there!" I gasped. "That copse of trees."

We bolted through the trees, glad to put something between our backs and the guns of our enemies.

"Where to now?"

"I know the very spot," I said, breaking into a run once again.

The prince kept pace with me, though he almost lost his bonnet and wig as we ran. "But we'll have to keep ahead of them for a bit longer."

"Go, lad, and I will follow," he said.

Then we were both quiet, saving our breath for the run.

Another musket boomed somewhere behind us. The redcoats must have stopped to reload. Every reload gave us extra time.

"Where is this place?" the prince gasped. "Is it soon?"

"Ahead," I replied as we sprinted up a steep rise.

We threw ourselves over the top and went sliding down the scree on the far side. Waiting below us was the one thing that might yet save us: the still, grey, peaty waters of the Gloaming Pool.

"What are we doing here?" the prince asked, his voice rising in confusion. "There's no cover. They'll see us as soon as they top the rise."

"Nae," I said, pulling him by the sleeve, which—in any other circumstance—could have cost me my head. "Just come with me." I dragged him over to where the hollow reeds grew.

Grabbing two reeds, I tugged them out. "We'll hide *under* the water. Ye can breathe through this." I handed him a reed and stepped into the pool, wading out to where it was deep enough to hide us, in a patch of other reeds.

Prince Charlie followed. "I understand," he said. "It's a desperate game, but perhaps the gamble will win." Quickly, he took his bonnet and wig off, stuffing them down the front of his shirt. "And I suppose we're as well drowned as shot."

Now I could hear the soldiers scrambling up the slope, calling to one another. I prayed that the ripples in the pool would fade before the redcoats got to the top of the rise or they'd guess at once where we were.

"Lie down!"

I took a deep breath, placed the reed in my mouth, closed my eyes, and slipped under the water. The chill of night was still on the pool and it wrapped me up like folds of ice. I felt the prince sink down close by and we lay together on the muddy bottom.

Now I opened my eyes and saw that there was about a foot of dark water above us, breaking the light into wavy threads, like a rainbow that's come undone. The reeds were just long enough to pierce the surface and allow us to breathe.

Then I heard the voices of the redcoats, as if through a rough piece of plaid. They sounded very far away.

"Damn you, Hawks! You said they came down here."

"They did, Sergeant. Sure as death they did."

"You idiot! Look about. The place is deserted. There's nobody."

"They must have gone another way," said the third voice. "Through those rocks back there."

I prayed silently, *Dear God and St. Andrew, dinna let them come too close!*

A soft splash hit the water.

I gulped and nearly lost the reed. My fingers clutched the muddy bottom of the pool as I struggled to keep still. *Breathe,* I told myself. *Breathe.*

Then a fish swam by my head, its tail flicking my cheek as it passed by in a flurry of bubbles.

Let them believe all the ripples are trout, I prayed.

There was so little air coming through the reed, it was hard to keep my head clear. I fought to stay calm, to take small, slow breaths.

Now the wound in my arm began to throb, my temples were pounding like a drum. I was hot and frozen both at once, the fire in my lungs struggling against the chill of the water. Then I felt that sickly pain in my brow that told me a fit was coming on.

A fit? Oh, God! I thought. *Surely that will be the end of us.*

I thought about Mairi falling into the Gloaming Pool, thinking the Fair Folk were waiting for her. Was I to die in the same way? Perhaps it was what I deserved.

Suddenly the motes of light on the water's surface seemed to merge together and I saw my sister's face. Her voice, like a ripple, played over my ears.

"Ye've done me nae wrong, Duncan. Things happen there's nae help for it. Nae blame, either." The touch of the water felt like Mairi's small hands stroking my cheeks, soothing me, taking away the pain. "Dinna look back and be sorry," said the voice. "Look forward and be brave."

Somewhere in the world beyond the pool Hawks cried, "Hoi, there!"

A musket fired and a bullet punched into the water a few feet from my head. In that instant Mairi was gone.

"What are you doing, you fool?"

"I saw something move in the water."

"We're here to catch men, not fish. That was a trout jumping."

"I'm going down to take a gander."

"Look!" the third soldier exclaimed. "There's somebody moving about there, high up in the rocks where I said they'd gone."

"It looks like a girl."

"The way these rebels dress, in those silly skirts, I'll wager it's the boy. And the other one will be with him. Come on, after them!"

I waited as long as I could bear it, to be sure they were gone. A musket shot in the distance told me they were. I pressed my hands to the bottom and pushed up.

Dripping with weeds and mud, I dragged myself to my feet and looked round for the prince. I spotted him a few feet from where I had just been lying. He was still under the water—pale, lifeless, and still.

39 ❧ FAREWELL

An awful fear clutched my belly. I plunged in with both hands, seized the prince by the sleeve, and hauled him up. He broke the surface, coming into a sitting position, and opened his eyes. Spitting out the reed, he began a frothy coughing and stared at me blankly for several moments before recognition sparked in his eyes.

"Yes, I remember now. Young Duncan. Are we safe?"

"The redcoats have gone," I replied. "They saw something else to chase."

I hardly dared think about what that *something* was. Surely it was too mad to suppose it was really Mairi. And yet, I thought I'd heard one of them say it was a girl among the rocks.

I shook the thought from my head. Taking the prince by the elbow, I helped him to his feet.

"What happened to ye, sir?" I asked. "For a moment I took ye for dead."

"It was so odd," he answered dreamily. "I felt I was back in my own bed in my father's palace in Italy. But the sheets were ice and the mattress stuffed with snow. It was cold and warm at the same time. I didn't want to get up. I fancied I could just lie there and sleep on forever."

"This *is* an enchanted place," I said. "Strange things happen here in the Gloaming Pool."

"Stranger even than a prince caked in muck?" He looked down at his clothes and began laughing.

I put a finger to my lips, urging him to be quiet. "We'd best be away from here while we can," I said, wading out of the pool. "We canna be sure they willna come back." But whether it was the red-coats I feared or something worse, I wasn't sure.

"A moment," said the prince, noticing the torn sleeve of my sark and the deep wound on my arm that was starting to bead with blood again. "We cannot leave that unattended." He took off his scarf and tied it snugly about my wound.

"Och, it's nae so bad," I said, trying hard not to flinch as he pulled the scarf tight. "The bullet cut the skin, but missed the bone."

"Nevertheless . . . " said the prince. "Nevertheless."

We started westward toward Loch Lochy, clinging to whatever cover we could find, and watching out for the redcoats. Our clothes dried slowly and we were both shivering with cold. I hated to think about the trail we were leaving. Even a child could have followed it.

"Do you think we'll come across the others?" the prince asked, breathing hard.

"No until the loch itself, if they're being as canny as we," I replied. I was out of breath, too.

"Well, there is no help for it then," he said. "We must do the best for ourselves."

We spoke no more after that.

By noon we'd reached the hills that rise to the south of the River Gloy. The country beyond was open and exposed, so we took shelter among a cluster of boulders to wait for the night. A small wind was puzzling around the rocks and for a little while rain clouds threatened. I hoped we wouldn't get wet again. We were only a few hours dry. But the good weather held and the sky cleared.

In the scramble to escape, the prince had come away with no supplies. I brought out my own food and offered it to him, though it was little more than a handful of oats, and that badly used by our time in the pool. Of course we didn't dare make a fire.

"It's hardly worthy," I said quietly.

Prince Charlie waved away my apology and chewed up a mouthful of the cold, mushy oats as if it were a shank of the finest beef. "I've learned to get by on humbler fare." He smiled at me. "Food so generously given is as good as a banquet."

I smiled back to see him put such a brave face on misery. All the while I was in a kind of daze, thinking about whom I was eating with.

"If I were a prince," I said at last, "I'm no sure I would take it so well."

He shrugged and took a swallow of water from my flask. "I think, Duncan, I've learned more these past months than in all the years I studied lessons with my tutors."

"Learned what, sir?" I asked. "To be dirty and cold and scared?"

He laughed. "I have learned to understand the quality of my people's hearts." He put his hand on his chest and there was a kind of pride in it. "I have dressed as a prince and a servant." He paused. "Once, I was even dressed as a girl."

"I heard that story." I grinned. "No a pretty girl, either."

He chuckled. "Quite ugly, actually."

Then he gestured at his kilt. "And I have dressed as a Highlander. I find I do as well with it as any of the best breeches. I hope to God to walk the streets of London with it yet."

"And I hope soon to be free of these breeks, these trousers, forever," I said fervently.

"Let us shake on that, Highland Duncan," the prince said. His hand touched mine.

The prince's touch.

If I had expected some lightning shock, some clap of thunder, some instance of healing, I was sorely misled. It was only a man's hand holding mine, well-callused from his time in the heathery hills. But magic or not, in that moment it felt good to be—in some small way—his friend.

Once the sun had sunk low enough in the sky to offer us shadows, we set off again. I got us over Glen Roy without further run-ins with any redcoats, and headed us down the slopes in the gathering dark.

The loch was a dark mass ahead. To the southwest we could see the distant suggestion of high-peaked mountains. On another day, in other circumstances, I might have enjoyed my first look at such a pretty place. But this was not the time nor place for admiring the view.

The cove where we were to meet the rest of our party was one the prince had visited earlier in his perilous journeys, and now it was he who became the guide.

We traveled stealthily through the twilight, keeping to the trees whenever possible. Up close, the loch was a deep blue with clumps of brown grass and wads of fallen leaves clogging the shore.

We would walk a few steps, stop to listen for any movement, then go on. Dark clouds scudded across the sky, for the moment hiding the moon.

At last we came to a curved stretch of beach sheltered from view by a willow grove. As we crept toward the water, we were stopped in our tracks by the sound of a pistol being cocked.

To have come so far to be killed at the last? I drew in a deep breath, put the prince behind me, and waited.

"Is that a friend who passes?" inquired a voice we both knew.

"Angus Ban!" I answered. "It's me. Duncan of Glenroy and . . ." To be safe I added, "And a companion."

The rest of our band emerged from the trees, welcome shadows. I counted them and not one was missing. Not even Lochiel.

"I'm glad to see you all safe!" exclaimed Prince Charlie.

"We took a few nicks," said Cluny McPherson, "but nothing worse. When they're tracking through the heather, the redcoats are nae good with their aim." He laughed. "Unlike Iain here, who can hit a redcoat as easily as a rabbit. Though they're no so good eating."

They started to laugh but Angus Ban hushed them. "Lochiel's men have found us a boat and stowed it in the bushes. It's a wee bit leaky, but the only one no destroyed by the English." He pointed to the far side of the willow grove. "I'd advise ye, sir, to get aboard and be off."

I saw some of the men hauling a long rowboat out of concealment and sliding it into the water. The prince saw it, too, but he took me aside for a final word. Shielding me with his body, he slipped the lion brooch out of his pocket and pressed it into my hand.

"It's all I have to give, Highland Duncan," he said, "and too little for the service you have done me."

"I canna think that it should come to me, sir," I said, trying to give it back.

The prince refused to accept it. "If you won't keep it for yourself," he said, "then keep it for me. Till I return."

I thought about that. "If yer determined, sir, I'll keep it till then." But even as I spoke, a sudden chill in my head warned me that he would never return, never sit upon the throne. That was just a story he kept in his heart, to give him the courage to see his journey through to its end. And a story all of Scotland would keep to see us through to ours.

I lowered my eyes so he couldn't know the thought in them. Then I pinned the brooch beneath my plaid so that it remained out of sight.

At that, the prince, his hand on Angus Ban's arm, climbed into the leaky boat, bending low. Lochiel and his brother and all of his men were already seated. There was one place left, at the back, for the prince.

With a grunted command from Lochiel, the men dipped their oars into the dark loch, and they were away. The clouds parted for a moment, and the moon shone down full on them. Then the clouds returned, the light disappeared, and the boat slipped into the shadows and was gone.

I stood on the shore with Angus Ban, Iain, and McNab. We didn't wave or call out or make any movement, just stood and watched them go.

After a while, I asked, "Will they be in time?"

Angus Ban sighed. "If God and St. Andrew make it so." Then he turned to McNab. "Well, it's back to the rocks and caves for Iain and me, McNab."

"Aye, it's an uncomfortable thing, this business of being free," McNab answered wryly.

"And what about ye, Duncan?" Angus Ban asked. "Is it a rebel's life ye'll have?"

I thought about it, about living up in the hills with the men.

About chasing through the heather and scrambling about the rocks. I thought about the cave where the beautiful widow Keppoch kept her small court. I thought about dodging the redcoats and killing them when we could.

Then I stared through the murk and over the dark loch. The prince's boat was no longer visible, but I knew he was going back to where he belonged, to the other side of the water, where the Fair Folk and the goblins dwell.

"Nae," I replied. "There's still much to be done in Glenroy. My family has more need of me now than any prince."

Angus Ban looked at me somberly. "But if the prince calls ye again?"

"If he calls, he shall no find Duncan MacDonald of Glenroy wanting." But I didn't really think he'd be back. There was too much to lose and too little to win for him now.

Angus Ban gave me a man's handclasp, and then a pocket filled with fresh oats to speed me on my way.

So I returned to Glenroy, dodging groups of redcoats till I came to my own home once again. I had a long night and a day to think about all that had happened.

It's a hard thing to separate what's real from what's fancy. Did I really hear Mairi's voice and feel her ghostly touch as I lay in the Gloaming Pool, or was it my heart telling me the things I wanted to hear? Did the redcoats chase her ghost up and over the hill, or was it some poor live lassie they found on the other side?

I do know that the fits have come upon me less and less often since then. And when they do come, they pass more easily. Mairi's touch? The prince's? Or have I just outgrown the sickness, like a childhood pox safely past? I suppose it hardly matters why.

I can't really look into the future. I don't know what will happen to the Scotland I love. But I believe my people will survive and I along with them. We'll have songs and tales of courage to sustain us through the hard years. And whether there are princes or kings come again to our shores, whether there will be more battles or more mad, heroic charges doesn't really matter. Our spirit will survive— not by the sharpness of our swords, but by the sharpness of our wits.

Truly, we'll be wolves no longer, but as the tinker said once long ago, we'll survive like the foxes, their children.

These are the people who are real: Bonnie Prince Charlie, the Keppoch MacDonald, Angus Ban, the widow Keppoch and her children, gentle Lochiel, Cluny McPherson, the "butcher" Cumberland, King George, Duke William, Atholl, and all the named generals on either side.

These are the people who are fictitious: the villagers of Glenroy, individual soldiers fighting at Culloden, the tinkers, the individual redcoats chasing Duncan and his friends through the heather and the servants in the widow Keppoch's cave.

And while there is a Glen Roy, there is no village at the top of it named Glenroy. Since we invented that village, we peopled it with heroes, and farmers and a miller and a farrier, too. Like many villages across the Highlands of Scotland, it sent most of its men off to fight for the Stuart and to die in the bloody massacre known as Culloden.

The basic story of the raising of Prince Charlie's flag at Glenfinnan, the terrible defeat on Drummossie Moor, the awful and relentless bloodletting by the rampaging English troops, and the prince's desperate flight through the heathery Highlands of Scotland always just a step ahead of the redcoats—that is all true. True, too, is the picture of Highland life with its feudal clan system, where men owed their land and their fighting lives to their laird or chieftain, who, like the Keppoch MacDonald, could call them out by sending forth the burning cross, the infamous *Creau toigh*, "The Cross of Shame."

As to the ending of the story: Four days after crossing Loch Lochy, and six months after the defeat at Culloden, Prince Charles Edward Stuart, age twenty-five, was on a ship bound for France. He never set eyes on Scotland again.

His attempt to recapture the united throne of Scotland and England for his father had been a madcap adventure from the start, made possible only by his own determination and charisma, and by the wild courage of the Highlanders who followed him. Most of Scotland did *not* support Bonnie Prince Charlie, and only a few of the clans actually joined him, including the Camerons and the MacDonalds. Yet he won two major victories over better-trained and better-armed troops, and he was poised at one point to march right on into London. In fact, King George and his court were already packed and ready to flee. Whether or not Prince Charlie's generals were right to force a retreat back to Scotland is a question that is hotly debated to this day.

If the defeat at Culloden had been the end of the story, Charles would not be the legendary figure he is today. In fact, he would probably be despised as the man who brought ruin to the Highlands, for the defeat at Culloden meant the end of a way of life. The power of the Highland lairds was broken. And the English worked hard at destroying the Scottish religion, language, and education, and they managed to put an end to the clan system as well.

Yet the courage and endurance Prince Charlie displayed in escaping his pursuers—living for five months in the Highlands, crossing the heathery hills not once but many times—that courage lives on in the imagination of the Scottish people. So do the stories of

Flora MacDonald (in whose company he dressed as a maid) and others who risked all that they had to protect him. It is amazing to note that not one of the impoverished Highlanders sold the prince out, not even for the astonishing sum of thirty thousand pounds offered by the English, a fortune in those times.

In his last few days in Scotland, Bonnie Prince Charlie did indeed journey from "Cluny's Cage" to Loch Lochy by way of Glen Roy. The adventure Duncan shares with the prince is mostly fictitious—though we have borrowed a number of incidents from Prince Charlie's actual five months in hiding, such as the prince peering out of the bothy and surprising a visitor, and the "privy council" conversation, among others. Of course, the time in the Gloaming Pool is made up whole cloth. However, it is typical of the hairsbreadth escapes the prince experienced during his flight through the heathery hills. Angus Ban MacDonald did accompany Charles on some of these travels, but we have inserted him into this part of the adventure in the place of John Roy Stuart, and hope that the Stuart clan will forgive us that small change.

Alas, once back on the continent, Charles led an unremarkable and even dissolute life until his death in 1788, drifting from place to place with no prospect of ever recapturing the glory that was once briefly, his. It can honestly be said that he left the best part of himself in the Highlands.

A note about Highland dress: In the eighteenth century, poor Highland men like the Glenroy MacDonalds would have worn a sark, or long linen shirt, and a kilt made up of a single piece of woven woolen cloth that could be gathered together and held up with a leather belt, a length thrown over the shoulder. Though often barefoot during the spring, summer, and fall months, on a march they would have worn either shoes of untanned hide or—when expecting to go long distances—cuarans, which were like boots that reached almost to the knees, shaped to the leg and kept in position by leather thongs. Knee-high stockings often supported a *sken dhu,* a knife. The bonnet or woolen hat was where the clan badge would be pinned.

The tartans at this time for the poorer folk would have been simple checks of two or three colors, not the more defined clan tartans we know today, though they were often distinctive by districts. So the MacDonalds in a particular location might have similar recognizable patterns, but certainly never as elaborate as the ones we see today. The wools would have been colored by natural dyes from plants, roots, berries. But since they would have been worn every day, after a while the colors would be faded.

There really was a proscription against the wearing of kilts and tartans, the playing of bagpipes, and the speaking of Gaelic, all to break the spirit of the Scots and the clan system. The men really were forced to wear the hated trousers instead of their kilts. This all happened through the Disarming Act of 1746, half a year later than we have it in our story. The Act was rescinded in 1782 and to some extent, kilts came back into regular use in the Highlands after that. However, the fancy tartans with the clear clan affiliations we see today are really a nineteenth-century reconstruction. The beginning of the "tartan revival" was in 1822, when King George IV, visiting Edinburgh, brought it back into fashion.

A note about the speech: Highlanders generally spoke Gaelic. Their chiefs would have also spoken Scots (a form of English) as well as some French and Latin, because they were educated. The Lowland Scots would have spoken Scots-English. The English spoken by the English was close enough to Scots-English for them to understand one another. We have distinguished all the Scots—both chiefs and Highlanders—with a more archaic form of language: *dinna, couldna, wouldna, ye, yer,* etc. The English in our story speak without these archaisms. It is a literary shorthand only.

Some of the Scottish words used in this book:

bairn—young child
bannock—a round, flat cake or roll
blether—to talk nonsense
bloody—a word often used as a curse
bothy—a rough hut
breeks—trousers
byre—barn
claymore—the old Scottish two-handed sword
craw—crow
cuaran—a boot reaching almost to the knee
cushie doo—pigeon, dove
daft/daftie—crazy, a crazy person
dirk—a knife used in battle
dyke—stone wall, boundary marker in fields
fash—to bother, worry, distress
greeting—weeping
havers, haverings—dreamy nonsense
laird—the lord or leader of the clan
loch—a Highland lake
neeps—turnips
pibroch—particular kind of bagpipe tune
porridge—oatmeal
sark—long shirt

shieling—summer pasture for cows and sheep
skelp—slap or smack with palm of hand
sken dhu—knife carried in a man's stocking top
targe—shield
wee—small, little

Scotland has a very rich tradition of folktales and we are pleased to be able to include some of them in our story. The tale Granda tells to Duncan can be found in slightly different form in *Folk Tales of the Highlands* by Gregor Ian Smith. The tale Duncan tells the prince is adapted from the version in *A Kist O' Whistles* by Moira Miller.

Finally, the Keppoch branch of the MacDonalds generally spell their name "MacDonell." We have used the more familiar spelling to emphasize their kinship with the other branches of Clan Donald, which was the most powerful of all the Highland clans.

Bonnie Charlie's now awa',
Safely owre the friendly main;
Mony a heart will break in twa,
Should he no' come back again.

Will ye no come back again?
Will ye no come back again?
Better lo'ed ye canna be,
Will ye no come back again?

—Scots song by Lady Nairne